Edge of Square Nine

'For those who first met Hannah in *The Magic Mooncat*, it will be intriguing to find her now in the moral maze of modern living. Most people will recognise their own journeys from Square Nine.'

Ann Widdecombe

Edge of Square Nine

Lois Fenn

The Third in the Lincolnshire Trilogy

Crow's Nest Books

First published in 2013 by Crow's Nest Books
18 Westgate, Ruskington, Lincs, NG34 9ES
www.loisfenn.co.uk

Distributed by Lightning Source
The right of Lois Fenn to be identified as the author of the work has been
asserted herein in accordance with the Copyright, Designs and Patents
Act 1988.

British Library Cataloguing in Publication Data
A catalogue record for this book is available from the British Library

ISBN 978-0-9542884-3-3

Typeset by Amolibros, Milverton, Somerset
http://www.amolibros.co.uk
This book production has been managed by Amolibros
Printed and bound by Lightning Source

THE AUTHOR: Lois Fenn is a retired teacher with two sons and two daughters, six grandchildren, and nine great-grandchildren. Her lifestyle is reflected both in the wartime background and country life of *The Magic Mooncat*, and *Cobwebs in Time*, and that reflection is continued in *Edge of Square Nine*, the third novel in the Lincolnshire Trilogy.

In this third novel of the trilogy, Lois Fenn produces a cocktail of events skilfully bound together through her deep understanding of family relationships. She closely identifies with her leading protagonist yet allows herself the freedom to create fictitious, larger than life characters in a wholly believable way.

Of *The Magic Mooncat*

'The *Magic Mooncat* convincingly evokes the innocence and the ignorance of a past age.'

Ann Widdecombe

The Magic Mooncat won the David St John Thomas prize for Best Fiction 2003/2004

Of *Cobwebs in Time*

'Holds one's attention from beginning to end…a superb sequel to *The Magic Mooncat*…such depth of feeling bringing the characters to life.'

Sue Hodge

www.loisfenn.co.uk

Dedicated to all the people I love and have ever loved.

The Story so far...

Hannah Flynn is evacuated at the age of nine from Hull to Lincolnshire with her best friend Sally Blenkin. She experiences many changes with foster parents after the death of her mother but Willow Cottage remains a constant in later years.

She trains as a teacher but after meeting her childhood friend, Jack Clayton, she marries and they have four children; a son Mark, a daughter Rachel, another son Simon and a daughter Emma. Rachel marries Stephen and Karl and Kirstie, the twins, are born. Simon marries Marie, but after three miscarriages they decide to adopt three-year old Alice.

When Alice is nine years old, her seven-year old cousin Leigh joins the family at Willow Cottage, after the tragic death of his parents Mark and Sarah. He is a very sensitive child and he and Alice form a lasting bonding.

The friendship is renewed between Hannah and Sally.

Emma becomes a single mother with the birth of Poppy and takes up employment at Daisy Cottage Nursing Home, where Ella, the old housekeeper at Willow Cottage, is spending the remainder of her days, and where Hannah meets the owner of the establishment, Daisy Buckerfield.

Jack dies from cancer, leaving Hannah to reorganise life at Willow Cottage, with the help of Simon and his wife Marie.

Rachel and Stephen are divorced and Rachel continues to bring up the twins on her own, until she meets and marries the new vicar of the Parish of Norbrooke.

Jane Dry, a care worker at the nursing home, becomes a good friend and an "Aunt" to the younger generation. She marries Clive Spryfoot, a fruit and vegetable wholesaler.

Molly Petch, the biological mother of Alice, makes herself known and a journey to Ireland to stay with her leads to the amazing discovery that she is acquainted with Patrick Flynn, an uncle Hannah did not know existed.

Now, with your memory refreshed the story continues...

Acknowledgements

As with the previous two novels of the Lincolnshire Trilogy, I owe a great deal to my two sons, Andrew and Ian, and daughters, Lisa and Karen and their families for their continued support.

I would like to thank Ann Widdecombe for supporting me from start to finish, both in my writing and personally, with such warmth and generosity, sharing time in her busy life.

My thanks also go to Sue Hodge, who we all remember as Mimi in *Allo Allo*. Sue works hard in the theatre bringing great enjoyment to the public, and in her efforts to keep 'theatre' alive. I greatly appreciated her comments on my second novel in the trilogy, i.e. *Cobwebs in Time*, and the value of her role in such a successful wartime comedy as a link with the original wartime background of *The Magic Mooncat*.

I have experienced the value of 'air time' on both Radio Lincolnshire and Radio Humberside, but my special thanks go to Howard Leader, who has interviewed me a number of times on his weekly Sunday Show, and made me feel so relaxed.

I greatly treasure the letter I received from the late Richard Whitely. It is handwritten and offered me a choice of quotes for the cover of *The Magic Mooncat*.

1

The Whispering Tree

'What upsets me is that Sally Blenkin knew before I did.'

Daisy Buckerfield had anticipated her friend Hannah's words after the abrupt telephone call a half an hour previously and now waited for her to continue, knowing what was to follow, but not daring to admit it. Instead, she attempted an air of innocence and ignorance, reaching forward from her chair to reposition a Chinese Lantern in her dried flower arrangement.

'Of course it's Leigh's.' Hannah waited for some reaction, staring expectantly at Daisy.

Daisy obliged, taking her attention away from the vase and registering what she hoped was a look of surprise.

'Really! When was this then?'

'Apparently about seven weeks from what I can gather. They decided to keep it a closely guarded secret. All of them. Not just Alice and Leigh.'

'Perhaps they didn't want you to worry. You have been a little bit under the weather just lately.' Daisy patted her friend's arm in an attempt to reassure her, drawing her hand back quickly as Hannah jerked away.

'There's nothing wrong with me! What do you mean? They don't think I can cope. Getting past it, am I? After what I've done. We could run rings round them, Daisy.'

'I'm sure we could, but I don't think they think of you in that way.'

'Well, it's the secrecy that's doing my head in and how could those two be so irresponsible! It doesn't seem to matter these days does it? No plans, no money, no intention of marrying. Like mother, like daughter I suppose.'

Daisy was surprised by the bitterness in her voice. She knew that Hannah had taken a liking to Alice's biological mother Molly Petch when the relationship had come to light a couple of years ago, even though it had put a lot of strain on Marie her daughter-in-law and the adoptive mother of Alice.

'I'm sure that Alice was not influenced by Molly. Don't you think the problems she had as a single parent would have discouraged rather than encouraged? I'm sure they got carried away. We've all been there, Hannah.'

'I suppose so but I don't like this modern world all the same.'

'Emma seems to manage with Poppy and she's a single mother. She's as happy as the day is long.' Daisy hesitated, stopping herself from commenting on Emma's earlier conversation when she had registered good-humoured surprise at her mother's unusual lack of ability to 'suss things out'.

'Emma's different. She's got her degree and her head screwed on. I haven't given up on Emma yet. She's destined for more than this.' Hannah waved her arm to encompass the office of the nursing home and beyond.

Daisy shrugged. She knew that any possible criticism of her friend's offspring would bring immediate denial. Instead she said, 'How about a cup of coffee? I'm trying a new brand. What you need is a blast of caffeine. I swear it's the only thing that keeps me going these days.' She stood up and went into the small adjoining room, which housed a kettle and an array of packets and jars in readiness for a break in the work routine.

'Where has all the magic gone, Daisy?' Hannah called. 'Those two are caught up in a material world now. They seemed so different. All that imagination and sense of wonderment. They were such lovely children.'

'But it's all still there.'

'I'm not so sure. Too many stimulants. These kids all getting their kicks from God knows what. I worry about Rachel's two. I did think after her marriage to Justin, they would steady down. They did for a bit but she's worrying herself sick over them again. They can't wait for the nightclub scene. Mind you, I'm worried about Rachel as well. She has taken on the role so seriously that she seems to be deadly earnest about life with no sense of fun. It's all Mother's Union and raffle prizes these days. Not that I have got anything against the church but we all need a laugh sometimes.'

Daisy nodded and sighed. She was feeling her age after a night of little sleep with only one night shift carer and several very poorly old ladies needing attention. She was not in the mood to enter into a long discussion on the whole of Hannah's family. Her friend was beginning to irritate her with her determination, it seemed, to find nothing good about the day not even apparently the coffee. They had both lapsed into silent contemplation as they sipped the hot coffee. Hannah dunked her ginger biscuit into the steaming liquid, and sighed as it disintegrated, until after a moment or two of fishing out the soggy remains she finally sat back and abandoned the whole business of the morning break.

'Well I don't want you to think that I am pushing you out, Hannah dear, but I am shockingly tired and have a hundred and one things vying for attention.' Daisy stood up, scraping her chair and jolting her friend's attention away from family concerns.

'You ought to delegate. I'm sure this place could manage without you more than it does.'

'It probably could but I like to be at the helm.' She nearly followed it with a comment about it keeping her young, but changed her mind, not wanting to encourage Hannah's train of thought back in that direction.

Hannah stood up, reaching for her bag. 'Is it OK if I have a quick word with Emma? I've got some mags she needed for some project Poppy's doing. I don't suppose she has mentioned Alice and Leigh.'

'Oh no. Not to me. I had no idea.' Daisy knocked the vase of dried flowers over and cursed inwardly.

She heard Hannah complaining to Emma about family secrets and strained to hear Emma's reply, catching '…it's their business, Mum' and 'Don't get so upset…' She could visualise the hug as Emma's voice became muffled, and then the closing of the door. Minutes later she watched through her office window as her friend accelerated away down the nursing home drive towards the lane leading on to the busy Lincoln road.

❄

Hannah was regretting her outburst. She had a feeling that Daisy had been in on the secret and she had given her the satisfaction of feeling superior. Immediately, she pushed those thoughts from her head. Daisy was such an old friend, helping her through years of loneliness after Jack's tragic death, and she had solved Emma's problems, giving her a job at the nursing home and accommodation in one of the small units at the rear of Daisy Cottage. She reproached herself for her insensitive comments about expecting more than secretarial work for her daughter.

'Why can't I be happy for them all?' She spoke out loud, a habit she had acquired in recent months and had at first rebuked herself for, but which now she did quite regularly with no compunction. What did she want instead? Just to be treading water? The status quo until she died? That was wrong, she knew, but somehow she was tired of moving on, yet feeling guilty if she did not keep up. Why could she not accept that she had had her life and be content to stand still; to retire into the background? She did not want to compete, did not want to interfere or take over. 'So what do I want for goodness sake?!' she exclaimed, suddenly braking to avoid a pheasant that made a dash across the road in front of her. She wanted to be included, but also to be left alone – wanted not to feel guilty at wanting to be left alone but yet feeling offended at being left out of things. They could not win could they, this family of hers? Why did life have to be so complicated? But then hers and Jack's married life had been just as complicated. The difference was they had no elders telling them what to do.

It seemed like going back into another lifetime, she mused; in fact someone else's lifetime. Jack was estranged from his biological parents after evacuation and both of his foster parents had died. Her mother and grandparents had been victims of a German land mine and her only known relative, her mother's sister, had started a new life in Australia. The nearest she had to a relative, as a young adult, was a lady who was the housekeeper in her evacuation days at Willow Cottage. Dear Auntie Ella. She never interfered, although in her old age she did cause concern as her dementia increased. That was all to the good as it happened, Hannah thought. Another joining up of dots, leading her to Daisy Cottage Nursing Home, and to her friendship with Daisy Buckerfield. The idea of continuation was reassuring and her thoughts allowed her memory to wander back into those days before her marriage, when she was a young schoolteacher, shy and naïve, and in love with a married man. It had been a time to move on, and life had obligingly provided her with new dots to join together in the shape of her old school friend Sally Blenkin. After a weekend spent in each other's company, Sally had persuaded her to confront her unhappy past in her early years as an evacuee, and she later returned to the village of Cragthorpe where she discovered that Jack Clayton had inherited his foster parents' business as the village shopkeeper.

Jack had often resurfaced in her thoughts as she grew up, but the disturbing memories of that early billeting had suppressed any desire to return to that locality. She recalled how she had dreaded an encounter with Elsie Porter, her first wartime foster mother. Poor Elsie had become deranged after that dreadful episode with her husband Tom. Hannah shuddered with the memory of his presence in her bed. Her mind still veered away from it after all these years, although later discoveries did allow her to forgive Elsie's cruelty. As it happened such an encounter was never to take place. During the first minutes of that reunion with Jack, he had announced that Elsie had taken an overdose with fatal consequences. Her feelings of relief had been followed by ones of sadness as he had continued with news of Mrs Knight's funeral. Dear old, strange old Mrs Knight, Hannah thought, her hands tightening on the steering wheel. People would think she was crazy to put so much importance on a white pot cat with big yellow eyes. She could picture it now sitting on the windowsill in the old lady's cottage. Mrs Knight had explained that it was a link with the spirit world and would bring special dreams to those who believed in it. She knew that Alice and Leigh had always been tuned in so to speak. They had been part of the story; part of what she called 'the big picture'. Of course, Jack believed in the magic of dreams and in his early years had been influenced by the mysticism that led back to those childhood evacuee days. But, in latter years, before his tragic death from cancer, he had become impatient with what he described as her 'being away with the fairies' beliefs. Emma, her younger daughter, was more given to flights of fancy, and quite prepared to investigate the paranormal, but ultimately it all returned to her grandchildren, Leigh and Alice.

She slowed down automatically as she approached the zigzag twists in the road, not requiring to be made aware of the hazard but nevertheless noting that the road sign appeared to have been hit by a previous vehicle. She clicked her tongue in disapproval, back with her earlier thoughts of the irresponsible behaviour of young people. Why couldn't Leigh and Alice have kept their relationship at a spiritual level? Although they were not blood cousins, they had grown up like brother and sister. Now Alice had joined the ranks of teenage pregnant single girls and no amount of soul-searching or spiritual enlightenment was going to negate that. An abortion was out of the question. The sanctity of life had always been upheld in their family. Besides, Marie, Alice's adoptive mother, was a practising Catholic and such measures were forbidden. Poor Marie. She had never even had to consider termination and a flouting of the church rules. After three miscarriages pregnancy was highly unlikely, and, in any case, as an almost certain health risk ,would not to be welcomed. How ever do she and Simon keep their relationship together, Hannah mused, with the threat of complications hanging over them, and Marie's continued dismissal of methods of birth control?

A flashing light on the dashboard brought her thoughts back in to the present. 'Damn,' she muttered, for the petrol gauge was on red. It meant making a detour to a filling station in Lincoln. She dare not risk leaving it until a later time with no facilities close by. As she headed into the outskirts of Lincoln she left her remonstrations and memories behind, focusing on increasing traffic and adhering to the thirty-mile-an-hour speed limit. After the freedom of driving on the comparatively empty Lincolnshire country roads, it was so easy to break the law. She topped up her tank, and, sighing with relief, headed out of the traffic and back in the direction of the village of Norbrooke.

However, her thoughts soon returned to family matters and on a sudden impulse she wrenched the steering wheel hard over at the entrance to a narrow lane, the tyres skidding and wailing as if in protest at this sudden turn of events. The lane was potholed, and little more than a so-called green lane. It was maintained by the local farmer, and was used on the occasions when he moved his sheep closer to the farmyard or needed to reach arable fields out of reach of the public highway. It petered out just beyond a small wood and consequently was not used by local ramblers who preferred a well-linked route in their weekly schedule.

Hannah was familiar with the rough surface and the sharp twists and turns, and drove slowly, avoiding the deep potholes made more apparent by the sunlight reflecting on their watery contents; evidence of a recent shower. Here and there it was necessary to pull on to the grass verge to avoid groups of holes which threatened to cause damage to her car suspension, but then a new hazard presented itself in the form of displaced stones, once part of the crumbling neglected field wall and almost hidden in the long grasses.

She sighed. This was not a good idea, she thought. The road surface had seriously deteriorated since the last time she had ventured along it and turning around could prove to be difficult. However, the thought of the pleasure she always experienced as she walked amongst the trees in the little wood gave her the determination to continue, and she remembered that the road widened sufficiently to point her car back in the direction of home after the next bend.

The sight of the little wood always excited her, and almost took her by surprise as it had done on her first visit. Then, she had likened it to a kind of Brigadoon, that magical place in the musical fantasy that materialised for one day and then vanished for a hundred years. Now she focused her awareness on that apparent new sighting, gripping the steering wheel and leaning forward in her seat.

There it was, in its summer array. Little more than a spinney, yet encompassing so much life within its boundaries. Snowdrops and aconites followed by primroses and blue bells were a prelude to the vigorous growth of summer, before the harsh winds of winter laid bare the branches, revealing new patterns and textures to delight the senses.

Evidence of some tree felling drew her attention to an area cleared of vegetation and for a moment she caught her breath, releasing it slowly in a long sigh. What if it had gone? The beautiful black poplar she had claimed as her tree. From the first moment she had seen it, she had marvelled at its strength and beauty not knowing what it was until she later identified it in her tree book back at Willow Cottage. Apparently, the Romans planted the Black Poplars in civic squares where each one could spread out its branches in vigorous growth and provide shelter in the resulting shade. Belonging to the aspen family of trees, the leaves quivered and rustled in the slightest breeze and Hannah had christened it The Whispering Tree. She lowered the window, breathing in the woodland smells and brought the car to a halt.

The little pathway through the wood was now well-trodden, its space no longer threatened by invading brambles which had snagged at her socks on previous visits. Further evidence of clearance was apparent in the piles of dead vegetation on either side, and her anxiety increased. But then there it was – her tree. It stood on its own in the small clearing that she had labelled 'The Happy Glade' in memory of a favourite childhood book.

She breathed in deeply and walked over to it. She had a sudden urge to make contact, spreading her arms around its trunk and pressing her face into the bark. The physical pressure of her body against the tree, the awareness of the texture of the bark under her fingers, and her quickening pulse, produced in her a surge of emotion and a physical longing to be with Jack; just to hold his hands. She had the love of her family, the hugs and kisses, but only Jack could hold her hands and give her such a feeling of security and belonging and living. She closed her eyes, reaching her fingers around the trunk and exploring the surface. She felt that the tree knew her loneliness and she stayed in its embrace, two life forms merging into total absorption. She was now aware of being part of the whole with no separation, and a feeling that it could last forever; the passage of time of no consequence in this act of unity. However, the material world became manifest again, dictating its rules of survival as her limbs began to stiffen with fatigue. Now, with her eyes open, she studied the bark, allowing her gaze to travel up into the branches where the leaves rustled in the sudden breeze. 'It's our secret,' she said. 'Don't whisper it to the world.'

She walked back to the car and sank down into the driving seat, shivering as an icy chill travelled up her spine, and knowing that she must ground herself. She took some deep breaths and wriggled her toes before switching on the ignition, going into reverse gear and pointing the car back along the twisty lane. Yet the image of the tree remained in her mind, and now in the clear light of her day-to-day life, she began to feel a little foolish.

Did she really want a companion? Tree hugging was a poor substitute. She recalled Emma's story, entitled 'I Remember Mama', inspired by a lovely old black and white film. Obviously, she had based it on her mother's life with some flights of fancy, particularly in the last chapter when a man appears on the horizon, and they all live happily ever after.

'But is that what I want?' Hannah asked the dashboard. 'Look at Daisy and that historian Maurice Mackinson.

She was reminded of Emma's description of them in a kind of 'new speak' she called it, with Orwell in mind. Emma had remarked that Daisy and Maurice were an item. When did item come into the frame? Why not a couple? Why couldn't they stay in the plural? An item indicated single status. Fastened at the hip. The words came into her head, reminding her of past discontentment, and she visualised the time when she and Jack had quarrelled, hearing herself declaring that they were not fastened at the hip. She had wanted to escape; have the freedom to follow her own interests and become the Hannah she once was. She now knew that was impossible. There was no turning back time. It was still valid to put away each 'she' like a Russian doll, one inside another inside another. So was this the final 'she'? And should she be prepared to become an item like Daisy?

She sighed and braked, leaving the narrow track behind, her mind now focused on the drive home. She noticed how green the fields were with grasses grown long and lush after the recent heavy showers. She always marvelled at the proliferation of nature at this time of the year, never tiring of the glowing colours and the abundance of energy around her. However, such a surge of joyous appreciation was marred by the sight of the sign that announced the entrance to Willow Cottage Garden Centre and displayed its hours of opening. Now, gripped again with a flagging of her spirits, she noticed how shabby and neglected it looked and the grass, so attractive in its lushness in the fields, presenting an unkempt look, offputting to potential customers. Jack would have spruced it up, she thought. Her dear Jack for all his shortcomings was a stickler for first impressions. Simon was a lot like him in looks, more so as he got older, with his brown hair and green eyes, and he had a great rapport with nature, but these were different times. He spent long hours doing weekly orders, filing invoices and organising delivery schedules. Demand for plants had become so great that the traditional home growing from sowing seeds to pricking out and potting on had long since been replaced with a weekly supply being obtained ready grown and for instant sale from one of the large nurseries in the county. Hannah sighed as she glanced across towards the greenhouses, remembering how she and Jack had spent hours in the humid warmth with the smells of damp compost and the satisfaction of encouraging a strong future existence for each tiny seedling. The tangy smell of tomatoes followed and then the heavy perfume of the chrysanthemums in the autumn, linked with the spate of winter funerals and Jack's ability to provide wreaths.

Now, more profit seemed to be made from the vast array of gardeners' aids including fertilisers and pesticides together with a large selection of tools and fancy goods. They were housed in a covered area in the adjoining field – the sunken field as it was known, and a reminder of a brick-making business in the last century when clay was dug out. It was now part of Simon's plans to expand the business after his father's death. Hannah pressed her lips together as she remembered the arguments she had had over the sale of pesticides. But in the end she had given up, still not convinced of the benign efficacy the labels assured, but too tired to argue. In any case it was not totally her business anymore, and she loved her son too much to cause discord.

She left her car in the drive, her feet crunching through the gravel, and entered the house by the side door that opened up into a room known as the front kitchen. In days gone by it was described as the servants' hall, and Hannah's bedroom was originally a servant's bedroom. The access to this small bedroom was through the stairs door and up a winding staircase. When Hannah was a child in her days as an evacuee, it had been Auntie Ella's room, and always smelt of her cooking, a favourite being her scones. Hannah maintained that the scones were like ghosts haunting the kitchen stairs, and the family had once had a debate as to whether it was possible to evoke an actual smell, or was it based on new recognition each time?

She struggled up the narrow staircase and sank down on to her bed taking in a few deep breaths before she leant forward to rub her legs, easing her feet out of the rather elegant shoes she kept for best. They were comfortable for driving and for sitting for a while, but after a couple of hours her toes had had enough of the constraints and made it quite clear that they needed to escape into her so called 'granny slippers'. She caught sight of her reflection in the mirror and her longing for the past returned. So many 'Hannahs' she thought. Each one locked up in memories; so many memories and no one to share them with. Loving and giving, that seemed to be the order of the day. She had done plenty of that, but what about taking? She wanted to cry and closed her eyes squeezing back the tears. 'What the hell's the matter with you?' she whispered, peering at her reflection. She wanted to be young and fertile again. That was it! The sudden realisation solved everything. She envied Alice. It was as simple as that. Underneath all the criticism was an overwhelming sense of bereavement. She was remembering now how she mourned the menopause. She would not have welcomed another pregnancy, but as the menstrual cycles had finally come to an end, she recalled her sadness at the choice being taken away. The grandchildren had eased those feelings to a certain degree, but it wasn't about children, she thought. It wasn't even about the sexual act. But it was about her body, her needs, and her emotions. Just to be special. But then she had had all of that. It was time to move on; to leave the physical and explore those unmapped areas of her mind. After all, she mused, Mother Nature had set the deadlines for a reason.

She remembered pointing out to Alice one day after the young woman's flippant remark about old age, that she would be a grandmother herself one day, and Alice had replied that she had no intentions of being a grandmother. She would have to be a mother first she had declared, and that was the last thing she wanted to be.

'Famous last words,' Hannah muttered, wriggling her toes into the fleecy linings of her slippers. Well, she decided, her self-pity now shifting to a wry kind of spitefulness, as old Auntie Ella would have said, all the chickens come home to roost, and if it came to that she did not want to be a great-grandmother just yet either! She had far too much to do than to sit back and be the matriarch.

The weeks and months that followed were punctuated by the so-called high days and holidays with plenty of low days thrown in. As usual, Christmas was a great distraction for winter blues and this year the annual planning included the listing of infant requirements, although Hannah's wartime philosophy of make do and mend had encouraged many items from previous childhoods to be packed away for future use. No one offered to buy anything major at this stage however. This was considered to be tempting fate and Hannah recounted the story of how her first pram was kept at the shop until after the birth, a custom accepted by parents-in-waiting and shopkeepers alike.

Alice was becoming increasingly moody, flopping her length on the settee and flicking through the television channels or wandering about and sighing, her face seemingly rarely moving from its disconsolate state. She hated being pregnant, she told her mother when Marie chided her for her lack of civility.

'It's worse than having a young teenager in the house,' Marie complained to her husband Simon.

Indeed it would seem so. Alice's light-hearted disposition was replaced with the moody sulks one would associate with a fifteen-year-old girl in the throes of hormonal turmoil. She slammed doors after heated arguments with anyone who fell foul of her fits of misery and spent hours in the bathroom and bedroom using all the hot water, and trying on clothes which did not fit, thus adding to her list of grievances. It did not help for her grandmother to remark that the first one was easy and how would she get on if she had two or three more trailing at her ankles.

'The length of time she spends in the bath is unbelievable,' Hannah told Sally during her weekly telephone call with her friend. 'It's almost as though she is trying to escape from the skin she is in. All she wants is to go to university with no attachments. Not even to Leigh it seems. As for him, he is so obsessed with his school work that they just seem to be miles apart already.'

Sally grunted and muttered something about it all coming out in the wash, changing the subject to her plans for a Spring holiday somewhere in the sun. Hannah was not listening and soon said her goodbyes and made her way to the kitchen and the business of preparing an evening meal. The weariness of life seemed to be on re-play. She had been here before, and had got the scars to prove it!

2

All the Chickens (come home to roost)

Alice stared at the window, aware of the dark clouds moving across in front of the sun and creating shadows on the cream painted walls of the small hospital room. She had been left alone to monitor her labour pains, with instructions to press the buzzer if she noticed any sudden changes. She sighed and unclenched her fingers. The buzzer had left a deep line etched into her hand, and had caused the only sensation of pain during the last ten minutes.

She was also aware of her heart pounding in her chest. It seemed separate from the rest of her body, dominating and demanding. What was her baby hearing? Her thoughts wandered to the CD of so called womb music, which apparently soothed new babies, the sounds relaxing them into a kind of foetal state of mind. Worlds within worlds, she mused.

'You're here rather early, dear,' the nurse had commented. 'Don't worry though. Just relax and try and grab some sleep. You'll be glad of it later. Remember, I'm not far away. They are all different, these little ones.'

Alice nodded. Her son was going to be very different. She turned on her side and closed her eyes, her mind wandering away from herself. Leigh had promised to drop everything and come. Easier said than done, she thought. His school exams were paramount, and in any case she knew that she could not rely on him for any practical help. He put his faith in a power that seemed to give him all the answers he needed, and although Alice went along with most of his beliefs, she still preferred to keep her feet on the ground when it came to very earthly matters. Having a baby is as basic as it gets, she thought to herself, already caught up in feminine reasoning, with the first signs of bitterness for the situation in which she now found herself.

A sudden pain jolted her thoughts back to the present, and she squeezed her fingers into the alarm, listening as the bell sounded along the corridor. She had not noticed the layout of the place when she came in. She was too involved with her condition and her fear of the unknown. She had assumed that the earlier discomfort meant that she was in labour and that it would soon all be over. But this last pain was the beginnings of reality. She knew that, and felt desperately alone, longing for the touch of Leigh's hand or the reassurances of her mother. But then her mother knew nothing of childbirth, she thought, because she was not really a mother, not in the biological sense, and at a time like this that was a crucial ingredient to understanding all the complications of giving birth. She knew from past conversations that Marie had suffered much of the pain of early labour during those unhappy times before the inevitable miscarriage but with the arrogance of youth she dismissed such 'ancient' history, as if the older generation couldn't possibly understand anything of the world in which she lived. Even her grandmother was of no help. 'You just forget,' she explained once when Alice broached the subject. She spoke of the old days when it was a taboo subject and of how she was told that it was like being constipated, which statement fuelled her grand-daughter's youthful arrogant thoughts, but then confounded it by adding laughingly, 'A bit more than that of course but it is only a day in your life. The rest of it is a lifetime of commitment.' Alice remembered how a shadow seemed to pass over the features of her elderly relative and she was reminded of the loss sustained by Hannah of her son Mark and her husband Jack.

Another pain dragged down into her groin, and she writhed, drawing up her knees in an attempt to extricate herself from it, at the same time releasing her breath into a long moaning sound which seemed strangely remote from her reality. She clutched at the pillow, hugging it against her.

'Come on, dear. Try to relax.' The brusque tones of the midwife coincided with a release from the pain. 'You're getting there, dear. Just take deep breaths and try to put yourself beyond it. Do you know what I mean?'

Alice nodded. Together with Leigh, she often practised relaxation, 'watching' the breath entering and leaving the lungs, and visualising spiritual energy moving into every cell of the body. She always experienced great comfort from these exercises, feeling somewhat self-righteous when she compared herself with those who she considered to be on a lower level of understanding. Now she tried to moderate her breathing, fear producing bursts of adrenalin tightening the muscles under her ribs.

A doctor arrived with the midwife and they talked out of earshot for a brief time before the man left and the midwife turned her attention back to the frightened girl in her care.

'Am I all right? Why was he here?' Alice's voice came out in almost a whisper.

'Don't worry, dear. We may have to give you a bit of help. Nothing to worry about. It happens sometimes. Perhaps a lazy baby or contractions not strong enough yet. Try to relax and I'll pop in again soon.'

Marie Clayton, Alice's adoptive mother, sat in the waiting area watching the comings and goings of the hospital staff. She had mixed feelings about her role in all of this. Her daughter had made it quite clear that she could manage on her own. Since the time that Alice had met her biological mother Molly Petch, Marie's relationship with her adopted daughter had altered and, as she described it to her husband Simon, it was like treading on egg shells most of the time. She had not welcomed the news of this pregnancy, not only because Alice had only just completed her school course and intended to follow on with a degree in English and further teacher training, but her relationship with her cousin Leigh was, in Marie's opinion, incestuous. They had grown up like brother and sister. She'd once voiced her disapproval to Simon and he had dismissed it with a reminder that they were not really cousins, but the uneasiness persisted and now as she stared unseeingly across to the nurses' station she gave a deep sigh.

'Is it your daughter, duck?' The voice came from a large lady who was occupying a chair on the other side of the room. She had tried to make contact several times with a nod and a clearing of her throat as though she was about to speak.

Marie nodded, and that was sufficient encouragement for the woman to burst into further conversation.

'Takes you back doesn't it ducky? I remember my first. I was terrified. My mother told me it was like having a bad period! Can you imagine? Still, it's hard to remember really. Is it your first grandchild? Is she your eldest?'

Marie nodded, leaving the woman not sure of her answers. Yet her reticence did not discourage further questions.

'Do you know what she's having? I can't get my head around how they all want to know what they are having. I've already got three grandchildren, two girls and a boy and this one's another boy they tell me, so you can see I've got my hands full, especially as this is my daughter's baby and she is still living at home. It's not the same with somebody else's daughter is it? You know what I mean?'

Marie nodded again. She wanted to explain that she herself had no recollections of giving birth and that Alice was her adopted daughter. She had a spiteful desire to enlighten this woman, imagining her discomfiture. Announcing that Alice was her adopted daughter was a kind of trump card that she could play when she was depressed and craving for sympathy. She had done it recently, she remembered, shuffling uneasily on the hard seat, her face flushing in recall. The words had burst out when the nurse asked her about family support. 'A daughter,' she had replied, 'But she's adopted.' The nurse had hurried on disregarding what she perhaps read as self-pity, reassuring her that Alice was still her daughter and explaining that many breast lumps were benign and it may well be a harmless cyst. Marie smoothed her hand over her right breast seeking out the now familiar irregularity close to the nipple, and sighed. That was on another agenda, and an issue that she was keeping a secret until her next communication with the hospital.

The woman was still chattering away. Having exhausted memories of her first labour, she had launched herself into the emergencies of the third one. 'What a curfuffle,' she was saying. 'I had a home birth that time. You know they reckoned it was a good idea but I said to our Marlene, you get into the hospital ducky, even if it is a long trek. Do you live far away? I don't know how some folks manage without transport.'

Marie nodded again, which seemed to satisfy the woman.

Alice moaned, as the contractions began in earnest. She was caught up in that huge wave of self-awareness which lifts one beyond the ordinary into a surreal kind of place; a dream-like state. During the months of waiting she had maintained that nature intended women to experience every facet of labour, but as the contractions strengthened and her baby began its journey down the birth canal, she was grateful for the gas and air like a drowning person reaching for a life raft. She clung hold of the nurse's hand, longing for her mother Marie and obeying instructions to push and pant, knowing that all this would pass, yet seeming to be caught up in it forever.

The series of events that followed during the next hour would never be in her recall. Her unconscious state induced by medication ,and her own inability to cope with the great difficulties that had suddenly manifested, was to become a vital component in her indifference.

She regained consciousness in unfamiliar surroundings, unable to equate with the reason for her being there. The so-called amnesia after childbirth was premature. She tried to sit up, becoming aware of the tube connected to a plastic container and dripping blood into her body.

She turned her head and saw her mother Marie standing at the end of the ward. She appeared to be in deep conversation with the ward sister. They both looked towards the young woman and stopped talking for a moment before turning their backs in what Alice considered to be a rather secretive way, as though it was nothing to do with her.

✳

Marie followed behind the ward sister who seemed to do everything at twice the speed of normal. Her earlier words had almost tumbled out and Marie had found herself watching the nurse's lips without comprehension. She tried to recall those words now. Something was not right. The baby had been transferred immediately into intensive care not only because of the difficult birth, but – what did she say? – Congenital abnormalities. What did that mean?

'Mask and gown dear. Can you put them on and the gloves?'

She looked down at the tiny form and a sob choked in her throat. She was later to describe her as 'a poor little lop-sided creature'. But now she was speechless, only staring and shaking her head in disbelief. Questions sprang into her mind but were left unspoken. Why had this happened? Why had it been left undetected with all the modern methods of screening? Why was this union cursed? She knew the answer to that, her brain reminded her; an unnatural relationship and witchcraft. In the olden days this child would have been smothered at birth.

'They can do wonders with plastic surgery now dear.' The nurse patted Marie on the shoulder. 'She's a strange little thing but what a fighter!'

Marie shrugged and turned away. 'Does Alice know?' she asked.

'No. She was too poorly. In my opinion it should have been a section but when a baby turns last minute like that so to speak, it is hard to make a decision.'

'So why was this child injured so horribly? Surely somebody could have made a better job of it. Who was responsible? I want the name of the doctor.'

'No no! You've got the wrong end of the stick, Mrs Clayton. This is congenital not birth induced. It isn't always easy to monitor a baby. It does depend on the position in the womb. All seemed to be well – organ functions and digestive tract. She has a very strong pulse.

Come on dear. I think you need a cup of tea. You can sit quietly for a while in the visitors' room.'

Alice strained to hear the sound of her mother's footsteps retreating along the corridor. Then in sudden recall, she put her hand down to her stomach. Somehow it felt different yet it was still swollen. It must still be there, she thought. Surely I would be almost as flat as a pancake now. She winced with pain suddenly aware of the damage and the repairs as her flesh pulled against the stitches. She was remembering now; the terrible struggle to give birth; the pummelling of the stomach; the agonising pain of it all, and how in the midst of unconsciousness she had found herself hovering above her body in what she would later describe to Leigh as a near death experience.

The young nursing assistant had hurried over to give reassurances and begin a series of checks on her patient's condition. 'You'll feel better soon,' she whispered. 'You've had a bit of a tough time, but you'll feel a lot better after you've had the blood transfusion. Just lie still. The buzzer's here if you need me.'

The feel of the buzzer in her hand took Alice's thoughts back to the beginnings of her labour. Where was her baby? Why wasn't he here with her? She looked down the ward again. Her mother and the ward sister had not returned to the 'station'. She relaxed her head back into the pillow, and sighed. Did she care about the baby, she asked herself. Did she care whether it was dead or alive? Did she care whether it was hers and Leigh's son or was it a girl, not a part of their visualisation?

Hannah stared down at the tiny form in the cot. Leigh had drawn in his breath and she waited for him to react in some way. However, he did not speak, but allowed his breath to become a sigh as he released it from his body. They watched in continued silence as the little girl puckered up her face seemingly in protest, and Hannah had the overwhelming feeling that this tiny misshapen creature already sensed that she was facing a cruel and unfeeling world.

3

Family Ties Unravelling

Alice announced that her daughter was to be called Elphine. She had read it in a book and had earmarked it for a girl's name; the only one at the end of a list of boys' names. Leigh agreed to anything.

'I'll leave it to Alice,' he said.

Hannah recognised the indifference. It was as apparent as if he had said that after all it was her baby. His studying was paramount, and with all the family around him any sense of responsibility towards the child appeared to be nil.

Marie did not like her daughter's choice of name. She considered that it sounded like a character in a fairy story, and when Leigh abbreviated it to Elphie her disapproval increased. She would like to have given her a saint's name, feeling that the child, already disadvantaged by her deformities, needed protection. She wanted her granddaughter to be christened in the Catholic faith, and raised up with an awareness of the teachings of the church. She had allowed the family to influence her in Alice's case because of the inconvenience of travelling to a Catholic-funded school, and for the fact that the state of her own health and both of their working schedules had made it difficult for her to attend church on a regular basis. Now she felt that she was being punished; a kind of a divine visitation upon the next generation. Ultimately, she blamed her mother-in-law with her involvement in what Marie called 'the occult'.

All this visiting of fortune-tellers, and then there was that session with that board thing, she thought, as she sat at the kitchen table preparing the vegetables for a beef casserole. Alice and Leigh had borrowed it from a friend a few months ago, and decided to test it out up in their bedroom. To be fair, Hannah did not know about it, but it had been her influence in the past with all the rubbish about the Mooncat that had encouraged them, she reasoned. What was it called? Her mouth formed around the sounds. 'Wee jar.' It did not make any sense to her. All she knew was that it was supposed to connect with people who had passed over into the spirit world. Apparently messages were spelt out on the board by the glass moving to individual letters. She had not witnessed it but she knew that Leigh and Alice had returned the board the next day and had refused to comment on the outcome of their attempts to probe into the unknown.

Now, in retrospect, Marie began to link all of the problems of the last months to that incident. Alice had changed from a confident young woman into a complaining sulky teenager. Hannah had blamed her state of pregnancy and her frustration at putting her education on hold, but Marie sensed a more sinister explanation, and when the baby was born with crooked limbs and irregular facial features she declared it to be the work of the devil. She decided that all of her prayers were needed, and she made no objection to responding to Elphine's cries at any time of the day and night, moving the carry cot from room to room as she did the daily chores.

No one else made any objections to this arrangement. Alice appeared indifferent to the needs of her child, and was in the habit of staying in bed late and wandering around in her dressing gown until midday. Leigh was in the throes of A levels, and Hannah was intent on him gaining good grades. Underneath all of these day-to-day issues it seemed to be of a common yet unspoken census that Marie as the grandmother should step in at this difficult time and build some bridges, so to speak.

Marie was still having difficulties with relationships. The idea that the relationship between her daughter and Leigh was incestuous would not go away, and the fact that she herself was not a mother in reality nagged into the deepest corners of her mind, reminding her of her parents' fulfilment and dedication to their faith and her own apparent failure. Now, this strange little misshapen child was not really her granddaughter. She had confessed to Hannah one day in a rare moment of shared reflections on life, that she felt like an intruder in the family. Hannah had tried to reassure her, maintaining that blood did not matter, but she knew that it did, and knew that it really mattered to Alice. It was accepted that her daughter wanted a son who would carry on the Clayton name and give a kind of respectability to the family line. A daughter reminded her of her biological mother Molly Petch and the 'father unknown'. Marie knew that Alice valued hers and Leigh's mutual grandmother. Hannah's rank was now great-grandmother for real, Marie thought, her mouth twisting into a hard line of jealousy.

Elphine began to cry; a strange mewing sound that seemed to come out sideways, Alice had commented, when it was first noticed.

'Don't say such horrid things,' Marie had remonstrated, turning to Hannah for support.

However Hannah was nodding in agreement and Leigh was remembering the times when he visualised sound as making strange shapes and angles, and words appearing like pictures in his mind. He had not thought about it for a long time, but he knew that this powerful gift of visualisation helped him to retain knowledge of the written word; a big advantage when it came to memorising the language of chemistry and physics.

Marie looked at the clock. It was a gentle reminder that a bottle was due. Alice had declared from day two that she was not breast feeding her child. The initial pain that she said made her toes curl was not going to continue when there was an alternative, and in any case she wanted her slim figure back as soon as possible. Marie sighed as she made up the feed, remembering her daughter's protests and her own feelings of inadequacy. How she had longed for a child at her breast; the sustaining of life; the sharing and the dependency. Alice was three years old when they had adopted her and although Marie was a devoted mother she often felt cheated. There were no stories of the trials of a pregnancy to share, no glorying in the triumph of conquering pain, no early photographs of mother and child and no use for her breasts other than as an indication of her sexuality. The recent scare that had put her on a yearly check-up register for breast health issues had only encouraged her to dismiss further her role as a woman, and now all sexual advances in the bedroom were taboo.

She watched as her granddaughter sucked hungrily on the teat, the fontanel throbbing, causing her fine reddish blond hair to rise and fall. She no longer needed to agonise over her irregular features. She was as she was; a little crooked girl. It would not be possible to level the eyes or straighten the curvature of the spine. That had been made clear by the paediatrician after her birth, although future problems with walking may necessitate calliper splints, he had said. Marie sighed, and the sudden rise and fall of her chest prompted the child to stop sucking and open her eyes. The recognition was there in those bright blue eyes. A sob caught at Marie's throat, and she fought against the urge to crush the child to her chest.

It was a powerful love affair; unconditional love was how she described it to herself, comparing it with her feelings for Simon. Recently, she had moved into the small bedroom 'to be with Elphine', she had explained. It would allow Alice and Leigh to get a good night's sleep and Simon's snoring was keeping her awake.

Initially, it had saddened her that Alice seemed to have abrogated all responsibility for her child. It seemed that her daughter was intent on entering university at the end of the summer, and was concentrating on restoring her figure to its previous shape ready to don the student uniform of jeans and a variety of tops. She had already secured a place at Newcastle, Leigh's preferred goal for medical training. Marie did not concern herself with his goals. She blamed him entirely for complicating her daughter's life, even though she was happy to facilitate their expectations by offering to bring up their child until they were free to accept responsibility. As far as she was concerned, he could take all of his problems to his grandmother.

Leigh stared at the sheet of paper in front of him, and mentally ticked off the headings. This was his final year at school, and everything depended on his exam results. He had achieved excellence in all of his course work and previous tests, but he knew that any failure would affect his choice of a university course in medicine and he could not bear to be parted from Alice. She would be starting her degree course in September and already he was anticipating a sense of loss.

He doodled with his pencil in the margin of the paper and sighed. Everything had changed since Alice became pregnant. Nobody seemed to laugh much these days, and Alice was so dismissive of the unhappiness of other people, especially of her parents. Having a baby seemed to have changed her from a caring, sensitive girl into – what? He could not describe it. The sparkle had left her eyes and she walked around as though she had all of the burdens of the world pressing down on her shoulders.

When had it all started? She had seemed to be happy and excited to be pregnant. It had been their delicious secret for a few weeks, but then as all the family involvement and organisation swung into action, they were both made aware of the ramifications. A sense of insecurity now clouded their joyous anticipation and they sought out reassurances from their spiritual experiences, discussing the significance of their dreams and of telepathy, pushing reality to the backs of their minds. It was as though they were playing a game, he thought; a big game of pretend as they had done as children.

Experimenting with the ouija board was very regrettable. A friend at school had offered to lend it to him and somehow it seemed to offer some answers for the future. Instead it brought back the past. He frowned at the memory of it; the crawling sensation that travelled up his spine; the trembling in his fingers as they pressed on the glass tumbler in the middle of the board. It had pointed to M, seconds after they had begun, and then S. They recorded these letters as his friend had advised, speculating as to whom they could refer. Could it be Marie and Simon? That would not make sense. They were supposed to be communicating with incarnate beings. They nervously returned their fingers to the glass.

'We do not understand M or S. Could you please give us some more letters.'

Leigh remembered how Alice's voice was hoarse with nervous tension, and how they almost lost contact with the glass as it zigzagged across the board. M.O.T.H.E.R. there was a pause, then S.A.R.A.H followed, the glass almost leaving the board in its apparent urgency to communicate.

'Is that your mother? She was Sarah, wasn't she?' Alice's voice was shaking.

Leigh's thoughts were back in the past when he was a little boy of seven years. He had suppressed that nightmare for years. The sound of her opening the knife drawer and her tread on the stairs. The screams coming from the bedroom where his father was in bed with her friend Julie. The footsteps on the stairs and the slamming of the front door. It had seemed to be someone else's nightmare during all the happy years of growing up in Willow Cottage. Suddenly, she had entered his world again; this woman whom he had loved so much but who seemed to hate him.

'Let's leave it,' Alice had said. 'We don't need this.'

He had agreed, leaving her to return the board to its box.

They had never mentioned it to each other again, but he felt that it was a turning point, and the love and compassion he had felt for his mother over the years in spite of everything was now replaced with the fear of her return into his life. He dare not attempt to communicate with his sister. Her death apparently had triggered his mother's breakdown. Lucy had made contact through his dreams when he first came to live here, but those childhood experiences had been replaced with worldly concerns, and his mind had focused on twentieth-century knowledge in the field of science.

Now they had this little daughter, so handicapped and such a bone of contention in this family of mixed relationships and beliefs.

He tried to return his concentration to his study plan, but his mind was on Alice and her dreams for the future that did not seem to include their child. He could not talk to Marie. She had made it quite clear that he had ruined her daughter's life, and Simon seemed to have abdicated from family life, concentrating on his role as breadwinner and dodging the accusations.

He could hear Elphine's screams resounding up the staircase. All he could feel was guilt.

'Post natal depression.' The doctor said the words in a flat unemotional voice. He was not their usual doctor. That gentleman was on holiday and a locum had been brought in. Marie recognised the bored indifference and a note of criticism; one which she shared for this irresponsible generation. He may just have well have said something like 'Serves you right, you silly little girl, and what do you think I am going to do about it?' She tried to block this impatience, knowing that Alice was very depressed. Whether it was hormonal or the result of frustration one could not say. She squeezed her daughter's hand and waited for the doctor to continue.

Alice made no response. She was not even making eye contact. Instead she freed herself from her mother's grasp, and pressing her hands on the top edge of the doctor's desk leant forward in readiness to stand.

There was silence except for a scratching of pen against paper.

'Come back in a month.'

They stood up. Marie said 'Thank you doctor.'

Alice said nothing.

Her state of depression seemed to Hannah to affect the whole household, and it was with a great sense of relief that the cold spring days gave way to the early summer when everyone could enjoy some sunshine and cast away those winter postnatal blues.

4

The Magic Mooncat

The seasons came and went, each one registering successes for the two students and the promise of ever-increasing business opportunities at the garden centre. The employment of more staff gave Marie the freedom to devote her time and energy to the raising of her granddaughter.

For Marie, time was measured now with an infant clock; the first sounds; the first real smile of recognition, rather than the flutter of facial muscles which Hannah pronounced as merely wind; the reaching out of the fingers; the bouncing and flexing of limbs. Each new accomplishment was a milestone in the tiny child's journey, and a treasured memory for Marie, before the heartache began.

Elphine, in spite of her handicaps, appeared to be healthy, with rosy cheeks and a good appetite. Her red hair had grown into curls, and she was constantly being told that she was very pretty. Only strangers stared at her lop-sided little face and noticed how she struggled to walk, lurching unevenly behind the baby walker. By the time she was three years old she was still not talking unless she did not want to do something which was expected of her: then her vehement cries of 'not dinner' 'not sleep' or just repeated 'no, no, no' were followed by high-pitched screams, stamping of the feet and flapping of the arms. This became a daily event, and Hannah with her keen interest in child development after her teaching days, already had suspected a level of autism. But then, as the months went by, Elphine began to communicate, surprising everybody with her sudden ability to create coherent sentences. A kind of echo speech had briefly preceded this when she repeated everything. However, it soon became apparent that the child was storing a vocabulary 'almost like making her own dictionary', Hannah remarked. As her language skills developed, the tantrums became less frequent. Yet Marie knew that her little granddaughter was very vulnerable and she was loath to let her out of her sight.

However, it was obvious to everybody that Alice and Leigh still regarded her as a sibling rather than their child. Indeed Alice did not cast a backward glance at her little daughter when she waved goodbye, and Elphine, in her turn did not shed a single tear. Alice's only concern, it seemed, was to qualify as an English teacher and then find employment in the Newcastle area in order to continue to share her life with Leigh. His degree course was five years in duration and as Alice was a year ahead of him, and her course was a year less, she would have two years to wait for him to qualify. No one voiced the opinion that this relationship would not last, but Marie's body language said it all; the little shrugs; the raised eyebrows; the meaningful glances at words of dissent.

Gradually everything fell into a routine disrupted only by regular visits made by Marie and the child to the hospital. Apparently there was some concern for the development of internal bodily functions, with pressure on the kidneys and bladder, and any plans for plastic surgery to improve her looks were quickly put on hold. The doctors were mixed in their opinions. Some warned of serious complications, whilst others were more optimistic. Nevertheless, no one could promise that the child would reach adulthood. The late development of communication skills was correlated with possible hearing problems, but Marie had always understood the sounds and gestures, thus strengthening her authority over the child. However, she was still frustrated. In spite of being given free rein in the general upbringing of her granddaughter, the religious controversy continued.

Alice did not want her child to be raised in the Catholic faith. She had made this plain right from the months before Elphine was born. Both she and Leigh had become pagan followers, believing in Mother Earth rather than the Holy Mother.

'It's like witchcraft,' Marie explained to Rachel. 'Here she is, nearly four years old and still not entered into the church. I worry that her life could end soon. The doctors are not very forthcoming about anything. You would think Hannah would say something and as for Simon..well!'

Rachel nodded in agreement. She had come on her monthly visit to see her mother, reminded by the letter M on her appointments calendar.

'Why don't you suggest that she is baptised at our church? It would keep it in the family and perhaps they would accept it as a kind of compromise.'

Marie stared at her sister-in-law. She could not believe that Rachel would stoop so low. What was she suggesting? That it did not matter – that her faith did not matter. She must know that the Catholic faith was the only one as far as she was concerned. Rachel had really changed since she married a Church of England clergyman. She had always been an ally in what, for Marie, had become a battle against the Clayton clan, and she respected her strongly held principles on the role religion played in life, but now here she was saying that she should compromise.

'I don't think that is a good idea,' she said coldly. 'They might just as well have Elphine baptised in the woods on May Day.'

Hannah came into the kitchen just in time to hear her last words and did not improve the situation by suggesting that it would be lovely if Rachel could organise something. 'It's just down her street,' she said. 'We might as well use our family vicar. Not many people can lay claim to one. And we shall soon have a doctor and a teacher!'

'I don't believe this! Don't include me in the cup of tea session. I have better things to do.' Marie stamped up the kitchen steps and slammed the door behind her.

'Oh dear! I obviously said the wrong thing there. But the health problems are paramount, don't you think? And I really can't see what difference it makes in the eyes of God.' Hannah sat down heavily on a kitchen chair, pressing her elbows on to the table.

'Well of course it makes a difference!' snapped her daughter. 'Our family is Protestant and always has been. Marie has joined this family and should accept our way of living. And I really think you ought to make it quite clear to Alice and Leigh that their pagan beliefs are equally unacceptable. You don't help, you know, Mother, with all this fortune-telling nonsense. Can't you be a normal grandmother?'

After Rachel had stayed for her hour-long 'appointment', as Hannah described it later to Daisy, the sun shone through the clouds, and a decision to get some fresh air into her lungs persuaded Hannah to walk along the back lane where the land rose above the village. Now, as she turned to look back at the little settlement, the silence only broken by the sound of a lorry engine on the main road, the feeling of separation from everyday life focused her mind on her blessings. Rachel meant well. At least now she had a purpose. Her first marriage had demoralised her, pushing her into a state of constant fear. But was it a good exchange? Perhaps she needed direction, not like Emma who was happy to organise her own life with her daughter Poppy.

What was an ordinary grandmother like? Was it like second childhood, to be seen and not heard? Should she sit in a corner and knit, and get to bed early to be out of the way? Suddenly, a dark cloud passed over the sun, and she shivered in the breath of a flurry of cold air. She had forgotten how the wind could be bitingly cold at this level.

One morning, a few weeks later, Marie was on her own with Elphine and enjoying the peace and quiet. Alice and Leigh were making the most of the last weeks of their summer holiday lounging in their bedclothes upstairs, and Hannah had taken a short break with her friend Sally Blenkin who ran a small publishing business in Hull. Simon had made an early start on organising the daily routine in the garden centre. It was still a busy time, although the initial rush of selling bedding-out plants was replaced with a steady trade in perennials and shrubs.

Elphine was sitting on her special chair with its attached table, scraping up the remnants of her cereal, whilst Marie was intent on clearing away the breakfast dishes in readiness for a walk down into the village. A gurgling sound drew her attention away from a patch of sticky marmalade on the tablecloth.

'Goodness! Are you choking, darling? I think you've had enough of that. Let Grandma put it in the sink.' The words came out in a gabbled nervous way. She had always been afraid of anyone choking after an episode once with Simon in a restaurant that had ended up with them going to the A and E department at the local hospital.

However, she breathed more easily as she saw that Elphine was laughing and waving towards the window. Was Simon out there, or one of the workers? She looked back at the child who was leaning sideways and pointing. Was it the wretched cat that had caught her eye, Marie wondered? There was no one else outside. She glared at the white pot cat sitting on the windowsill and, hoisting it by its neck, she repositioned it on top of the old chest of drawers, turning its big yellow eyes away from the sight of the child.

Elphine's attention had returned to the cereal bowl, putting her fingers into the remnants of her breakfast and then sucking them noisily.

'Dirty girl!' Marie exclaimed.

Elphine laughed, her face lighting up with mischief.

Marie turned away back to the task of washing up, jetting the hot water on to the liquid detergent in the bottom of the bowl. She sighed, allowing the frustration to return. Washing up was a boring chore made even more distasteful by the state of the old kitchen sink. As old as the ark, was how she described it to Simon. She longed for a modern kitchen with a stainless steel sink, a dishwasher and fitted units. She was tired of preparing food on the old scrubbed top table and storing an assortment of things in the even older chest of drawers. This was Hannah's idea of a kitchen not hers. Simon had promised to make some changes when they had taken over the business and part ownership of Willow Cottage after Jack had died, but apparently he had great plans for the business, and the house would have to wait. He'd grown up in it of course, so as far as he was concerned it was home. He had compromised with a new electric cooker to be used when the coal- fired range was not lighted. How visitors admired the range, describing it as charming and so quaint. 'Huh,' Marie grunted, with a sudden picture of choking smoke and blackened hands. They could have it with pleasure.

Suddenly Elphine gave a high-pitched squeal, and Marie turned to see her once more waving both hands in the direction of the pot cat as if trying to gain its attention and annoyed that she could not see its face. To a stranger this would not seem to be sinister in any way, but to Marie it represented the occult; devil worship she called it. She marched over to the chest of drawers and once more grasped the cat by its neck.

'You can go back in the cupboard,' she declared. 'It's my kitchen. If Hannah wants it she can keep it somewhere else, but for now it can stay behind closed doors!'

Elphine watched, her little face changing from joy to anguish. She began to scream, kicking her feet against the legs of the chair. Her sudden cry frightened Marie. It sounded to be so full of pain that she thought the child had jagged her throat with the handle of the spoon. Bending over to investigate, she felt a sharp stab as Elphine thrust the spoon into her face.

Marie snatched the spoon away and threw it across into the sink.

'That's naughty! You do not do that. That is so naughty! You really hurt Grandma!'

Elphine's head sank down and she pressed her chin into her chest, her shoulders drooping.

This sudden flash of anger was alien to both of them and Marie would look back and realise that it was a turning point in her granddaughter's awareness of her own powers.

Surprisingly, Simon noticed the disappearance of the cat on the kitchen windowsill when he drew the curtains across later that day. In spite of his apparent indifference to matters of the household he did notice changes and the absence of the familiar outline against the failing light immediately drew comment.

'Oh that,' Marie replied to his queries of the whereabouts of the ornament, 'I've put it in the cupboard. Elphine is constantly waving to it and it really bugs me.'

'Mum won't be happy about it when she comes home.'

'I thought this was our house. It's my kitchen, even if it is grotty. That cat is ugly anyway, and all that nonsense about it being magical!'

'Oh, you know what Mum's like. We all go along with it to please her. Even Dad used to, although I've seen him actually stroking it. He used to say that Mum was away with the fairies, but that is really what he loved about her. She has had so many setbacks, and we all just want things to work out now. We are very lucky, you know, not to have a huge mortgage.'

'It is four-way, don't forget, and we are the ones ploughing in the profits.'

Simon sighed. He knew that his two sisters with rightful shares in the property and business were decidedly sleeping partners in the arrangement.

'Well, Mum does her bit bless her, and surely we can allow her to regard this as her home, even though you have taken over from her. Please don't cause any upsets when she comes back from Sally's.'

Marie shrugged and set the table for supper. The child's sudden aggression had upset her more than she would admit. Now, with betrayal seemingly coming from all directions, her mind sought out memories of happier times when she did not feel so under-valued. It was easy to visualise the grandeur of the four-star hotel where she and Simon had spent a wonderful weekend. He had organised it as a surprise for her after the trauma of a third miscarriage. That was years ago, she thought, a sense of bitterness competing with the pleasure in the recall. Of course, adopting Alice and enjoying the act of motherhood was very fulfilling, but the recent years of giving up their holidays to help at the garden centre during Jack's illness and then moving in to Willow Cottage allowed no space or cash for fancy meals in restaurants, never mind four-star hotels.

Simon settled down to watch the television yet his mind was

wandering back to the long silences during their evening meal. Marie's attitude towards life had changed noticeably since the birth of Elphine. Admittedly, she had never really settled down to living at Willow Cottage. He loved every corner of it and as the manager of the garden centre his attitude was all embracing. His mother had always been part of the scene. In fact, he mused, it would not be Willow Cottage without her.

Although he had promised Marie that the kitchen and bathrooms would be updated as soon as they had settled their previous affairs and set a budget for business expenses, he was loath to alter a stick or stone of the place. In fact he loved the old-fashioned shabbiness of it. The old house did not mind the cracks and the peeling paintwork. In its long history there had been many attempts to rejuvenate it and these in their turn added to the character of the place like the patina on an antique. A modern kitchen, in his opinion, would be like an open sore and taking away the tongue and groove wainscoting from the downstairs bathroom would not only risk opening a kind of Pandora's box but would create a space with little or no charm.

He sighed and tried to return his attention to the crime drama on the television, but he had missed a vital part of the plot and the sudden cries of Elphine brought his attention back to family matters. What a mixed blessing it was to be grandparents. His concern for his wife was now replaced with feelings of irritation. Alice had no business to offload her responsibilities onto her mother, even though Marie seemed to welcome them. They were only kids themselves, he thought, but the modern world seemed to be programmed for young people. If they wanted something they had to have it. There was an unreasonable urgency about their lives as though they did not have enough time to wait. Everything had to be experienced now. He thought of his own youth when sex seemed to be a great mystery and it took huge amounts of courage to approach a girl, never mind go to bed with her. But then he had led a very sheltered life and brushing against the more worldly attitudes of his colleagues at the horticultural college had widened his point of view. Even so, his marriage to Marie had been a minefield of emotions and misunderstandings. Marie's strong Catholic beliefs regarding birth control had led to constant fears of pregnancy in the early years of their marriage when he was struggling to get work, and they depended heavily on her income from the clerical work at the local surgery. During the early weeks of her first pregnancy, he remembered guiltily how he had prayed for it to be a false alarm. The miscarriage six weeks later was a relief for both of them, if they had been honest with each other. But then it seemed to have set its pattern, and over the next five years two more miscarriages brought Marie close to a life threatening condition and the advice to avoid conception.

He could hear Leigh and Alice arguing in the kitchen, their voices rising in anger, and not wishing to be a part of it he reached over to the hatch door located low in the alcove shelving and pulled it into its closed position. He smiled as the voices stopped, imagining their consternation at being overheard, yet his face remained for the most part set in tension, emphasising the hard lines that of late were becoming a permanent reminder of the advancing years each time he looked into the mirror. Those two would soon be more usefully employed, if that described students these days, he thought. They were on a kind of count down to the end of the summer vacation and then it would just be the four of them again at Willow Cottage. Two camps, he speculated – Marie and the child and he and his mother.

He reached for the channel changer, flicking through the programmes, his eyes resting briefly on a preview of a romantic drama. Marie was looking forward to it he remembered; fantasy, sex, virtual reality, where did it all leave him? She had long since left the marital bed. He frowned. Now he was beginning to think like a marriage guidance councillor. But then no amount of advice would put back the spark in his marriage. She had even accused him of attempted rape.

'For Christ's sake, I'm only forty-five', he muttered. What would she be like after the menopause, when she could no longer conceive? No doubt they would both be past it by then. He stood up dropping the television remote controller on to the floor, and went to the sideboard cupboard housing an assortment of bottles of alcohol, some unopened and others partly consumed. Since his father's death from cancer, Simon had tried to resist the urge to indulge in any form of stimulant, although the occasional drink at social functions or at times of stress proved to be very enjoyable, and friends and business acquaintances still presented bottles of wine and spirits that found their way into the sideboard cupboard.

He sought out the half consumed bottle of brandy and slowly unscrewed the top before selecting a tall glass tumbler and pouring out a generous quantity of the liquid. He raised the glass to his nose and smelt the alcoholic fumes before taking first a sip and then a gulp. He shuddered at the raw strength of it, but then gulped the remainder down and closed his mouth tightly over the sensation. After the initial shock to his system he could feel the warmth travelling into the depth of his stomach and he poured himself another large measure. A third one accompanied him back to his chair, where he settled down with the retrieved controller in his other hand and viewed the local news channel with little comprehension or enjoyment. He no longer cared what the world or his wife was doing. He was in his own little world and no amount of harassment during the next hours of the evening would persuade him to leave it.

When he awoke he winced with the pain of stiffness in his back as he pulled himself forward in the chair. The grandfather clock was announcing the passing of one hour after midnight and he realised that he was shivering in the low temperature with little heat coming from the dying embers in the grate. The central heating system was not turned on until late September and in any case its use never extended beyond eleven o'clock in the evening. One table lamp was emitting a dull light from a sixty-watt bulb and the large galleried room was hung with shadows. Simon struggled to stand up, his body swaying under the effects of the large quantity of brandy and his physical discomfiture triggering a feeling of guilt and fear. He felt vulnerable, knowing that he would have been observed and found wanting.

The stairs creaked under his uneven tread and he strained to make out the position of his bedroom door on the landing aided only by the moonlight entering through the thin curtains. He sensed her observation of his actions, knowing that she did not actually need to see him. Each other's movements were so familiar, and he in turn visualised the tight line of her mouth and the hunched up posture in the bed. No doubt her concern was with the sleeping child he thought as he carefully located the doorknob and slowly pushed open the door.

Marie raised herself up in the bed, leaning back on her elbows and listening to him opening the door. Her chest ached with tension, a hard knot of contempt for him already there in her thoughts. 'What a coward!' she mouthed into the darkness. This was all about his mother and yet if she was here he would not dare to be so self-indulgent and set such a bad example. 'That cat stays in the cupboard,' she whispered. 'This is my house, and I will have my kitchen as I want it.'

Suddenly ear-splitting screams ripped through the silence. Marie's heart leaped, beginning to pound its beat in her chest. She lunged at the light switch, knocking over a glass tumbler of water in her panic and struggling to pull the covers back from her legs. As she reached the bedside she could see the little girl, mouth open wide and staring with wild eyes towards the wall. Her hands were shaking in an uncontrollable frenzy and her legs lashed out against the quilt, pushing it down to the bottom of the mattress.

Marie pulled the shaking screaming child towards her. 'There, there. There, there,' were the only words of comfort she could offer, as she struggled to hold the writhing body.

'What's the matter with her?' That was Simon's deep voice raised against the shrillness of the screams filling the room and escaping beyond it.

'Well, it's pretty obvious, isn't it?' Marie had now rocked the child into a state of shuddering sobbing, holding her tightly against her chest.

'What do you mean? Is she dreaming?'

'No. It's you, isn't it? Coming to bed at this hour and waking everybody up.'

'Come off it. I hardly made a sound,' Simon protested. 'Do you need anything? A cup of tea to calm your nerves.'

'No. Just a good night's sleep thank you and for God's sake don't snore. I can hear you through a brick wall.'

'Oh well. Happy dreams!' Simon closed the door slowly behind him and returned to the loneliness of the king-sized bed, wrapping the duvet around him and pressing his face into the plump pillow.

Apparently, Alice and Leigh slept through the nocturnal drama with an enviable and perhaps youthful ability to shelve their worries and relax, although it seemed that each one had dreamed of disturbing events outside reality with amazing similarities.

Alice had found herself in a huge derelict building where sets of stairs came to dead ends and the lifts travelled sideways, whereas Leigh was trying to find a railway station in a maze of underground tunnels. Both talked of the fear of being followed by an unseen sinister being and of the relief of returning to the light of another day.

Marie was expecting them to comment on the absence of the Mooncat on the kitchen windowsill, but they were so caught up with remembering details from their dreams that they did not seem to notice the empty space.

Simon drank his coffee and ate half a slice of toast before muttering that he was expecting a delivery of compost and some help would be appreciated. He sighed at the lack of response and scraped the chair legs noisily across the quarry tiles. He sensed his wife's continued disapproval. The apathy of the two young ones seemed to be part of their growing-up stage when anything amounting to hard physical labour was to be avoided. He mounted the stone steps and went into the narrow hallway, slowly closing the door behind him and making a mental note to lubricate the creaking hinges. He could hear the sound of their voices again; Leigh's deep tones and Alice's shrill laughter. No doubt he was in everybody's bad books, he thought grimly. For God's sake, can't a man have a drink occasionally? The question bounced around in his head over and over as he went into the office and sought out the necessary paperwork and the daily work schedule for the student who would be presenting himself for work experience later in the week. He checked the details. The student's name was Max Browne. He enjoyed this yearly link with the horticultural college, giving him an opportunity to refresh his teaching skills. He was contented enough to manage the garden centre but sometimes missed the educational aspects that had been part of his everyday life at the college before the death of his father.

5

Sunshine and Showers

Hannah watched Sally applying her makeup; layers of heavily tinted cream eventually masking the aging lines around her mouth and eyes as much as was possible on a sixty-seven year old skin. Although she no longer smoked, years of indulging in the habit had left their mark. She still kept her hair in the same shoulder-length style, with regular visits to the hairdressers for the application of peroxide to mask the grey roots and the occasional added streaks of copper and bronze hair dyes. In spite of, or, as she claimed, because of all this, she managed to look good and her ability to wear anything from old jeans to the most expensive ball gown and still turn heads was a talent that Hannah had always envied. Now, she stood at the mirror in her short dressing gown, her long slender bare legs extending beyond the hem of the garment and her toenails emblazoned with a bright red nail varnish.

It was their third day together in a week's planned break that had begun with a celebration of their birthday on September 9th, both reaching the age of sixty-seven. Apparently Sally needed to take stock of her wardrobe. Hannah was amazed at the contents of the two wardrobes in her friend's bedroom. They were both already filled with what to her sensibilities were enough clothes to last for at least the next twenty years. Sally had laughed at her incredulity and declared most of them to be ready for the charity shop. Hannah nearly admitted that very often her clothes came from such places, but checked herself and instead commented that someone would be glad of them.

It's not that I can't afford to buy new clothes, she reasoned to herself a short while later as they were heading for the town centre and the department stores, but she would rather spend her money on antiques or books. Clothes had never come high on her list of priorities, although Sally's flare for looking elegant had always rankled from the days of their youth. Besides, she loved a bargain, and enjoyed nothing better than doing the rounds of the charity shops opening up on town high streets as other small shops battled with high rates and competition from the trendy large stores.

However, two hours later found the two friends both struggling with plastic carrier bags and hurrying back to the car park. A parking ticket would be a bitter blow after such an enjoyable spending spree. Sally flung herself into the driving seat and switched on the engine, 'ready for a quick get away', she gasped, leaving Hannah to bundle the bags into the back seat and twist her body into the passenger seat. They drove triumphantly past the car park attendant, a surly-looking individual in a peaked cap and navy blue uniform, who had reached that end of the row of cars, notepad in hand and 'out for the kill' Sally muttered. She explained to Hannah as they headed away from the town centre that he was the most disliked attendant of them all, so tightly did he adhere to the clock, and a number of irate people had verbally threatened him. Indeed one man who was two minutes late in reaching his car had actually punched him on the jaw. The news had quickly spread around the city and the aggressor was treated like a local hero; such acclaim a small yet treasured sweetener to the bitterness of an imposed fine for disturbing the peace.

'We have the same problems,' Hannah said. 'Well Lincoln does, I suppose,' she added, realising that she was becoming caught up in the everyday negativity that irritated her. Her legs were aching after two hours of wandering around the shops in the large shopping centre. Much of the time had been wasted in a kind of pining for their lost youth, she thought. Many of the shops catered for the under forties or more extremely for those with 'no boobs and no bums' as Sally described them. She had been tempted into buying a rather expensive jumper with a low neckline and baggy raglan sleeves and now was regretting it, wondering what she would team it with and when the occasion would arise for wearing it. Perhaps she could give it to one of the family for a birthday present, she thought, and spent the next ten minutes trying to visualise whom it would suit.

Back in Sally's house in Anlaby, the bags were emptied out onto the settee. Sally continued to enthuse but Hannah volunteered to make some tea, staring out of the kitchen window at the small back garden mostly laid to gravel as she waited for the kettle to boil. She sighed; her thoughts back at Willow Cottage, where the view of open fields and the abundance of vegetation never failed to please her.

They chatted on over hastily prepared egg and chips, and a banana split to follow. The mixture lay uneasily on Hannah's stomach whereas Sally declared it to be tasty and just what she needed. The topic of Daisy's love life resurfaced. Hannah commented that on reading between the lines it would seem that Daisy was getting very serious about settling down with her gentleman friend Maurice and described her friend as a born victim.

'You've been reading too many novels,' Sally jokingly replied. 'And it isn't in one of mine. The public like the happy ever after theme, you know.'

'I don't know how you write about romance when you are a declared spinster.' Hannah gripped her stomach as a spasm of indigestion caused a sharp pain.

'It didn't stop the Bronte brigade did it? Anyway, it's like the old adage about teachers. Those who can, do. Those who can't, teach.'

'And that's not true either!' Hannah shook her fist and grinned.

'I can't imagine you being a strong disciplinarian.'

'No. I was more cut out to be a mother I think. I do wish Rachel could be happy. I still think she would be better off on her own like Emma. She is so content as a single mother.'

'And I'm content as a spinster in spite of my mother's little digs. That reminds me. I'm supposed to be going to visit her when we get back from our little jaunts. You wouldn't like to stop off on the way with me, would you? You haven't seen her since the kids were little. She amazes me really and I don't know how much longer she can live on her own. The lads keep hinting about me being the one with more space but I couldn't cope. I can't do with all these 'oldies' and in any case she wouldn't hear of it.'

Hannah laughed. 'We're not exactly spring chickens ourselves are we?'

'I know! There is no need to remind me, but you know what I mean.'

'I'm sure most people feel irritated by signs of old age. We none of us see ourselves as others see us.' Hannah was suddenly recalling the smiles exchanged at breakfast time one day last week when she had voiced her opinion about tea-bags and the effects of the dye which stained the cups so badly. She realised that she had voiced that opinion on the previous day and reacted to their smiles by spreading the butter on the toast with such savage vigour that she had knocked against her cup resulting in tea splashing some of its contents into the saucer. 'Clean cloth.' She heard Ella's voice clearly in her head, her mind back into the time of her childhood as she wistfully visualised the embroidered teacloth and compared it with the comparative vulgarity and tackiness of the piece of oil cloth which could be wiped over constantly, and in her opinion encouraged sloppy table manners.

She realised that Sally was waiting for an answer. 'I'll come with you if you want a bit of moral support. I think your mother is great for her age.'

'She likes an audience. She can be all sweetness and light but for some reason I get into her firing line. She's always been the same. The boys of course can do no wrong. Do you remember when we were kids before we were evacuated? It was always me who had to wash up and do the errands. They used to get things wrong on purpose I reckon.'

'Well, who knows? Perhaps it toughened you up. She has to admit that you have done well for yourself and she certainly benefits from your success. The flat is just right for her with the warden at hand. She could be isolated on a housing estate or in a nursing home by now.'

Sally pushed her hair out of her eyes. Hannah studied her friend as she rested her chin on her cupped hands and stared at the window where the rain beat a steady rhythm on the glass. She was looking more tired than usual, she decided, and stretched out her hand in a reassuring gesture.

'What?' Sally jumped, returning her attention to the conversation. 'Sorry, I was miles away. Back in the past in fact. Thoughts of Paul just flitted across my mind. It's all your talk of Daisy needing a bloke.'

'I never met him, did I? You had gone your separate ways when we met up in London, and then our plans to share a flat were upskittled. You went to Manchester, and I met up with Jack. I often wonder if I would have done that if you had not persuaded me to confront my past. I still have bad dreams about Elsie Porter, you know, even though I have understood more as life has gone on. She terrified me, especially when she gave me mouse pie. All these events or lack of events shaping our destinies. I used to think it was all planned. I don't know what I believe these days. Somehow it is like a new life since Jack died. I can't believe it has all happened to me and Jack seems to have existed in someone else's life. A different Hannah – do you know what I mean?'

'Not really. I have always been me. I suppose my years in Australia seem a bit remote now, but I don't feel like a different person. I think you are still in a stage of bereavement, and not accepting that Jack has died. Perhaps you are like Daisy and need a new relationship. Anyway, where are we going to go tomorrow? The weather forecast should be on soon. If it is going to rain we'll go to York and if not we'll head off for sunny Scarborough, shall we?'

Hannah suddenly felt depressed, and she could not think why she did. It must be all this talk of the past, she decided. She had really looked forward to spending time with her old friend, indeed her oldest friend. Yet somehow she did not belong in this kind of life. She felt that she was merely passing time. Why did she always have to achieve? Simon had asked her that a while ago, she remembered. 'Why can't you enjoy the day-to-day experiences and relax?' he had continued, when she had complained of feeling tired. It was he who had suggested that she rang Sally.

Perhaps they wanted her out of the way. Just lately, in fact she speculated, since the birth of Elphine, there had been an uncomfortable feeling in the house. Marie was such a moody person and Simon could not seem to put a foot right.

'A penny for them!'

Hannah turned to look at her friend, suddenly aware of her voice and the realisation that she was expecting an answer. 'Sorry! I was miles away. The seaside always reminds me of the week I spent in Sheringham with Jack before he died.' She looked down at her lap, avoiding Sally's penetrating gaze and reproaching herself for using such emotional blackmail to excuse her bad manners.

'Well, let's make it York then.' Sally's voice was suddenly shrill with embarrassment and a hint of impatience. 'We can always just chill out somewhere and find some place to have a meal. We don't need to do the tourist bit if you are tired.'

'No. Scarborough will be fine. Why don't we have a few days away? Day trips can be so tiring.' Hannah was regretting her attempts to excuse her lack of enthusiasm. It would be good to walk on the sand and breathe in the sea air away from the crowded city streets and the buildings that rose so high blotting out the horizon, she thought.

They sat after their evening meal looking at the brochures Sally had collected on her last visit to the Tourist Information centre. After some debating, they decided to avoid the city and follow the route from Beverley, skirting the beautiful hilly landscape of the Wolds and across to Bridlington. The weather forecaster, after the six o'clock news, had promised a short period of bright sunny days, apparently a mini Indian summer.

'Make the most of it,' he advised.

'We certainly will,' they answered in unison, laughing at their timing with their thoughts back once more into the realms of the closeness of their childhood friendship.

Before they had sunk into total weariness, a vague timetable had emerged from the brochures scattered across the coffee table. They decided that they would spend an hour in Bridlington, regaling themselves with coffee and cream cakes before travelling north east along the coast road to Flamborough Head, recalling the white lighthouse and the breathtaking views of the chalk cliffs whose contours were slowly being changed by the eroding action of the tides. Apparently, according to a friend of Sally's, a 'must see' tourist attraction in these parts was the large sea bird colony at Bempton Cliffs. She had enthused over the magnificent views down the sheer cliff sides from the safety of specially selected and maintained areas where visitors could observe the habits and characteristics of a number of species. From there it would be a relatively short drive to Scarborough where they could seek out bed and breakfast accommodation for two nights, giving them time to renew their acquaintanceship with this seaside town and the opportunity to travel on to Whitby with its abbey set high on the hill overlooking the busy harbour, and its intriguing connections with Count Dracula.

It was a long time since either of them had travelled so far north and enjoyed the simple pleasures of looking for fossils, eating fish and chips out of paper bags or indulging in large ice-cream filled cornets, licking the escaping drips away with the practised skill of children on a day out at the seaside.

Indeed, they were already behaving like a couple of children giggling at the silliest happenings remembered from the past or from more recent times. Sally was pleased to see that the signs of stress, which had manifested in deepening lines around her friend's mouth, were being over-ridden by the laughter lines around her eyes, and they talked into the early hours both invigorated by each other's company and the anticipation of two or three days in this great escape from home and family.

When they arrived in Bridlington on the following day, after a pleasant drive through the green fields away from the major coastal route, it seemed that half the population of the East Riding was of like mind, taking advantage of this late summer heat wave and descending on the east coast resorts by the car and coach load. Consequently, parking the car was a major problem and, after driving around for over half an hour in ever-widening circles with not a single space in sight, they abandoned Bridlington and took the road north to Flamborough Head. Here, parking was no problem and they were soon taking deep breaths of the invigorating sea breezes, which circled around the lighthouse. It all appeared to be as they had remembered it; the famous white lighthouse, a solid reminder of the dangers to shipping in these coastal waters, and the ancient cliffs carved into shapes pleasing to the eye; a contrast to the flat beaches and eroding coast line in the south of the county.

Bempton and the famous Bempton Cliffs were next on the agenda and the village cafe offered a welcome cup of coffee and the promised cream cakes. The path to the cliffs was well signposted and groups of people were coming and going, with no one, it seemed, in a hurry to move away from this delightful area made even more appealing by the welcome heat wave.

The two friends kept up a running commentary as they wandered along the narrow mud path, stepping over the grasses and other native plants reaching out across the man made space. The varieties of grasses were observed and outwardly named by Hannah, and Sally tried to share her enthusiasm, although the conversations of other people caught her attention more readily. It was not long before they reached the first viewing area on the very edge of the cliff face. A stout fence marked the boundary for the safety of the public but it was possible to extend one's head beyond it and look down the sheer drop to the sea below. The sky was azure blue without a cloud to mar its intensity of colour and the whiteness of the birds, swooping and circling, either contrasted with that blue or suddenly became less visible against the background of the white cliffs. The noise and movement of this restless gathering caused such a conflict between the audio and visual senses that some people protected their eyes by the wearing of dark glasses, or put their hands over their ears in an attempt to focus their attention on individual species.

'You should be here earlier in the year. June is the best time,' a lady advised, stepping aside from the telescope sited close to the fence. 'We are always assessing the numbers in their thousands. There are six different species of sea bird, which choose these cliffs as their breeding ground, including puffins. Sadly you won't see those at this time of the year, but it is still a wonderful sight isn't it? Are you on holiday or just out for the day?'

'We are not sure really. We may find somewhere to stay the night or we may just head off back to Hull. It depends on the weather and how we feel after a day of tramping around,' Sally responded looking towards her friend for confirmation.

Hannah nodded her head and smiled. 'We are retracing our footsteps from many years ago although this bit is new ground for us. We must try to return in June. I would love to see the puffins.'

'Well don't leave it too late for accommodation. This weather has got everybody out by the looks of it.' A man had joined in the conversation and they turned their attention away from the lady, intrigued by the gruff tones of the elderly gentleman standing behind them.

'I accommodate guests in my inn if you decide to stay for a night or two and I have a room there just right for you two ladies. That is if you don't mind sharing.' He fumbled in his jacket pockets pulling out an assortment of keys and what appeared to be shopping lists before struggling with a small book that was being restricted by the confines of his pocket. 'There we are,' he gasped, his voice hoarse and barely audible.

The two friends leant forward with some expectancy as he turned the pages of what appeared to be a very old diary. They were yellow and creased with some corners folded over perhaps to mark special dates.

'Here we are,' he said. He shielded the page from their curious gaze and read the information recorded on it. 'Delightful room with four-poster bed and superb views of the sea .The bathroom is, as they say, en suite and there is easy access to the dining room down one flight of stairs.'

He looked up, regarding them quizzically as if to register their reaction and they both obliged with 'That sounds nice,' followed by embarrassed giggles at their rather child-like unison of speech.

'So, that's solved your problem. Now you can go off for the rest of the day and we will have a meal ready for you at seven o'clock or later. Don't worry about time. My other guests come and go as they please.'

'Thank you. That's very kind of you but we can't give you a definite answer, can we, Hannah?' Sally turned to her companion, her eyes narrowing to convey some doubt and distrust of this strange little man in his rather shabby jacket and baggy trousers.

Hannah was smiling with gratitude, it seemed to Sally, as she thanked him and promised to give his invitation some consideration as the day progressed. 'You must give us directions to your place,' she continued.

'Of course. Here's me expecting you to know, although you seem like the kind of person who would know.' He gave Hannah what Sally later described as a sly grin and ferreted in his pockets again, extracting a stub of a pencil and yet another old shopping list. Using his diary as support he carefully wrote the name of his establishment. 'There we are,' he said, handing the paper to Hannah. 'It's between Bridlington and Filey. Watch out for a cluster of cottages and then a lane opposite that leads down to the sea. It is well signposted. You can't miss it. You will like it.' He turned to Hannah again.

'Yes, I do like old places. They have such an atmosphere like going back in time.'

Sally laughed. 'She's always back in time,' she said, tugging at Hannah's arm.

'It's not far along a lane and has a view of the sea from the cliff top. I get lots of visitors. Some stay for a long time all wanting peace and quiet. I don't welcome children or dogs. Not that I've got anything against them but folks need a good rest sometimes especially after a busy life, and I must get on, but I will see you later.' He doffed an imaginary hat and started back along the path towards the village, now, from the rear view, appearing to look even more eccentric in his dress and manner.

'Goodness me!' Sally declared. 'Where did he spring up from? What did he write?'

She snatched the piece of paper from Hannah's hand and read the words aloud.

'The Mermaid Inn! Is that it? It took him long enough to write it, and what strange handwriting! I think we will give that a miss.'

They watched the birds circling and swooping against the background of blue sky for another ten minutes and then slowly made their way back to the car, Hannah again focusing her attention on all the grasses and wild flowers now producing seed in varying shapes and hues from gold to reds and browns, and remarking on how wonderful it was to view Autumn in such glorious sunshine and how prolific nature was in its preparation for next year's growth. She seemed to have forgotten about the strange offer of accommodation, and Sally, reassured by this, pushed the memory of the incident to the back of her mind. An hour later they set off for Scarborough, soon reaching the turn off to Filey. However, in spite of her professed indifference, she was somewhat relieved that they did not see a signpost pointing to The Mermaid Inn, although there were several groups of cottages en route on the left hand side. It did not seem long before a road sign indicated that they were now in Scarborough. But then the search for a parking space began all over again.

'We'll ask the Parking Angel for a space,' Hannah said, as with flagging spirits they began a tour of the next car park; the third one so far.

Sally giggled but obliged, putting one hand on top of the other on the steering wheel as if in prayer.

They had now turned into the final avenue, their eyes scanning the rows for a space.

'There's one! Quick! Before someone jumps ahead of us! Thank you, Polly. I don't know why I didn't ask you before.'

Sally skilfully steered the car into the narrow space and sighed as she switched off the engine. 'Who on earth is Polly?' she asked.

'The Parking Angel of course. And she is not on earth. She must have a name, otherwise there's no feeling behind it.'

'Oh. OK. I should be used to your strange beliefs by now. I don't know about you but I am ready for something a bit more substantial like fish and chips. Then we could have a walk along the sea front.'

Much time was consumed in waiting in long queues for a midday meal, and the proposed walk along the sands was shelved in favour of a quiet rest on a seat along the promenade, where, as Sally enthused, they could 'watch the world and his wife' go by. However, a black rain cloud gathering in size and blocking out the sunshine drove them to seek shelter in the shopping area. Hannah sighed. They had not come on this journey north with more so-called retail therapy in mind. They wandered aimlessly around a gift shop jostled by other people escaping from the threatened rain or desperately seeking out something 'cheap and cheerful' for the folks at home.

Sally pointed to novelties, commenting on their prices or giggling at their vulgarity, but ten minutes of struggling to avoid elbows and shopping bags persuaded her to follow Hannah back outside onto the pavement and the heavily falling rain. They hurried into an amusement arcade, staring dispassionately at the slot machines and wincing at the jarring cacophony of sounds that accompanied the various games in progress.

As of like mind they stepped back into the rain, and without uttering one word turned in the direction of the car park. Initially, they had forgotten how far they had walked away from it, and by the time they reached the car they were out of breath. They sank back into their respective seats, their wet clothes clinging to their bodies and decidedly dampening their spirits.

'So. What shall we do? This rain seems set to last. So much for our "Indian Summer".' Sally tapped her fingers along the rim of the steering wheel.

'We'll give it a chance to brighten up. It may just be a shower.'

Sally switched on the radio. It was the news followed by the latest weather forecast that warned of rain in Scotland, spreading south later. Sally's comment that those lot down in London knew nothing about anywhere north of Watford made Hannah laugh and from then on they competed in saying silly things and becoming more and more hysterical.

'After another half an hour of watching the rain running down the windscreen, their conversation becoming spasmodic and their bodies beginning to feel cramped in their damp clothes, they decided that it was time to move on in the direction of Hull and to abandon all ideas of Whitby, the Abbey and the whole 'Dracula Experience'.

As they travelled south they could not believe how quickly the sky seemed to empty of that threatening leaden grey, and their voices became more animated again, their backs straighter.

'Let's try Filey. Have you ever been there?' Hannah was looking in the guidebook.

'I remember our Gavin taking the kids to Butlin's holiday camp one year. They were very enthusiastic but then kids always are. What does it say?'

'"Filey has a long sandy beach set in a wide bay. The beach is edged with a long promenade.

'"To the north of the bay Filey Brigg juts out into the sea and has many rock pools to explore."'

'Sounds like a good place to stretch our legs.'

Hannah paused to examine the small map, screwing up her eyes against the brilliant sunshine now flooding into the car.

'Well, go on then. What's the town like?'

'This sounds interesting. A bit of history for you. "Filey's name means five leys, a clearing of forest and meadow. The oldest building is the museum on Queen Street built in 1696. For most of its history it was a fishing and a farming village. When seaside holidays became popular it was always regarded as a quiet refuge away from busy Scarborough and it still has that reputation, although for over forty years it was a centre for thousands of holiday makers who stayed at Butlin's holiday camp. Now, its clean environment and peaceful atmosphere encourage visitors who want to get away from it all."'

'Right! Filey here we come then. Look! Next turning left. How's that for timing?'

Sally wrenched the steering wheel down with her left hand, at the same time braking hard. The tyres squealed as if in protest for such unusual treatment and Hannah's high pitched yells of alarm, in combination with the high revs of the engine, were enough to put a horse to flight in the adjacent field.

The two friends were back in high spirits.

'That poor creature! You nearly gave it a heart attack,' Hannah gasped. 'Please don't do that again or I'll be having one.'

Filey was as delightful as the brochure promised. The sand was as yellow as the ochre in an artist's palette, they decided, and the sea as blue as it could ever be on this northeastern coastline. The tide was coming in and they walked along the edge of the water, dodging the incoming waves and pressing their bare feet into the wet sand. Occasionally one or the other would stoop down to pick up a shell or interesting pebble, dropping most of these 'treasures' minutes later in favour of others of differing shapes and colours, which caught their attention. When they had retraced their steps back to the familiar bricks and mortar of humankind, they decided to return the few favoured trophies, grown warm in their tight grasps, to their rightful place amongst the millions of others worn smooth by the action of water over aeons of time.

'Whitby is the place for fossils,' Hannah remarked, dropping the stones one by one as they walked towards the promenade. 'I am getting quite a collection, although I do kind of cheat, and buy them.'

A delightful little tearoom provided them with fresh leaf tea and delicious sandwiches on a plate of assorted salad. They indulged in more cream cakes, the second that day, but used their mutual birthdays as an excuse for such indulgency.

It seemed that no one was in a hurry to move on and another hour passed with a second pot of tea and a conversation full of nostalgia, each looking back over the years and recalling their childhood when evacuation from their native Hull had made such an impact on their young lives.

The sound of chairs scraping took their attention away from their reminiscing, and they looked across to the young woman who was busily sweeping up crumbs into a dustpan and giving her remaining two customers what they soon realised were meaningful looks.

'Sorry. Are you closing? We have been lost in another world I think. We'll get out of your way.' Hannah struggled to her feet, her limbs stiffened from over an hour and a half of resting.

'We closed ten minutes ago. It's ten past six.'

'Goodness me!' Sally explained. 'How time flies when you are having fun. How much do we owe you, dear? That was a delightful little meal.'

The sky was becoming heavy with greyness and it was obvious that the threatened rain had decidedly moved south and they would be caught up in it again.

'I think we'd best head for home, don't you?' Sally slid her hand companionably into the crook of Hannah's arm.

Hannah nodded. She was tired. They had covered a lot of ground she thought, in spite of or because of the weather and she could think of nothing better than to sit back and leave the driving to her friend.

The rear and wing mirrors reflected various parts of the sky in a pattern of greys and ever diminishing patches of blue. Hannah commented that it was like a race against the elements, seeking sanctuary before the skies opened up their deluge of rain.

'Something like that,' Sally responded, her voice weakening with fatigue now, and the tiredness showing in the sag of her shoulders.

6

Selina and the Mermaid

According to the last road sign, they were five miles from Bridlington travelling on the A165, and there were indications that the turn-off to Bempton and Flamborough was a mile ahead.

'Only about forty odd miles to Anlaby now I think,' Hannah said, running her finger along the red, yellow and green roads wandering over the page of the map.

At that moment the car gave a small shudder and then a moaning sound, slowing down to crawling pace in spite of Sally's foot pumping the accelerator pedal. It shuddered again as it navigated the next bend and then came to a halt.

'That's all we need. It can't be fuel. The tank's still on half.' Sally turned to look at her friend, who was pointing along the road to an old signpost somewhat hidden in the hawthorn hedge.

'There it is. Look!' Hannah yelled. 'The Mermaid Inn! What a coincidence!'

There was no choice but to seek help, and they struggled to push the car on to the safety of the verge. The lane on the left was little more than a cart track but impressions made by car tyres in the mud were evidence of recent traffic activity, a fact that the two companions found reassuring. They got their overnight bags from the boot and set off in the direction of The Mermaid Inn. At first a sense of urgency governed the speed in which they strode along, but when no sight of a building appeared beyond each bend in the twisting track, their energy began to fail.

'Must stop for a minute,' Hannah gasped.

'We'll soon be overpowered by these bloody nettles!' Sally was not a country lover at the best of times, and the vegetation growing in the verges contained stinging nettles and thistles some of which seemed intent on reaching out to attack her ankles. 'It can't be much further, surely!'

'He did say it had a view of the sea. When I think about it there was quite a space on the map between the road and the coast until that turn off to Flamborough. We'll perhaps be able to see beyond the hedge in a minute. It will be good to get inside. It's turning really chilly.'

Her expectations came into fruition as they rounded the next bend. There on the right, along a narrow pathway through a wilderness of vegetation, was an ancient building. They both stopped walking and stared at first in relief and then in amazement. This was nothing like they had expected to see; both with a conventional image of a village public house etched in their memories. They expected 'old worldly' but this seemed to be 'out of this world'. It looked to be an abandoned cottage, yet a lopsided sign displaying the painting of a mermaid languishing on a rock in some watery place, identified it. The roof was of old red pan tiles stained green in places with the dripping of water from the branches of an overhanging sycamore tree. The sag in the line of the roof ridge suggested decaying failing timbers and the window frames were desperately in need of a coat of paint. The main structure appeared to be built of small red brick, although little of that could be seen beyond the heavy growth of ivy.

As they stared with a mixture of consternation and morbid fascination, the front door was opened, and the man of their previous encounter at Bempton Cliffs waved his arm vigorously, firstly in greeting and then as a gesture to join him. He seemed to be older and more eccentric in his dress than Hannah could recall in their previous, rather brief relationship, but it was decidedly the same voice.

They made their way slowly along the path leading to the door, casting quick glances at each other and at the rough surface beneath their feet, avoiding the potholes. Hannah allowed her gaze to travel up to the bedroom windows, dark with shadows, imagining eyes watching from behind the grimy glass and recalling The Listeners, a favourite poem of her childhood.

The man stepped aside to give them access and they now found themselves in a narrow hallway, the walls part boarded and part roughly plastered. Hannah could barely distinguish between the many pictures of all sizes hanging against the rough plaster with very little space between them. Instead her eyes focused on a stag's head mounted in a space above a doorway. The strange staring blankness in its glass eyes made her hold her breath and draw closer to her companion.

They had no choice but to follow the man into a surprisingly spacious room where a huge fire blazed in an inglenook. The atmosphere now was of comfort and conviviality. A long settle piled with plump cushions invited visitors to settle down and toast their weary bodies in the heat from the fire. Clusters of lighted candles, their flames flickering in the changing air currents and casting strange shadows on the whitewashed walls, were stationed on small tables in each corner of the room. The floor, dismal in its quarry tiled surfacing, was covered here and there with straw-coloured rush matting stained with spillages, yet not detracting from the general ambience. Hannah gasped, 'Wow!' and Sally's face was now registering pleasure in place of anxiety.

Their host pointed to a table opposite to the settle. 'It's all ready for you, my dears. Take a seat and I will organise your luggage. Did you leave your car round the bend? If you give me the keys I will park it closer for you.'

They explained that it had broken down at the beginning of the lane, and they would need some help in the morning if any of his other guests could oblige.

Sally watched his reaction, feeling that he was not surprised by their news, but then reproaching herself for entering Hannah's world of strange beliefs. He was perhaps a man whom nothing surprised or perhaps his face did not register his reactions. However, her state of anxiety had returned and she left Hannah to describe the frustrations of the day.

The meal followed with no choice other than to partake of the three courses; tomato soup, beef and dumplings with assorted vegetables, and fruit cocktail. With little appetite after the earlier indulgencies of the day, the two companions were not impressed. They agreed that, apart from the fruit cocktail and the soup, obviously both canned, the other savoury items had freshly come out of the microwave.

'I hope that was OK for you, ladies. My wife is a dab hand with her dumplings, aren't you, dear? And you can't beat her tomato soup in these parts. A nice cup of coffee now?'

His voice came from the adjoining room, presumably the kitchen.

They were grateful for the coffee, albeit of the instant variety, and retired to the comfort of the settle watching the flickering flames reaching up to consume the large log in the fireplace. The changing light patterns were reflected in a large pink mirror secured on the opposite wall. It was very handsome they decided, with an etching on one side of a mermaid amidst rocks and waves echoing the inn sign over the front door. They chattered on about the varied experiences of the day, and the car problems confronting them on the morrow, their faces registering both happiness and anxiety. For a while the normality of the evening was reassuring, but when the grandfather clock announced by its heavy chimes that it was ten o'clock, their attention returned to the present time and the sleeping arrangements. They had heard the sounds of his footsteps in the room above them when he had taken their luggage upstairs, and although they were ready for sleep, they were reluctant to leave the comfort and the familiarity of the lounge.

Their host appeared 'dead on cue', Sally muttered, her lips pursing, and they followed their host up a narrow staircase to a small landing on the first floor. A door was open revealing a large bedroom, the décor fitting the description that he had given them on his first contact at Blempton Cliffs.

'There we are then. This room is always warm, being as it is above the living room fire, and the bed is comfy. The bathroom is through that door. I hope you sleep well, ladies.'

'Thank you Mr – sorry we don't know your name, do we?' Hannah turned to Sally for some support.

'Constable,' he replied. 'Jabas Constable. My name was over the door but I don't suppose you noticed. My wife is Selena. You may meet her later. She is resting now.'

'You will need our names of course for your records. I am Hannah Clayton and my friend here is Sally Blenkin. Will you need any more details?'

'No, my dear. I know you will not be doing 'a moonlight'. Not get far, would you? But don't worry about your car. I will sort it all out in the morning for you. My other guests are not back yet. I hope they do not disturb you, but some people are noisy.'

He closed the door and they heard the latch drop into place.

'Did he give you a key?' Sally leaned forward to examine the door. 'Oh! It's only an ordinary sneck! There doesn't appear to be a keyhole. Hannah! I'm getting a bit scared! Can we put something against the door? I don't think I am going to sleep a wink. This room is so creepy.'

They carefully transferred a small coffee table from under the window, placing it against the door and putting their luggage on the top.

'That should stop anyone from coming in. Or at least it will alert us,' Hannah whispered.

They slowly undressed, the act increasing their feelings of insecurity, pausing to look around at the furnishings and décor and commenting on the signs of neglect. Hannah gingerly pulled back the top covers on the large four-poster bed. A patchwork counterpane and an eiderdown, reminiscent of her childhood, covered a worn blanket and off white sheets. The pillow liners, unusually huge and apparently stuffed with feathers, were encased in equally off-white pillowcases. A canopy jutting out above the head of the bed consisted of ornate fittings draped with what appeared to be pink muslin, although years of dust had removed its first blush of colour. Floral patterned drapes hung at each corner post, secured by twisted loops of gold braid.

Hannah chose the side closest to the window, first drawing back the heavy brocade curtains to allow moonlight to enter the room. Sally stared nervously towards the door as she climbed into the bed imagining someone's hand on the latch attempting to push away the obstacle of the table and luggage. She giggled hysterically when Hannah knelt down and peered under the bedsprings.

'I'm always doing that,' she said. 'Goodness knows what I would do if there ever was somebody under the bed.'

'Die of fright I shouldn't wonder. Do you remember "The Listeners"? Walter De La Mare? It began with, "Is there anybody there?" said the Traveller." The Listeners were a host of phantoms.'

'Oh for goodness sake, Hannah!' Sally pulled the covers over her head and drew her knees up away from the damp coldness of the sheets.

In spite of their fears, they both were soon asleep, their minds shut off from sight and sound, and it was not until the clock below was proclaiming four o'clock that Hannah left sleep behind and returned once more to reality.

She half sat up, pressing her back into the feather pillow. She was aware that the darkness appeared to be vibrating. It was as though the room was made up of many moving particles and she stared at it in fascination, rubbing her eyes in an effort to clear her vision. The vibrations still continued and in the strange light she was aware of the furnishings around her and the sound of her friend's breathing. She knew that she was not dreaming. Suddenly the atmosphere changed and now she could see someone close to the window. She hardly dared to breath, not wanting to attract this creature's attention, and yet she was composed sufficiently well to observe the details of the intruder.

In the moonlight she could make out that it was the figure of an elderly woman in a red blouse and black skirt. Her grey hair appeared to be fastened back away from her face and, as she stood in profile, the outline of her nose, long and straight, and the set of her chin were clearly apparent She was holding something in her hand, and Hannah, her eyes now accustomed to the gloom, recognised a large bunch of keys. As she stared, she found herself wondering which doors the keys fitted and how this lady had entered the bedroom. She tore her eyes away for a second, ascertaining in the moonlight that the table was still in position against the door. The lady had turned and now Hannah could make out her other features; heavily browed, wide spaced eyes and a generous firm mouth. She appeared to shimmer as though she was covered in water. A crawling sensation travelled up Hannah's back as the dark brown eyes stared back at her.

Was Sally awake? She pressed her foot into the side of her friend's leg not daring to speak. Sally stirred and turned over, muttering disjointed words of protest. Hannah did not attempt to reassure her. Her throat was dry. In that instance she knew that this was Selina Constable and that she herself was the medium. She did not understand how she knew this. It had never occurred to her that Selina Constable was dead but now it was beginning to make sense. The old man was alone, his life desolate without the companionship of his wife. He wanted proof that she was still near to him. Somehow he recognised that she and Sally could help him and some power had guided or, it seemed, had manipulated them.

'I will tell him,' she whispered. 'I promise.'

She sensed words of acknowledgement. 'Tell him I kept my word.'

She shivered. That was what the traveller said in the poem. 'That I kept my word.'

As she watched, the figure seemed to disintegrate, small pieces disappearing until there was an empty space. Hannah felt a huge sense of bereavement. She did not want this link with spirit to end so soon. She had experienced similar events in her life and now realised that the vibrations were a change in the energy levels and the advent to spiritual contact. She would later compare them to the shimmer of a heat haze as she recounted this latest experience.

For a while she could not take her gaze away from that side of the bedroom. Had she gone to join her husband or was this their bedroom in her lifetime?

"Tell him I came." They needed a message carrier and she Hannah was that message carrier.

The hair was standing up on her arms again and she reached for the light switch on the bedside lamp not caring now if she disturbed

Sally. The forty-watt bulb produced a dim light sufficient to return the room to some normality and, even though the sight of the table pushed against the door reminded Hannah of earlier fears, she felt reassured by even this kind of normality.

Sally stirred and opened her eyes. 'What's the matter?' she whispered. 'Have you heard something? It isn't a mouse is it? This place is so creepy. Mice frighten me to death.'

Hannah frowned at her choice of words. 'It's nothing to worry about,' she replied. 'Somebody using a bathroom I think. Don't worry. Nobody can get in here.'

Sally muttered 'Oh. OK. Turn the light off then. That window looks really creepy with the curtains drawn back. Somebody could be hiding in the folds.'

'Don't be silly. There's nobody else here not even a mouse. Just close your eyes and go back to sleep.'

'Excuse me! I was asleep. Are you settling down? It will soon be time to get up.'

Hannah switched off the light, and put her head under the covers. She wished it was time to get up and yet she had a huge longing to explore that strange place between life and death.

However, nothing further distracted her mind and body away from its need to rest and the next time she opened her eyes the sun was shining in through the casement window and a blackbird was showing his appreciation of this fine September morning with his joyous song. It did not seem possible that such extraordinary events took place in this very room during the hours of night, yet it was all undoubtedly true.

The grandfather clock downstairs was noisily welcoming the day with its mid hour chimes. Twice, Hannah counted, so that was half past something. She reached for her watch. 'Goodness!' she exclaimed. 'Eight! Sally it's half past eight! Come on! Get up! We'll be lucky if there is any breakfast left.'

Twenty minutes later, after sharing the space in the bathroom and hurriedly dressing, they attempted to put on the kind of faces acceptable in the world outside of the privacy of the bedroom. Hannah knew her limitations. Curling tongs succeeded in putting some curl into her fine hair and a dab of cream and rouge compensated a little for the disturbed sleep and the stresses and anxiety of the previous day. However Sally had her morning regime. She would prefer to miss breakfast rather than show the world her 'night ravaged face' as she described it.

'For goodness sake, Hannah! You don't have to do that.'

Hannah had turned her attention to the bed and was straightening the bed covers.

'That's what we pay for. Don't be such a peasant!'

Hannah sighed and sat on the edge of the bed instead. This was all so mundane. Paints and powders and fancy clothes, she thought. They were such kind of surface things. She suddenly had a picture in her mind of a little pond skater skimming along on the surface of the pond. She had watched one a few days ago as she sat on the wall surrounding her 'tadpole pond'. This was her own little wildlife space where she could pond dip and watch the yearly progress from spawn to tiny little frogs, appreciating their role in the life of the planet. The pond skaters seemed to occupy an in-between space; needing both the water and the air at the same time, and not aware of the complexities of either. But then what do I know, she asked herself, and stood up at Sally's command to lend a hand with moving the table.

They tentatively opened the bedroom door and stepped forward on to the landing.

'Not a sign of anybody else,' Sally whispered. 'This house is as silent as the grave.'

Hannah's arms prickled at her description. 'I expect they are all out on the beach. It looks like being a lovely day. We are so late. Shall we bother about breakfast? We can always grab a coffee and a sandwich in Bridlington or go back to that little café at the cliffs.'

'You are right. Let's get the hell out of here. Our priority is getting the car sorted. Do you think what's his name will be able to help? There should be a garage around here somewhere.'

They went into the lounge calling out his name and then, with no response, venturing into the kitchen. There were no signs of recent culinary activity, not even the smell of coffee, and they stepped over to the window overlooking the back terrace. From this angle the path to the cliff tops was visible, and they could just make out the shape of a man standing staring out towards the sea.

'I'm out of this place,' Sally said. 'Come on. Let's get our stuff and go. We can flag somebody down, or walk to Bempton. It's only just down the road.'

She hurried back to the stairs, stumbling on the first step and grabbing at the banister rail.

Hannah waited in the entrance hall, her eyes now able to focus on the many framed pictures and photographs adorning the walls. She suddenly became aware of a portrait and the familiar features of her early morning visitor. It was an oil painting of a woman dressed in a red blouse and a black skirt. The name Selina Constable with the dates 1926 to1998 engraved on a small plaque were confirmation enough that she had indeed been in the ghostly presence of the innkeeper's wife.

Sally was back now with their luggage. They decided to leave their host some money on the counter with a note apologising for oversleeping and thanking him for his hospitality.

They thought that thirty-five pounds would be enough. Hannah took her diary out of her bag and tore out a blank page at the back. Using the wall as support, she wrote their message and then added, 'She said to tell you she kept her word.' She looked back at the portrait, her eyes meeting those of Selina Constable.

They walked quickly along the lane, able to avoid the encroaching vegetation more easily in the light of the morning sunshine. Neither of them looked back. Hannah wondered whether Sally had any awareness of being watched. She herself certainly did, visualising figures behind those dark windows observing their every movement. It was a great relief to reach beyond the first bend in the lane and leave The Mermaid Inn behind.

What had Selina promised? 'Tell him I kept my word.' Did she really say that or was it just that poem in her own head? Had they arranged to communicate? Had she made a promise? Perhaps she had threatened to haunt him. Perhaps he had been unfaithful to her. Perhaps she was explaining bumps and bangs in the night.

'Nearly there,' Sally gasped, cursing as the bag caught against her shin. 'I recognise that strange tree. It looks as though it has been struck by lightning.'

She was right about being nearly there. As they approached the next bend they became aware of the sound of traffic and then the sight of a lorry travelling past the entrance to the lane.

'Bless you, Elvis.' Sally yelled with excitement at the sight of her beloved car. 'You poor thing. Look at you – all wet. We'll soon get you sorted. Get in, Hannah. He may be better after a rest. Have you got a breakdown angel as well? One who is an Elvis fan?'

Hannah did not reply. She was not in the mood to trivialise angels.

Sally turned the ignition key, and the engine burst into life.

'Thank you breakdown angel, whatever your name is!' she exclaimed.

7

Modern Morals and Dilemmas

Hannah was pleased to be home, although she had to admit that it had been a stimulating break. She was disappointed to find that everyone was out. This was not unusual if extra help was needed outside, but it was late afternoon and there was not a customer in sight. She was longing to tell someone about her experiences at The Mermaid Inn whilst it was still fresh in her mind. Not that she was likely to forget, she reassured herself. She had resisted the temptation to confide in Sally. She knew that her friend would be annoyed that she had not been alerted at the time, or sometime during the next day before her return home. Initially she had not wanted to alarm her, but as the hours passed she could not bring herself to put the episode under scrutiny. She herself was having vague doubts in the cold light of day. There was such an atmosphere in the place and no sign of any other guests. Yet he had talked about them. Was he in some state of dementia? Was there only a host of phantom listeners? I'm back with that poem again, she thought. Could she have just been dreaming after all? That would be an immediate suggestion from her friends and family, but how did she know what Selina Constable looked like? They would say that without realising it she was aware of the portrait when she first entered the building. But she knew that she was not. Sally and Daisy would shake their heads and tell her she was away with the ghosties. She could just imagine them. Emma would understand, but she tended to approach it from an academic angle these days. Rachel, already well settled into bible study classes and other church organisation in her capacity as the vicar's wife, had only recently reminded her that investigating spiritual matters was best left to the experts. Marie had nodded her head in agreement, quick to point out that according to the Bible, communication with the spirit world was forbidden. So that left Simon, Leigh and Alice. Simon was trying to cope with all the complexities of the business, and Leigh and Alice were totally wrapped up in organising their futures. Oh well, she thought, perhaps it was all a series of coincidences. But then she did not believe in coincidences.

She shrugged her shoulders and reached across to the bookshelf for her current novel. She had started to read it on the day before her break at Sally's and now had forgotten what it was about. She started again at the beginning but could not concentrate and decided to have a walk around the garden centre instead. Simon worked so hard and just lately, in fact since Elphine was requiring more and more attention, he had received little support from Marie. The workload was reduced in September after the summer rush but there was always a lot of clearing up to do, and she felt sure that he would appreciate some solid down-to-earth help or a bit of tidying up in the general retailing area.

She wandered down through the entrance to the sunken field, as it had been known in the past. Apparently clay had been removed for brick making many years ago and the area now had a tendency to flood in wet winters. Simon had utilised it successfully by organising the building of a large prefabricated shed on ramps. He claimed that this was his contribution to the success of the garden centre after the death of his father. It was divided up into sections, each one specialising in gardeners' needs, but then at the end of August he had decided to compete in the Christmas market tempting people to spend money on artificial flowers, pottery vases and other fancy goods. Hannah had to admit that diversification was a good way to safeguard against financial problems. However, security was proving to be a problem, and so was the increase in insurance costs.

She found Simon in there talking to a young woman and, assuming that she was a customer, she wandered around to the other side and looked at the assortment of tools displayed on the shelves. She loved tools, especially when they were new. There was nothing worse than a blunt edge, she thought as she studied the quality and comparable prices and recalled how she struggled to tidy up the lawn edges with old shears when money was in short supply. Nowadays she was satisfied merely to look and to resist the urge to handle heavy tools. Of course she had her favourite spade and fork and her hoe and long-handled trowel. She smiled. The passion for gardening was not going to leave her in spite of the painful back problems she had endured, but she was a little more cautious these days, not being tempted to dig just one more row or tackle one more bed of nettles.

She glanced across at Simon again. It was obvious that he had not seen her. Perhaps he needed to be rescued. Some customers expected the staff to solve all of their problems. But then he seemed to be enjoying whatever it was they were discussing. His face was animated and Hannah thought that he looked more like his old self. She was very concerned about him these days. He very rarely smiled, but here he was laughing at something the woman had said, and she in turn was joining in the laughter. What a pretty girl she was. Hannah had always admired black hair, describing her own faded fairness as dull and mousy. Now, as she drew closer, she saw that everything matched. The young woman's dark brown eyes were fringed with thick dark lashes, and her skin was tanned. She looked the picture of health and was possibly in her early twenties, Hannah guessed.

It was very obvious that Simon did not want to be rescued. She knew his signs of embarrassment; the tightening of the lips and the avoidance of eye contact.

'Oh Mum,' he said. 'I didn't know you were back. Meet Maxine, or Max as you prefer it, don't you? Max is here for work experience. I was expecting a male student with a name like that. Sorry Max.' He patted her on the arm. 'My mother is an expert on all things garden.'

'I don't think so.' Hannah laughed at the idea, feeling embarrassed by his extravagant description of her and of his familiarity with the student. 'I am sure that you know a lot on the science side. I tend to go by instinct.'

'Don't listen! She's got all the knowledge one needs, Maxine, together with green fingers and thumbs, although growing doesn't come into much these days. It is really more about maintenance. People watch television programmes and come armed with lists of plants. Most of them want instant gardens. Max is studying propagation. I'm sure between us all we can give her some practical experience. Anyway, why are you back so early? We were not expecting you until Sunday.'

'Sorry, I should have let you know. It just seemed like a good day to travel before the weekend rush. The east coast is crowded. I think everybody is trying to get the last of the sunshine. Anyway, Sally and I were running out of conversation.'

'What! Don't you believe her, Max. They can talk the hind leg off a donkey. Mum has known Sally most of her life. I expect Marie will be interested in your escapades, although the kid seems to be the be-all and end-all of her life. She has gone out somewhere but I would have thought she would be back by now.'

He did not wait for a response and turned back to the student. 'Anyway Max,' he said, 'I will leave you to explore the pest control section. I had better get back into the greenhouse. Mike should be around if you need any help and Robert will be here until five.'

'I'll get back as well I think. Perhaps Marie will need some help with Elphine. I haven't come across Leigh or Alice either. Everywhere seems to be deserted.' Hannah wanted to step in between them.

'What? Oh yes it is quiet. Like you said, I think everyone is taking advantage of the sunshine and escaping. No, think again – we have some customers. Here's your chance to turn on the charm, Maxine. Talk later, Mum.'

Hannah walked slowly along the path leading to the house. A femme fatale, she thought. That young woman's body knew all the tricks. It showed in her eyes, her dimples, her pursed lips, the intimacy of her concentration, in fact her whole ambience. Simon was like a lamb to the slaughter and at a dangerous time in his marriage when Marie was obsessed with her granddaughter. Should she say something to him? It could be the last thing on his mind. Should she have a little chat with Marie and try very tactfully to tell her how unhappy Simon seemed to be? Should she warn her? It was none of her business, and yet it was her business. Simon was her son. Could she just ignore it? 'Wait and see,' a little voice said in her head. 'Never interfere between man and wife.' That was Jack's voice now. It had always been his philosophy on married life. But then she remembered his anger when Rachel collapsed in tears over the problems of her first marriage. He had immediately taken her side, even threatening violence. Still, he was very close to death at that time. A wave of sadness travelled through her mind and she wished he were here to advise her. But would he sympathise with his son?

She took a deep breath and quickened her pace. It could all be nothing. Perhaps she was reading too much into it. He was just being friendly, she told herself. After all, it had been his job to talk to students when he was a lecturer at the horticultural college. He must miss the life with his keen mind and lively sense of humour. Talking to students was what he had always done in the work place. Was he really fulfilled running a garden centre, or had he done it for the sake of his parents? Being an only son was a big responsibility.

She had reached the house now and could see Marie in the kitchen. Something made her stop walking and stare. It was the window. There was something different about the window. Something was missing. Of course, she suddenly realised. It was the Mooncat! She ran in through the door calling Marie's name. 'Has something happened to the Mooncat? Don't say he is broken!'

Marie turned to greet her, studying her hands intently whilst she carefully dried them on the tea towel. Without attempting to make eye contact she said in a low voice, 'Oh no problems. I have put it in the cupboard. I am thinking of doing some cleaning. The windowsills are in need of a good wash and a coat of paint. But probably, knowing Simon, a good wash is all that they will get. I didn't expect you back so early.' She looked up, anticipating disapproval, and was surprised by Hannah's response.

'What a good idea,' her mother-in-law enthused. 'I used to sometimes despair over this kitchen. I'm sure you must have dreams of all mod cons. I can give you a hand with the cleaning but my painting skills leave a lot to be desired these days. We can always put him back at night – the cat,' she explained. 'It really isn't good for him to be shut up in the cupboard and this is the only windowsill wide enough.'

Maria nodded, feeling that she was on safer ground yet somehow defeated.

'I had a wander across to the sunken field. Simon was there giving instructions to the student. Have you met her yet? It's a change to have a girl, but very refreshing in these days when it often seems that women's lib is floundering. She seems to be very bright.'

'He's not mentioned a student. Elphine has been so fretful and we are both very tired. She has screamed every night just lately. It could be those last molars. I remember Alice at this age. I had some terrible times with her, but not the screaming. She had fevers and saw things that were not there. Elphine does the same but her screaming is very wearing. Do you remember this age with your family?' Marie's question briefly reflected her enjoyment of shared motherhood.

Hannah did not respond to her question. Instead she asked, 'Can't Alice show a bit of responsibility while she is at home? I know I keep saying this and I know she has a lot of studying to do, but she must care about her child in spite of her condition. She was always so tender-hearted. I can't believe that she could have changed so much. We can't expect Leigh to do anything. He is little more than a child himself. Boys don't seem to be mature until about twenty-five.'

'There's nothing childlike about getting a girl pregnant,' Marie snapped.

Hannah sighed. It was so difficult to talk to anybody these days. 'I know. I expect they are all the same. I never put much faith in their ability to cope. Somehow, they don't recognise danger. Well Jack never did. As long as they were quiet, he didn't worry. I do think that we should get some advice, you know. Elphine has certainly got some issues which need investigating.'

'She has got an appointment next week at the hospital, and, like I said, she is getting those last molars.'

'I'd better unpack,' Hannah muttered.

She continued to worry about the child as she sorted out her washing and put unsoiled clothes back onto hangers or folded into a neat pile and returned to the chest of drawers.

Although it was obvious that Elphine understood everything that was said to her, and surprised them with her sudden bursts of coherent speech, she still made little attempt to communicate. Instead, she would revert to the 'echo talking'. Hannah sighed. Perhaps her behaviour was a passing phase; part of normal development and nothing to do with autism,

The next morning Simon noticed that the Mooncat was back on the windowsill but made no comment, eating his breakfast quickly and then leaving by the outside kitchen door. Hannah was painfully aware of the atmosphere. She helped with the tidying up and then made her way to the office to do her share of book-keeping. The garden centre was not open for business on Mondays, giving everyone a six-day week from Tuesday to Sunday. After the student had gone they would keep a skeleton staff on until the early spring. This was a good time for Simon and Marie to have a break, but over the last few years Simon had made every excuse, it seemed to Hannah, not to make any plans, and now that he had opened up the gift section no doubt he would be making excuses again.

Poor Marie, Hannah said to herself. Perhaps she could go to stay with her sister down in London. Marie had been excited when Bernadette moved to England. It had seemed like a million miles away to travel to Dublin, and the passing of each year added to their responsibilities. But apparently, with her dedication to the welfare of her granddaughter, a holiday was out of the question. Perhaps she would relent and allow someone else to look after the child. Perhaps Jane would stay at Willow Cottage. Clive could still do his vegetable round, and Daisy could take on a carer for a week or two in place of Jane.

Her feet had automatically found their way to the office during all of this deliberating.

'A penny for them!' That was Simon's voice. He was sorting through a heap of invoices on the counter top.

'I was thinking about you and Marie having a break. She is getting into a bit of a state with Elphine, but she won't let anyone else do anything. To be quite honest I don't think I could cope but I feel very guilty.'

'Why should you feel guilty? You have given a lot of time to grandchildren. She loves it. Nothing else seems to matter. Going on holiday with me would be the last thing she wants to do.'

'What about if Jane came for a week and she went down to London to stay with Bernadette? I'm sure Jane would manage. She is so good with children.'

'I very much doubt it, but you can suggest it. I won't even begin down that road.'

'Oh Simon! This is getting so complicated. If you and Marie are not careful, all of our futures could be affected, and Alice will not know whom to turn to. There's really nothing to stop you once this latest student has finished. What's her name?'

Hannah would have liked to comment on his familiarity with the student but hoped that she had been mistaken. However his next observations about Maxine's capabilities revived her suspicions. His eyes sparkled as he recalled her enthusiasm for her studies on propagation and the development of hybrids.

'Max is really going places,' he said. 'Those lads had better watch out this year.'

Later that day, during an escape from the weekly book-keeping to her friend's nursing home, Hannah expressed her concern for her son and his wife, omitting to mention her suspicions of possible infidelity and emphasising their need for some respite from work and child care. Daisy sympathised and agreed that she could replace Jane for a few weeks, providing she had some notice to reorganise the rote. Apparently, two of the carers were willing to do extra shifts and earn money for winter breaks in the sunshine.

'We could all do with that. How about it, Daisy? Do you fancy a week in the Canaries?'

Daisy laughed and shrugged her shoulders. 'Somebody has to

be at the helm. Not like you gallivanting off. How was Sally by the way? I bet you couldn't get a word in edgeways.'

Hannah was desperate to tell someone about their strange encounters with Jabas Constable and, in spite of her intention not to make Daisy her confidante, she heard herself describing the conversation at Bempton cliffs and how events had led them to the Mermaid Inn.

She knew as she watched her friend's reactions that Daisy would have a rational explanation for everything.

'But what about this lady's portrait in the hall? I didn't see it until we were ready to go. And why did he pretend that his wife was still alive?'

'Perhaps it wasn't a portrait of his wife. It could have been his mother, and you said that you walked along the hall when you arrived. You know very well that we see more than we realise, and dreams reflect the subconscious. It would make a good story if you embellished it a bit more, but that's all that it is. A series of coincidences and a vivid dream. What did Sally think?'

Hannah sighed. 'I didn't tell her. Selina had disappeared when she woke up. Anyway, lets talk about something else. Are you still going to the Readers' Group?'

Daisy giggled in what Hannah decided was a silly girlish way. Her friend had thoroughly irritated her with her attempts to rationalise everything.

'Actually, I've got some news for you and I am not dreaming. We've got a new member. You would approve I think. He is very distinguished-looking with a moustache and beard. No, not the ragged unkempt look before you wrinkle your nose up any further! Anyway, he seems to have picked me out to talk to during our coffee break.' Daisy giggled again, her voice shrill with embarrassment.

'Oh! What happened to Maurice then? Don't you think you should be cautious? This one could be after your money. You've already fallen foul of one gold digger in your life.'

'Hannah dear, Maurice was just a good friend and I have heard on the grapevine that Greg is loaded. Apparently he lives in a huge house on his own. He never mentions a wife and family. He could be suspecting me of being after his money. In spite of some people's opinions, I do not make a fortune out of providing care for the elderly, and I am getting elderly myself. Don't pull a face like that. We both come into the elderly description now whether we like it or not. Anyway, I thought you would be pleased for me.' Daisy's voice was now as petulant as her friend's had been moments earlier and they suddenly both felt the strain of criticism, a tangible crack appearing in their relationship.

'Oh well, it's your life, Daisy. I know you get lonely. Just be careful that's all. I intend to hang on to my independence as long as possible. I don't need you or Sally trying to pair me off with anybody. Don't tell your son that you are fraternising with the opposite sex. He will certainly be focusing on the pounds, shillings and pence, by what you have told me.'

Daisy shrugged her shoulders and shook her head. The corners of her mouth dropped back into their everyday creases. 'I will jump that hurdle when I reach it. I expect they will be as suspicious of Greg as you are. Anyway, it's early days.'

'Oh Daisy, I'm sorry. I just worry about you. I would be lost without you and Sally. It has been the three of us for years now. Like the musketeers. I couldn't have coped with Jack's death without your support.'

'But I am not going anywhere. Whatever happens in the future we can still meet up for coffee and I am not going to retire just yet.'

She stretched her arms out to embrace her friend just as the phone rang and her attention returned to the affairs of the nursing home.

Having re-established the events at the Mermaid Inn in the recounting of them to her friend, Hannah could not get the picture of Selina Constable out of her mind. Each time she visualised those brown eyes staring at her so intently, she experienced the crawling sensation travelling up her spine. What did it all mean? She longed to investigate the paranormal. She always had. The closest she had come to it was on the two occasions when she had visited Rebecca Lickis. Each time she had experienced a mixture of both excitement and apprehension, with guilt thrown in, she recalled. She had tried to satisfy her curiosity by reading various books on life after death, finding that some explanations satisfied some of her questions but mostly she remained with the same doubts expressed by Daisy and Sally and returned to her down-to-earth self, living her day-to-day existence.

However, this latest episode had strengthened her resolution to follow her own convictions and, later in the afternoon, when Marie disappeared along the driveway with Elphine in the pushchair, she looked in her address book for Rebecca's phone number. She dialled the number and listened to the ringing tone going on and on. Of course, she thought, she would not use an answering service. This would mean that she would have to return the call and she did not want to dilute her credibility by knowing personal details in advance. Perhaps she was away on one of her tours, or perhaps she no longer worked. It must be at least six years since she saw her. Perhaps she was dead. Hannah replaced the phone and went into the kitchen to make herself a drink.

After their evening meal the whole family settled down to watch the television. Looking around, Hannah sensed that each one was caught up in private thoughts, their eyes wandering away from the images on the screen, occasionally glancing at each other and quickly looking away. She suddenly felt lonely again. She was the odd one out, although it would seem by the atmosphere that everyone was single at this moment.

Later she helped in the kitchen, drying the dishes and putting them away in the cupboard, before carefully lifting the Mooncat out and placing him on the windowsill in his usual position, giving him a view of the driveway and the bordering willow trees. She patted him on the head and could sense Marie's disapproving looks even with her back to her. She deliberately did not draw the curtains across.

'I think I will have an early night, Marie. Say goodnight to the others for me.'

She opened the stairs door and made her way slowly up the twisted narrow steps, securing the bedroom door behind her and sinking down onto her bed. The rattle of the rings on the kitchen curtain pole made her jump. She visualised Marie's petulant expression as she trapped the Mooncat between the curtains and the window. She stared at her reflection in the dressing-table mirror, seeing the dark shadows under her eyes and the tired droop to her mouth. Right, she thought, it's time for some action. She struggled into her nightclothes wincing at the pain in her arm, which was rheumatism according to Daisy, and made her plans for the following day.

Perhaps she should drive to the village where Rebecca lived and enquire at the village shop, if it was still there of course. So many small shops were closing, she mused. Perhaps she would try phoning again in the morning. She struggled to undo her bra, once more grimacing at the pain in the top of her arm and minutes later relaxed under the shower, washing away the pollution of another day. Yet her anxiety for the family remained intact.

The clock ticked away the hours, until by three-thirty she felt further away from sleep than when she had first gone to bed. She reached out towards the foot of the bed where she always draped her dressing gown in readiness for nightly wanderings. Insomnia was a problem these days, and she was pleased that she had this part of the house to herself away from the main bedrooms. Even so, she trod carefully down the little twisty staircase and slowly opened the stairs door. It would be sensible to have a cup of hot milk. She knew that, but still dropped the tea bag into the cup in readiness for the boiling water. The kettle was making a droning noise as it came to the boil, adding to Hannah's sense of guilt. She clicked her tongue, impatient with herself and muttered, 'For goodness sake!'

Again, the idea of having a place of her own came into her mind. Daisy's plans to change her life had made her feel restless. The idea of leaving Willow Cottage appalled her, yet it was not the same now. In fact it had not been the same since Jack had died. This business of the Mooncat being put in the cupboard had wakened up her feeling of not belonging. There was no one to talk to anymore. What about Leigh? She had not shared her experiences and feelings with him. Somehow, these days, he and Alice had grown apart from the family. She saw little of them during term time and holidays were spent on studying and catching up with their friends.

She would confide in him before seeking out a medium, she decided, as she sipped the hot tea and ate a number of digestive biscuits.

The opportunity came sooner than she expected. The following Sunday Alice announced that she was going to meet up with an old friend from her school days.

'Is that OK with you, Marie?' Simon asked. 'Alice, your mother didn't get much sleep last night with Elphie. You look dreadful, Marie.'

'Oh thanks! That's cheered me up no end. Well I do feel about sixty this morning, but it's no good Alice doing anything. Elphine is poorly at the moment and she will only settle with me. The fewer people with her the better.'

'I could take her out for a walk. Leigh, do you fancy a stroll around the village? I haven't been able to spend much time with you, and you could take turns pushing the pram.' Hannah could hear her voice gabbling, and began to clear the breakfast dishes away.

'Don't worry!' Marie's voice rose with impatience. 'She will only go into a screaming fit. But you go for a walk, and take Leigh with you. It will be good not to listen to all that pop music. Goodness knows how young people concentrate these days.'

'I'll get out of your way as well,' Simon muttered. 'I must sort out Maxine's schedule for the final assessment.'

'Marie is really cracking up. What does Alice think about it all? I know you are under a lot of pressure with your studies, but Elphine is ultimately your responsibility.' Hannah took a deep breath and waited for her grandson to reply.

Leigh grunted, and looked across in the direction of the fields to the east of the village. After a few moments he responded. 'It's not as simple as that. Alice has offered to look after Elphie. It's no good me offering. You would think I had the plague. Marie is determined to go it alone, and there is nothing we can say or do. She is furious about us not wanting a Catholic baptism. We really don't believe in it, and she accuses us of witchcraft because we prefer to worship Mother Earth. We are grateful. Don't get me wrong. But we are not allowed anywhere near Elphie. You can see what she is like. Alice has given up trying.'

'I think the child has other problems. I know being physically handicapped is the major one but there may be something else. She could have signs of autism. Marie won't have it, but the screaming is part of it and she has been very late in talking, just repeating what she has heard. I think she is very spiritually aware and it has not helped that Marie is being so stubborn about the Mooncat. It may all seem very trivial and silly to her, but Elphine likes the cat. I've seen her expression change when Marie puts it in the cupboard.'

'I know. I noticed the speech problems, but suddenly she seems to be much better. We are trying to keep out of the argument. Marie blames our session with the ouijah board for the problems which Elphine has.'

'I didn't know anything about that. What happened then?'

'It spelt out Mother and then Sarah. The glass moved so quickly that it really scared us, and to be honest, although I always felt that I loved my mother in spite of what she did, I really felt threatened by her, as I did after Lucy died. We do follow pagan beliefs but that is not the same as spiritualism.'

'Oh well, you are not going to want to hear my latest experiences then.' Hannah sighed. 'I did feel that you would listen and comment.'

'Of course I am interested. It's just that I am trying to keep the peace with Marie and with Alice. Come on, Grandma. What have you been dreaming about?' Leigh put his arm around the back of Hannah and gave her a squeeze.

Hannah took a deep breath. 'It all began at Bempton Cliffs,' she said.

The recounting of her 'ghost story', as she now called it, lasted until they had completed their walk around the village boundaries and were walking back towards Willow Cottage. Leigh did not interrupt the flow of words but reacted with a quick catch of the breath or a tightening of his grip on his grandmother's arm during the passages that caught his imagination.

'Wow!' he exclaimed. 'What an amazing experience! What did Sally think to it all? Was she scared?'

Hannah explained that Sally had slept through it, and that somehow she felt she would have laughed it all away by declaring that it must have been a vivid dream resulting from the 'instant food' or the weird Jabas Constable.

'Daisy, as you can imagine, dismissed it all as a figment of my imagination,' she continued. 'Simon and Marie are too busy falling out and I've hardly seen Alice since I got back. So, what do you think then?'

'Well, it wasn't a dream. It was far too lucid for that. I mean the old man is obviously very switched on to recognise the level of your medium-ship. He was drawn to you, wasn't he? As you know, it is hard to communicate with someone when you want it so badly. That is why you need someone else to do it for you. I think it was a lovely experience for you. I am green with envy. It was pretty obvious that the place was empty apart from the three of you and of course The Listeners.'

'So, what do you think of me going to see Rebecca Lickis again?'

'Is she the lady Marie called the fortune teller?'

'Yes. She does talk about the future, but mostly she makes connections and who ever she connects with seems to give the advice or drops hints about things to come. I don't think she claims to tell you your fortune. I just feel that perhaps I need to move on but I don't know how to or where to go.'

'Oh Grandma! You don't have to move on. Willow Cottage is your home. Anyway, I thought you were going to spend some time with your cousins in America. All these relations you have acquired through your Uncle Patrick, are going to waste. Every year you talk about it. Instead, you spend all your time worrying about everybody else. I would like to go back to Chicago when I have qualified. In spite of bad memories, it is the place of my birth, and perhaps I need to lay a few ghosts.'

'I'm sure that you do, but perhaps I don't, and in any case you know what I am like with long flights. Anyway to get back to the spiritual side, I would like to see what your grandfather thinks. I hope Rebecca can make the connection. That is if I can get hold of her.'

But apparently it was still not the right time to seek out the services of Rebecca Lickis. Suddenly, more 'down-to-earth' problems were manifesting themselves, which, in a strange kind of way, were about to echo Hannah's wishes. However, it was not to be the holiday she had envisaged for Simon and Marie, and it certainly was not going to solve their marital problem.

8

Lost Brigadoon and Rebecca Lickis

On their return from the walk, Leigh had resumed his studies in his room, taking himself away from Marie's accusing stares. Meanwhile Hannah was telling herself to 'strike while the iron was hot' and to ring Rebecca. She reached for the phone at the precise moment when it began to ring loudly, causing her to jump in alarm. She snatched the hand piece from the stand and shouted, 'Hello.' She had become so flustered in that unguarded moment that she struggled to hear the quiet voice of the caller. 'Sorry. I can't hear you. Who did you say?' she asked.

'Can I speak to Marie? It's her sister Bernadette.'

'Oh, I'm so sorry. I didn't mean to shout. It made me jump. I'll go and fetch her.'

Hannah hurried into the kitchen where Marie was preparing vegetables for Sunday lunch. She looked up, her face immediately registering concern when Hannah told her that her sister needed to talk.

'Did she say why she's calling?' she asked Hannah as she hurried up the kitchen steps into the hall.

Hannah shook her head and waited in the doorway, hoping to glean more information from Marie's responses, but apart from the initial greeting, her voice was drowned out by Elphine's sudden laughter.

'Oh my God,' Hannah yelled, almost falling down the steps. 'I don't think you should be having that, darling. Give it to me, there's a good girl.'

She managed to extricate the vegetable knife from the child's grasp just as Elphine was about to stab a large carrot. The inevitable screams followed, bringing Marie hurrying back into the kitchen.

'For goodness sake! What have you done to upset her? How can I possibly go and help my sister when no one else can look after this child? Come on now. Grandma's here.'

Elphine continued to scream into the folds of Marie's neck, drawing her knees against the tight embrace, her eyes registering both distress and triumph it seemed to the watching Hannah.

During the inevitable sobs and shudders following this outburst Hannah waited, her brain formulating a plan of action. She recognised that there must be a plan. Suddenly she was focusing on the situation; seeing the complete picture, rather than small segments of family involvement. Poor Marie, poor Simon, poor Alice, in fact poor everybody, including this unhappy little girl marred by the circumstances of her troubled conception and birth, she thought. How easy it was for each one of them to shrug off their responsibilities by giving other matters priority and then declaring that there was not enough time, or that it was not the right time.

Well, she decided, this was the right time for everyone to take stock of the situation. Marie was heading for a breakdown in her state of health, and her marriage was in stormy waters. This call for help from Marie's sister, apparently needing some company after an eye operation, could be an intervention, divine or otherwise. She realised that she had to tread very carefully. She knew from years of experience that family issues were complicated and requiring much diplomacy. Now, as the outsider, generation-wise, she was the ideal one to negotiate some kind of peace settlement. She decided to drive to her favourite place where the big old poplar tree spread its branches and where she could embrace its stout trunk and allow the spiritual forces to work their special magic.

Half an hour later she stared in total disbelief at the ploughed land dotted with piles of logs. She remembered how there had been signs of a clearance in process before, but this was a mass extermination. Not one tree remained standing. The tears streamed down her cheeks and soon her chest ached with convulsive sobbing. She turned the car around pointing back along the lane and drove slowly over the rutted surface. She guessed that once the logs had been transported away the lane would also have no purpose along this particular stretch, and it would join the little wood as part of history rather than reality unlike the fabled Brigadoon.

She drove the car with no sense of purpose or direction. She could not face returning to Willow Cottage just yet. The last period in her time had worsened the situation, jumbling her thoughts and replacing her previous resolutions with dampening melancholy. All this spiritual stuff is getting me nowhere, she thought bitterly. Who am I kidding? Marie and Rachel were right. She should just try to be a good grandmother and leave go of the reins. Let them all sort everything out. She had done her bit.

She slowed down to avoid a stationary car and glanced at the row of houses to her right as she swung around to overtake. She recognised the tall privet growing along the side of the last house and the black gate across the front path. Without realising it, she had driven around in a circle and was now in the village where the reputed fortune-teller Rebecca Lickis lived. Such realisation jarred at her state of misery. She pulled into the side of the road trying to grasp the significance of the situation. But was it significant? She found herself in the place she had intended to re-visit. Was that significant or merely her brain subconsciously at work? At that moment a lady walking along the village street came into view. She had blond hair cut in a severe bob and was carrying a basket of provisions. In spite of the change in her appearance, Hannah recognised her as Rebecca Lickis. On her previous visit she remembered that the lady had long black hair, but years ago on that first encounter she had been as blond as she was now.

The sight of her pushing open the gate and disappearing from view beyond the hedge lifted Hannah out of her state of disillusionment. This could not be a mere coincidence she thought, quickly reminding herself as usual that she did not believe in coincidences. Something had led her here at the precise moment when Rebecca was returning home. She must act on her instincts before time passed by and this given opportunity was lost forever.

She reached for her bag and got out of the car, slamming the door behind her without her usual regard for its hinges or paintwork. Still feeling that time was of the essence, she ran across the road and pushed open the garden gate, almost tripping over the edge of the footpath leading to the front door. Her first instinct was to rap her knuckles hard against the door but rationality was returning and, taking a deep breath, she pressed her finger on the bell push. Minutes later she was looking into pale blue eyes with an immediate recall of Rebecca Lickis, no matter what the colour of her hair. She mentally flinched at their close scrutiny, and the facial expression that demanded an explanation.

'I..I'm sorry to disturb you. Do you remember me? I have paid you two visits in the past. But then I don't suppose you remember people with the number you see.' Hannah was gabbling in her usual way when she found herself caught up in an embarrassing situation. 'I'm sorry if this is a bad time for you. You must be very busy. Only my car seemed to head in this direction and there you were, and it seemed to be the right thing to do.'

'I'm sure it is, my dear. Come in and have a seat. I was just about to have a coffee. Will you join me?' She led the way into the small lounge, indicating the large leather armchair that Hannah clearly recalled sinking down into and had later struggled to be released from its grip. She sat down carefully, perching on the edge, not willing to relax; the memory of the desecrated spinney still uppermost in her mind, and the disturbing family issues following close behind.

She stared around the room, the contents not registering on her mind's eye. As on her previous visits, she was not particularly interested in the lifestyle of Rebecca Lickis. Yet, as her eyes wandered along the surface of the old sideboard, she found herself wondering whether her host was married with a growing family, and whether she could have any concept of the complexity of other people's problems. After all, she was not some kind of counsellor. What am I doing here? Hannah asked herself. She shuffled her feet on the deep carpet pile and looked anxiously towards the door.

'Here we are, my dear. I do remember you. You had Irish connections which have resolved themselves, haven't they? Well nearly.' Rebecca put the tray down on a small table and carefully handed a steaming cup of coffee to Hannah. 'Do have a biscuit or eat them all if you wish. I am on a diet.' She patted her stomach and gave a quick grin, her eyes crinkling at the corners and temporarily taking away the rather severe set of her countenance. 'If it is advice on eating disciplines you want you have come to the wrong place, but then I know you haven't. In your own good time, my dear. I will not count this as a reading, but merely as a heart to heart, although I must tell you that Jack is here to give you support. I expect you know that anyway.'

She listened intently as Hannah talked about her family, her attention moving from one person to another and back again. She made no comments, other than the occasional 'I see' accompanied by nods and the occasional pursing of her lips. The description of the tree massacre as Hannah described it brought a frown and 'Oh no. How terrible!'

Her reaction triggered another flow of tears from Hannah, and she picked up a box of tissues from the coffee table and offered them to her client.

'I couldn't believe it,' Hannah murmured between sobs, 'And then I just drove, without really seeing anything. You know what I mean? Then, here I was, and there you were. Actually, I have tried to contact you, but had no reply. I didn't know whether you had moved, or whether you were on a tour.'

Rebecca appeared not to be listening. She was staring at the window and suddenly Hannah was aware of changes in the atmosphere. She recognised the strange vibrations as spiritual energy. It was the same phenomenon she had experienced in The Mermaid Inn when Selina Constable had appeared. Rebecca turned to look at her. Her facial features had altered. There was a softening of the lines of ageing around her mouth, and Hannah was aware of a bright aura around her head. Another presence manifested itself now behind her.

She knew it was Jack and she knew that he was telling her to listen to Rebecca and that the dots were joining together. A huge surge of emotion swept over her, almost taking her breath away, and she sank back into the chair, closing her eyes and allowing the thick cushions to embrace her in their folds.

A sharp clearing of the throat brought her back into the realms of the material world. She opened her eyes and blinked against the sunshine now lighting up the room.

'Right, my dear,' her companion said. Her voice was strident, indicating urgency, and Hannah struggled to sit forward and pay attention.

'This is all about Elphine. She is the crux of every situation. Of course, it was all there before, simmering you might say, but she is the catalyst, and so our starting point. She is, what I call an in-between soul. She struggles between two worlds. Modern experts give it names. Autism, and Aspergers are two conditions often misunderstood and others talk about Indigo, Rainbow and Angels on Earth children. What many have in common are so called psychic gifts. I prefer to describe their condition as a linking with spirit. The fact that many of them seem to have amazing gifts in art and music for example is quite understandable when fundamentally it all comes directly from spirit. In the past they were known as child prodigies, or conversely idiots. Of course, some children have physical abnormalities which can hamper development, and although this would seem to be the case with Elphine, I can assure you that in spite of her difficulties, she is a very spiritual little girl and will develop special gifts.'

She absent-mindedly nibbled on a biscuit and stared into space.

'You have a white cat don't you. Ah! I understand. It's a Mooncat. An old friend of yours is telling me. It is her Mooncat, but she is letting you borrow it. She just popped in. Were you aware of her?'

Hannah nodded. 'She's my old friend, Mrs Knight. When I was a little evacuee she came to my rescue, but then I was moved on and I never saw her again.'

'That doesn't matter. She is still your friend and watching over you. Marie will not have the Mooncat on the windowsill during the day, will she? This is one issue upsetting Elphine. She communicates with spirit through the Mooncat. Of course Marie senses this but to her it is witchcraft and against her strict upbringing. Poor Marie! She is also caught up in such a tangle of truths and half-truths, feeling that she has lost her daughter and is in danger of losing her husband. So she is clinging to this child for her own sense of self-worth. She really needs the love of her sister to give her a boost and some respite even if it is only in the form of a good night's sleep.'

'I know that but it is hard to convince her. Alice and Leigh will be away again very soon, but Maxine Browne, the student, will not be finishing her work experience until December. It could be the wrong time for Simon to have a free rein with only me there to check him. I wish I knew what to do. I know that Jane would come and help with Elphine. She is an earth angel if ever there was one.'

'Don't worry. The first thing to do is to contact Marie's sister and explain to her that Marie does need a break from Elphine. Persuade her to ring again saying how much she needs Marie. Then, as your Jack says, all the dots will get joined together. By the way there are still Irish dots to join.'

'Really? In what way?'

'That's another story for another day. Time will tell.' Rebecca wagged a finger at Hannah and grinned. 'Right my dear, and that same Father Time is saying that you and I must part company. I have a client later on and I am starving.'

9

Another Serpent in the Nest

It seemed to Hannah that everything fell into place as Rebecca had predicted or more likely had known, she thought at bedtime, as she pulled the covers up to her chin and reached her feet down to the hot water bottle. Apparently she had been missed, and the anxiety showed on each of her family members' faces as she had joined them for their evening meal.

Simon had patted her on the shoulder before pulling out his chair, and Marie had managed a rather lop-sided little smile before passing her the vegetable tureen. Alice and Leigh obviously had been doing their best to guide the conversation onto lighter subjects, chatting about a mutual friend's experiences at a recent stag night and not really succeeding in impressing Marie with such tales of youthful exuberance. The sound of the telephone ringing had brought the conversation to an end. Apparently Alice was expecting a call, but as the fates had decreed, it was the next dot to be joined. Marie had quickly responded to 'Mum, it's for you,' and suddenly plans were being made. Marie was to join her sister the next day, and Daisy had reorganised her carers at the nursing home to allow for Jane to move in to Willow Cottage on one of what she described as her 'special little holidays'.

Alice and Leigh were full of enthusiasm. 'Aunt Jane will soon sort things out,' Leigh had said. 'Well, you know what I mean. She could always sort us out. She is a born nanny. And of course we shall both be out from under your feet, Grandma, on Wednesday, and the change of surroundings will do you good, Marie.'

Hannah gave a wry little smile at the memory of the expression on Marie's face. She felt sure that it would certainly do everybody else some good, but then the frown was back at the idea of Simon being given a free rein.

As was often the case, Hannah was a good judge of matters of the family, and indeed, Simon wasted no time in arranging a clandestine meeting with Maxine under the pretence of stock-taking in the gifts and tools shed. The freedom away from the scrutiny of his wife and yet the continued need for secrecy had heightened his senses, and he experienced surges of both sexual and emotional needs.

Hannah unusually did not notice the sparkle in his eyes. The process of helping Marie to pack her case and take her to the railway station to catch the southbound train occupied the whole of her attention. Jane was already sorting out the needs of Elphine. She had arrived at eight o'clock, full of life and distracting the child with her special brand of kindness and sense of fun. What a wonderful mother she would have made, Hannah thought, and not for the first time. Alice and Leigh hovered in the background, waiting for the day to settle into some kind of normality. Like Simon, they both viewed life without Marie for a while with pleasurable anticipation. It seemed to them both that they could do nothing right in her eyes, and the relationship with their child suffered in consequence.

Hannah waved goodbye at the station and returned to her car with a feeling of lightness in her step. She could not wait to be in charge. Not that I want to organise everybody, she thought to herself. It was just to be the housekeeper at Willow Cottage once more; to dust her furniture and possessions; to prepare her lunches and suppers; to stoke up her fire. The Mooncat can stay out all day now, she said to herself. He will like that and so will Elphine. It would be interesting to see if she calmed down. Just lately she had been very hysterical. Of course, Jane had a calming effect on everyone. Anyway, she mused, we will wait and see.

✳

Simon equally had breathed a sigh of relief as he waved goodbye to his wife and his mother at the gate of Willow Cottage. In that same moment the sunshine burst through the clouds and he shaded his eyes against the brightness. He planned to meet Maxine in the gift section where she would be checking and labelling the latest stock intake, and to invite her for a drink at the local inn as a prelude to what he hoped would be some intimate moments in the car before she returned to her college accommodation. Usually, a mini bus collected up the students from their work experience locations, but they could make their own arrangements if they worked into the evening. Maxine had done this on two occasions already, eating packed-up sandwiches and drinking bottled water. On the first occasion, Simon had found her in the greenhouse, and these few intimate moments albeit based on body language had led to another packed supper a week later with the increased familiarity of touching hands. He had driven her back to the college, feelings of both shyness and guilt overtaking him on both occasions. Now, in spite of his apparent freedom, he needed to put some restrictions on his behaviour. He reasoned that under the eyes of the local customers at the public house, he could justify his appearance with a young woman. It would seem very innocent to be seen discussing the work schedule and her college studies. Everyone knew him in the village. There may be a few raised eyebrows or some ribald comment, but it would all be taken in good part he was sure.

He wavered with the idea for the rest of the day. Perhaps it would be more sensible just to take her back to her room, but she would need something to eat. She was not prepared for a late session. He decided not to mention it to Hannah. No doubt she would invite Maxine to supper and volunteer to take her back. On the other hand he could organise it to look like a casual meeting at the local. He could go for a game of darts and she could be there already having sandwiches. What would be more natural than offering her a lift? It would avoid any awkward questions from the family. They would probably be pleased for him to get a bit of fun out of life with a game of darts and a pint of beer.

The last of his ideas pleased him the most, and later that morning he made his way to the gift and tools shed to organise a time for their meeting. He found Maxine engrossed in conversation with a young man. Her manner could be described as friendly, inducing a possible sale of a garden spade, but Simon, and obviously the young man ,found it to be sexually charged. She was an expert at manipulation, and as Simon approached, he sensed the hostility directed towards him from the stranger. 'Are you OK with that, Max?' he asked. She nodded and turned her back to him, successfully excluding him from a conversation that seemed to be all about the merits of this particular spade.

He wandered off towards the gift section, putting a vase straight or checking that the price labels were visible. He could hear her voice but could not make out the words. She seemed to be having a long conversation. How long could one talk about a garden spade, he wondered? The voices suddenly stopped and he turned to witness the young man walking away without the spade.

'No sale,' he called across.

Maxine gave a shrill laugh. 'It wasn't for him,' she explained. 'It was for his grandfather. He wanted something engraved as a sixtieth birthday present and his grandad is a keen gardener. In the end he decided to get him a tankard instead. Apparently he is a keen drinker as well. Has Marie gone then?'

'Yes. I'm sure it will do her good to get away, and do me good as well.'

Simon's face twisted into a grin, but the humour was not reflected in his eyes. He suddenly felt weighed down by guilt at his planned deceit. Maxine waited, expecting him to justify his last comment. When he turned away and began to stack up some packets of pot-pourri on the shelf, she tugged at his sleeve.

'How will it do you good then?'

There were shades of amusement, gentleness, and sexiness in those few words and he subconsciously recognised all of them. He knew that there was no escape. He could not resist her. He could feel the heat rising in his body and the quickening of his breathing. In the next moment he was squeezing her hand and pulling her towards him.

'Meet me at seven in the local. I plan to have a pint and a game of darts. I will tell the family that I am taking a catalogue to a customer. I will make a name up of someone in another village so that I have to use the car. You know where the pub is, don't you? Not far for you to walk.'

Maxine struggled to follow his logic. 'Why can't we just drive off miles away from here where nobody knows us? You've driven me back before.'

'I know, but Hannah will offer to take you home if she knows you are working late, and in any case they will all be pleased for me to go for a drink. They will give me their blessing. They know how Marie and I have been at loggerheads just lately. A night out with the boys is just what the doctor ordered you might say.'

10

The Whistle Blower

Hannah was not so sure of this proposed night out with the boys. She had always been able to recognise expressions of guilt on Simon's face from his early childhood and now the suppressed excitement was there for all to see. She gave Maxine a long stare as the young woman called at the office to report that she was being picked up by the mini coach in the village rather than at the garden centre. Something in the deliberation of her diction and the way her voice seemed unnaturally loud was a 'dead give-away' she decided as she later described it in silent communication with her thoughts.

It was well past midnight when she heard the sound of a key turning the large old lock in the front door. She had a terrible urge to jump out of bed and confront her son, but nevertheless she was reluctant to confirm her suspicions. After all, he was no longer a small boy to be admonished and his goodies rationed. She gave a wry smile at that thought. He was the one who should be rationing his goodies. But that brief attempt to lighten the situation quickly became overtaken by the all-pervading feelings of approaching gloom. She listened to his movements in the hall, and waited for the familiar click of the kitchen latch. However, the sounds faded into the occasional creak of the stair treads and of the old floorboards on the landing. No further sound penetrated the stout walls and she sank back down under the covers and closed her eyes back into a sleep mode. Yet she knew that a return to sleep was difficult with so many thoughts racing around in her mind.

The next day dawned with a feeling of calm in the air. It was difficult to explain such calmness with so many underlying currents in what, to all intents and purposes, was an unchanged routine. Apparently, everyone was reacting to this calmness. Elphine was all sweetness and light as Jane described it, sitting at the table and carefully eating her breakfast cereals.

Hannah sat at the head of the table in Marie's chair feeling that she was back where she belonged. Alice and Leigh were like a couple of kids she thought, as she watched them arguing about who was to have the novelty in the cornflake packet. If only Jack was here. Simon certainly was not, in mind at any rate. She studied his face, noting how much like his father he was becoming. But then Jack would never have betrayed my love, she mused.

Simon was suddenly aware of her close scrutiny and pushed his plate away from him.

'Have I overcooked it?' Jane asked, looking with concern at his half-filled plate.

'No. I'm not hungry. I must get on. We have a lot to do today. The Christmas stock is coming in and then there is all the millennium stuff. I need to check it all against our order sheets There is so much talk of crashing systems, I am doing a belt and braces thing.'

'I never did trust leaving everything to computers.' Hannah said. 'Still, what's the point of worrying. If the banks crash, we are all in the same boat. I'll give you a hand later, Simon, if that is OK with you, Jane? I have to sort out some stuff for the village jumble sale. Leigh and Alice, you had better get on with your packing and get rid of anything you will never wear again while you are at it. We all have far too many clothes.'

No one disagreed with her or perhaps actually agreed with her, she thought. Simon got up from the table and left the house by the kitchen door, walking quickly towards the tools and gift shed. Alice began to talk quite loudly to her little daughter and Leigh joined in. Their youthful exuberance covered an awkward silence, and left

Hannah wondering just how much they knew of the state of Marie's and Simon's marriage and to what level of guilt they felt for their part in it.

Jane began to clear the table. She reminded Hannah so much of dear Auntie Ella. Why had everything changed so much? What happy days she had spent at Willow Cottage in her childhood and then later when she and Jack left the village store, which he had inherited from his foster parents, and bought Willow Cottage to develop it as a garden centre. She had been very uncertain of that move; afraid of old memories, the trauma of Aunt Kate's death and the bitter jealousy of Uncle Harry's sister. Later, the good memories had surfaced, and she was back in her own little paradise with her four children and her husband. But suddenly it was all going wrong. She was on her own now without her partner, and her family were changing; now with modern values and standards she could not readily accept.

However, her older daughter Rachel was in a different kind of world, she thought. She still had traditional standards, but had moved over into a rather bigoted state of mind. Now as the vicar's lady, she viewed the modern world with a disapproving eye, labelling all young people as irresponsible, regardless. Her family links could only be described as tenuous. The twins Karl and Kirstie seemed suddenly to be out of tune with each other. It could be hormonal, Hannah reasoned. They were of different sexes after all, in spite of them being twins and having a lot in common. She had noticed on recent visits to the vicarage that the usual harmony between them was now replaced with constant, noisy, verbal intercourse, and all of the remonstrations from their mother seemed to fuel the differences of opinion. Justin was pretty useless in that department, she mused. The difference in age between him and her daughter had always worried her. He was set in his ways; a confirmed bachelor it would seem, and she had guessed from the start of their relationship that he needed a wife to give him social acceptance in this small Lincolnshire community with its rather narrow-minded rustic way of life. Apparently, in his youth, he had worked abroad at Christian missions where a single status was an advantage. Hannah sighed. How Rachel had changed, she thought. That happy carefree girl of…she paused allowing her brain to trace back the years. She remembered how she had fretted over this second marriage, wondering whether her daughter was destined to be happy or to be some kind of victim.

Elphine's sudden laughter brought her attention back to the kitchen. Jane had completed the morning chores and was repeating the nursery rhyme about Jack and Jill, accompanied by comical actions. She joined in, and Elphine looked from one to another, her expressions changing from anguish to happiness as the brief 'story' of the two children was recounted. Jane threw her arms around the child, hugging her so joyfully that Hannah wished she had some kind of device that could capture such love. A photograph was the nearest thing, she thought, but even that could not come anywhere close to holding the essence of it. What did people say? If only it could be bottled.

She relaxed back on to the kitchen chair and studied her companions; the middle-aged woman with early signs of aging showing in the deepening lines around her mouth and in her brow, and the little girl born with the imperfections which marred her complexion and the shape of her face. Jane had produced a nursery rhyme book from her shopping bag.

'I thought she might enjoy some of these. The pictures are good. It is one of mine from my childhood, a real treasure you might say.'

'That's a lovely idea. I have got a book from my childhood. It was sent to me on my fifth birthday from my grandmother in Ireland. Did I tell you that I found out why she never contacted us again? As you say, a real treasure. In fact it is called *A Child's Treasury*.'

Elphine was turning the pages. 'That one,' she demanded.

Jane began to read:

'There was a crooked man, who walked a crooked mile.

'He found a crooked sixpence beside a crooked stile.'

'Crooked, crooked, crooked.' Elphine repeated the word. 'What's crooked?' she asked.

Jane looked at Hannah, who hesitated before saying, 'It's something that is not quite straight.'

'I'm crooked,' Elphine said and laughed. 'I'm like the crooked man. What is a sixpence and what else was there? Start again.'

She commented on the stile at the entrance to the field at the back of Willow Cottage and laughed at the idea of a crooked cat and a crooked mouse. 'We live in a crooked house,' she declared. 'Willow Cottage has crooked bits all over it. I am the crooked girl who lives in a crooked house aren't I, Great-grandmother?'

Hannah and Jane looked at each other and Jane raised her eyebrows and tilted her head to one side in a silent comment on the child's sudden ability to reason and communicate.

Hannah was recalling her recent conversation with Rebecca Lickis, when she had described Elphine as a special child. She was reminded of her son Mark who had died so tragically, and of his son, her grandson Leigh. Mark had appeared to be very late in developing speech and apparently so had Leigh. Suddenly all the connections in the brain seemed to have been made and both of them had missed out the baby talk and moved into advanced syntax. She remembered how Leigh had the strange ability of seeing sounds like colours, and how acute his sense of hearing was. These days she could not recall him demonstrating any of these traits, but he had a phenomenal memory. Of course he was closely linked with spirit; something he did not talk about readily with the rest of the family, except of course herself and Alice. Now, it was all beginning to fall into place or as Jack would say, 'All the dots were joining together.'

She left Elphine in the capable hands of Jane, and went into her bedroom to make her bed and to sort out the promised jumble. Half an hour later she went in search of Simon, leaving by the old back kitchen door, and not noticing Rachel's small hatch back car parked on the front gravel. Consequently she was very surprised nearly to bump into her daughter as she rounded the end of the long greenhouse. Rachel looked unusually flustered, and was breathing heavily. She stopped and put her arms out, barring the way. 'Go back to the house. Don't go in there,' she gasped, her voice barely audible.

'Whatever is the matter?' Hannah had turned and was walking back along the path, half turning to look at Rachel, concerned at the flush in her cheeks and the agitation in her voice. 'You look as though you have seen a ghost.'

'Just get back to the house. Is Jane in the kitchen? We don't want her to get wind of it.'

'Wind of what? I expect she is doing the bedrooms by now. We can always walk into the village. Will that be far enough away?' Hannah's concern was being replaced with curiosity and slight irritation at Rachel's tone of voice. They had reached the area given over to herbaceous plants and shrubs where Mike Cross, the senior gardener in the business, was apparently 'having a good clear out'.

Rachel ignored his cheery wave, taking the earlier advice and hurrying her mother along towards the entrance.

'I was only joking,' Hannah gasped. 'Can't we just go inside? I'm sure Jane will be too busy to interrupt whatever ghastly secret you have to reveal.'

'I'm not taking any chances. Anyway we can sit down there, look, and you can catch your breath.'

She indicated the seat on the grass verge somewhat overgrown by tall grasses and cow parsley. Hannah cast a suspicious glance at it. In its position under a sycamore tree, it was never a particularly inviting place to sit, the surface inevitably littered with wet or decaying leaves.

'We'll try the next one.' Rachel strode on, her breathing more under control now but the agitation still showing in the stiffness of her shoulders.

They had almost reached the village street by the time the next available resting place came into sight. This was a length of tree trunk ornately carved with faces, animal shapes and sheaves of corn to illustrate the nature of the place. The parish council commissioned it in the previous year as a central focus of creativity, and it seemed like sacrilege to Hannah to use it as a seat. However, Rachel had no compunction in finding a smooth area and sinking down onto it. She patted a space along the trunk, and Hannah perched on it at a slight angle, shaking her head and sighing.

'Come on then. What's the big secret? I'm sure we are not meant to sit on here. It's a work of art.'

'Where do I begin? You are not going to believe this, Mother. I couldn't believe my eyes.' Rachel shook her head to emphasise her supposed disability. 'But I have got to tell you, because you have got to say something. He won't take any notice of me.'

'Is it Justin. Whatever has he done to you? Or is it Karl?'

'Oh Mother, for goodness sake. Why do you think I wouldn't let you go in the greenhouse? Why do you think we have walked this far? It's Simon who is causing all the problems. I was looking for you. You were not in the kitchen so I guessed you would be somewhere in the gardens. The greenhouse door was open which surprised me and I was just going to call out when I saw Simon at the far end. Oh gosh! This is so embarrassing! He was…well you know what, with a woman. I couldn't see her face. Just her legs.' Rachel's voice trailed off into a whisper. 'I turned and ran back along the path, and that's where I bumped into you. How could he do that with a customer? Has he gone mad or something?'

'Oh Simon. You stupid boy.' Hannah's breath was coming quickly with the exertion of the hurried walk and the agitation caused by her daughter's disclosure. She explained that he appeared to have developed an infatuation for a student called Maxine Brown. 'I hoped it was just a small lapse, and that he would come to his senses, but she knows how to manipulate and he is at a dangerous age. Marie hasn't helped with her obsession over Elphine, and her fear of pregnancy.'

'Of course! She is so obsessive about birth control, and all this business of having the child baptised in the Catholic Church.'

Hannah recognised the self-righteous tone in her daughter's voice and suspected that she would take some kind of sanctimonious pleasure in her sister-in-law's discomfort. But surely not like this, she reasoned. 'We must keep this to ourselves,' she said quietly. 'Don't breathe a word of it to Justin or allow the twins in on it. They are not exactly the souls of discretion.'

Rachel nodded and shuffled her bottom on the log, remembering how her children had been responsible for Alice learning of her adoption, and running away. It was a long time ago, but she knew that Hannah was remembering as well, hence her comment. Couldn't they ever forgive and forget, she thought bitterly.

'I will talk to Simon tonight when all the staff have gone. In fact I will make sure that he does not make plans again to go out. I don't think he will do that two nights in a row.'

Rachel leant forward to hear her mother's words, the last ones being almost swallowed up by the noise of a passing tractor. She did not ask her to repeat her words, suddenly wanting no further part in all of it, and stood up, intent on returning to her daily duties as the vicar's lady. Hannah eased her body off the hardness of the tree trunk, wincing at the pain in her lower spine.

'Why did you come, by the way? It isn't your day for a visit yet.'

'Oh that will keep. It was some fund-raising for the church roof. We wondered if you had anything of value you could part with for the cause. We are thinking of an auction.'

Hannah shrugged 'I'll have a look. They will wonder where on earth I am. It will soon be coffee time.'

They did not speak again, putting all their energy into climbing the small hill that led back to Willow Cottage.

Rachel declined the offer of a cup of coffee and half-raised her hand towards Jane who was looking through the kitchen window. She is too embarrassed to stay and risk coming face to face with Simon, Hannah thought. She knew with a sinking heart that the damage was done, and it was going to be very hard to put things right between brother and sister. They had always been good friends. Simon had defended Rachel in their younger days and was full of sympathy over her failed marriage, declaring outrage over the infidelity of her first husband Steve, and now here he was playing the same cheating role. Although Rachel declared that she had no wish to discuss the matter any further, Hannah knew that it would put a great strain on the rest of the family. Emma would soon pick up on it, she mused. She and Rachel were close, in spite of conflicting ideas on relationships and philosophy. Sibling love and loyalties had created a strong bond over the years. Perhaps that same bond with Simon would help her to forgive and forget.

There was no time like the present, she decided. The workforce usually took a break for coffee at around eleven o'clock, taking it in turns to man the till. She rang the big hand bell and began to set the mugs out on the table in the old back kitchen. This morning ritual went back to the years when she was an evacuee living at Willow Cottage with Aunt Kate, Uncle Harry and Ella. The only work force at that time was a garden boy, except for a brief spell when a land girl helped with the vegetable harvesting, she remembered. They were such happy days in spite of the war and the death of her mother and grandparents. She felt the tears pricking at the back of her eyes and turned to switch off the kettle, reproaching herself for her weakness as she had done on a number of occasions during the last few months.

She was not sure how she would broach the subject with Simon. Could she look them both in the eyes with the knowledge she now had of their earlier misdemeanours? Perhaps the student would not show up for coffee. She very often had a bottle of water with her, and continued with the work in hand. That would be a relief if I could get Simon to himself, Hannah thought. She spooned coffee into four of the mugs, her hand moving awkwardly and tipping some of the granules on to the table. She could hear voices and looked across to the side gate leading to the garden centre. There were three men and no sign of Maxine. They followed each other in, all dutifully rubbing their feet on the big old doormat. Hannah greeted them in turn, giving Simon a cursory nod.

Jane decided to join them, leaving the preparation of vegetables in the front kitchen and with Elphine following behind. Soon everyone was chattering about the changeable weather, the latest news, and the talk of problems caused by the millennium time change on computers. Jane insisted on a few minutes of silence from the adults as the child recited Jack and Jill, with comical actions bringing smiles to their faces in place of frowns. This seemed to be a signal for them to stand up, scraping the chair legs on the quarry tiles and stretching their spines back in to a working posture once more.

Hannah knew that she was sweating. She could feel the stickiness under her armpits and along the creases in her neck. She knew that she could not avoid this confrontation with her son. 'Simon,' she said, her voice sounding strangely alien to her, 'can I have a word?' She turned to go up the step into the hall, half-turning to see if her son was following her. She led the way into the living room, and told him to close the door. The fire was struggling to burn, and she picked up the poker to lift the smouldering sticks and allow air to feed the flames.

'Jane hasn't got the knack of it yet,' she said. 'Marie would have had it blazing by now.'

'So what do you want then, Mum? Whatever it is I really must get on.'

'I'll not keep you long, Simon. Rachel saw you and Maxine in the greenhouse. Do I have to spell it out?'

'Oh.'

For a moment he watched his mother stirring the flames before continuing with more subdued tones but now with a defensive air.

'So is Rachel going to spill the beans then? I bet she can't wait to don her holier than thou cap and punish Marie for being a Catholic.'

'I don't think this is the right time for you to get on your high horse, Simon. I have seen what is going on for sometime. It is pretty obvious, you know. I think the only person in this household who has not seemed to notice is Marie.'

'She doesn't notice me at all. Full stop. Have you any idea, Mother, what it is like to have an empty bed? Of course you do, but I mean in the past when Dad was alive. She has no interest in even a cuddle. She even puts her hands over her breasts as if she will be polluted in some way. How do you think that makes me feel?'

'Well, that's about her cancer scare, isn't it? You did know about that, didn't you? She is still not in the clear, poor girl. She has been advised to be vigilant, and she has six-monthly check-ups.'

'Cancer? She never told me. You see what I mean. She doesn't communicate with me any more.'

'Please think about how this will affect all the family, Simon. If Marie leaves, she will want to take Elphine with her, and that will cause problems with Leigh and Alice. I could not accept a relationship in this house with this girl and would have to leave, and you are going to end up with recriminations coming from all directions. The business would suffer, and no doubt when the infatuation is over and you come back down to earth, you will regret this possibly for the rest of your life. Don't forget that your father wished for the girls to have a share in the business. You have not done so bad. Nothing is ever easy. Yes I know you have worked hard, but so has Marie. It hasn't been easy for her to give up her modern house with all the latest furniture and come to this cottage with its old-fashioned décor and facilities. It was not hard for you because you have always been used to it but poor Marie would love to have a modern kitchen. Don't do this to her, Simon. It will destroy her.' Hannah took a long breath.

Simon did not speak. He had sunk down into the armchair, resting his head in his hands and staring into the fire. After a few minutes of silence apart from the crackling of the burning wood, he stood up and left the room.

Hannah heard his footsteps in the hall and on the steps leading down into the back kitchen. She picked up the coalscuttle and shook some small lumps onto the blazing sticks. Fire had always been such a comfort to her, and now the heat radiating out encouraged her to crouch down on the rug and absorb it. Jane was alarmed to see her in this position when she popped her head around the door minutes later. She was concerned initially about lighting the fire so early, and about her clumsy efforts to chop firewood, and now the sight of her friend staring into the flames renewed her concerns.

'Are you cold, Hannah? I'm sorry it is such a lousy fire. I'm hopeless with them. I'm used to clicking a switch on. Can I get you anything?'

Hannah turned around, and struggled to her feet. 'No thanks, Jane. I just had a fit of shivers, but I am all right now. It will be fine soon. I think the wood is a bit damp. It's a daily chore I know, but it's well worth it especially in the winter when we can escape the cold in front of a roaring fire.'

Elphine opened her eyes when she heard Jane leaving the kitchen. She had been pretending to be asleep, curled up in the big old armchair near the comforting heat from the kitchen range. She had sensed that the Mooncat was staring at her and pleased that he was facing into the room instead of in his usual position looking out towards the willow trees.

Hannah and Jane had been surprised at her sudden burst of coherent speech, but they would have been even more surprised by her ability to communicate by thought. Of course Hannah knew that the white pot cat was an embodiment of a link with the spirit world; that other level of awareness ever present and accessible beyond the material world. But she herself had only ever accessed his powers by proxy through dreams. Elphine did the same of course. Sometimes she saw strange frightening people in her dreams. She called these crooked dreams, and sometimes she found herself flying over the rooftops and sitting high in the branches of trees. Mostly she wanted to stay in her dreams forever, but on other occasions she was relieved to experience that familiar 'plop' as she returned to her physical body.

But then the Mooncat was a direct link for her with her spirit guides at any time of the day or night. She closed her eyes again as she heard the footsteps in the hall, and within seconds found herself in a garden where water cascaded down rocks, and beautiful flowers grew in all the nooks and crannies. She looked at her reflection in a clear pool and saw her face no longer crooked, but beautifully formed, smiling back at her. A little girl joined her, looking into the pool and laughing. She had a ballet dress on and began to dance, pointing her toes and moving in leaps and twirls across the lush green space on the waterside. Elphine knew that they had played together before and now they held hands skimming lightly a few inches above the tops of the flowers. Suddenly a young boy appeared, and she found herself in between them, each holding a hand and guiding her upwards into a beautiful blue space.

The atmosphere at midday as the family gathered around the kitchen table for lunch was strained to say the least. Jane was her normal pleasant self, but Simon did not speak throughout the whole meal and Leigh and Alice, aware that something must have upset him, were discussing their friends and giggling over what to Hannah's ears amounted to childish nonsense. She knew that they were doing their best to lighten the atmosphere, but the whole thing was irritating her. Jane began to clear away the plates, clicking her tongue at the quantity of food still on Simon's plate. Suddenly, Elphine threw her spoon across the room and began to wail. This seemed to be a signal for Simon to jump up and leave the room. Jane gathered up the screaming child and took her into the hall whilst Leigh, Alice and Hannah looked at each other and sighed in unison.

Throughout the rest of the day it seemed to Hannah that everyone was in a kind of role-play mode; going through the motions so to speak. Even Jane, who was not normally given to moodiness, appeared like a shadow of herself, mechanically completing her chores and spending time listlessly turning the pages of the nursery rhyme book for the attention of an equally dispassionate child.

Rachel had fared no better, and she had still been awake into the early hours of the morning. In spite of her anger at the irresponsible behaviour of her brother, she was not happy with the role she was playing as some kind of whistle blower. She knew that her mother was already aware of the situation and that fact both saddened and irritated her. How could she stand by and let it happen? But then what could she do about it? Marie was not the easiest of people to advise. Her sister-in-law had changed so much since the family had moved in to Willow Cottage. 'Extended families are a recipe for trouble.' That was what one of her parishioners had said the other day. She remembered debating this, and pointing out that everyone had a contribution to make whatever the age or relationship. She knew that her mother could be high-handed at times, and tended to forget that Marie was now at the helm.

Still, she thought, I've done my bit. She had moved across the mattress, as Justin flung his arm sideways, and she inwardly cursed his snoring. She was tempted to go into the small bedroom and escape from the incessant noise, but she was warm and the mattress on the spare bed was hard. Anyway, she grumbled to herself, why should I have to move? She drew her toenail under the sole of his foot causing him to jump violently and the snoring stopped for a moment, but then it began again with greater ferocity, and she pulled the covers up over her head.

She knew that Marie had left the marital bed, using the child as an excuse, but look what that had caused. She herself was not particularly interested in having sex with Justin. He had no skills in that department. At least Steve had had his moments, even if they were interspersed with violence. She could imagine that Simon was very loving. He had always shown her brotherly love. Poor Simon! Why did she tell Hannah? Perhaps it would have all fizzled out when Marie came home and it would soon be the end of term for the student.

Suddenly the snoring had become too harsh to bear, and Rachel, acting against all of her efforts to preserve harmony in her marriage, had flung back the covers, and left the marital bed.

Hannah needed to talk to someone. She knew that it would be pointless upsetting Emma. Emma and Simon were very close and she would make excuses for him, especially if she thought that Rachel was getting on her high horse, as she would probably describe it. Somewhat against her better judgement, Hannah rang Daisy, and arranged to meet her for coffee at their favourite 'watering hole' in Lincoln. As she replaced the receiver she regretted her impulse, but then consoled herself with the thought that there was no need to broach the subject of her son's misdeeds. She was just being sociable after all. It was good to meet up away from the work place from time to time.

Daisy was dressed in her new outfit. Hannah recognised it from her friend's description earlier during the phone call. The first ten minutes of their get together was used up with details of her journey to Leeds on a local coach, and how she had scoured the shops for matching accessories.

'You ought to come with me next time, Hannah dear. You really do neglect yourself. That family of yours should be sorting out their own problems without involving you. They had some lovely dresses in one big store. I thought about you when I saw them. Casual, you know. Just your scene.'

Hannah suddenly had the urge to justify her concern over her family, and her apparent lack of anything decent to wear.

'I really need some advice Daisy. I know that you think I should leave them all to it but I am so worried.'

Daisy shook her head and sighed as the events of the previous day were revealed.

'What does Emma think?'

'I haven't told her. I think she would probably side with Simon. Marie does seem to have alienated everyone just lately, and Rachel is so condemning of the single mother status since she married Justin. I know that gets up Emma's nose. Oh! I do wish they would all get on.'

'And I wish that you were not so involved. I didn't agree with them moving in, you know. They could have stayed in their own place and Simon could have travelled each day. It did throw Alice and Leigh together, didn't it, and look at the consequences of that. I don't know, Hannah. My advice is to keep out of it. How's Jane by the way? That replacement carer is a bit useless. How long is she staying with you?'

Hannah began to enthuse about Jane, listing her qualities as a child carer, and commenting on how she would have excelled as a mother. She described Elphine's amazing progress in her communication skills, recounting her conversation regarding the 'Crooked Man'. Her voice shook with emotion, and Daisy patted her hand across the table.

'Well. Let's hope Marie returns soon and sorts out her husband, and it would be nice to have Jane back with the team. Old people, that's her forte. I suppose we had better get on. Emma is covering for me. She's one in a million, that daughter of yours. I don't know what I would do without her. I just hope she doesn't suddenly decide to have a relationship and move on.'

Emma was pleased to hear Daisy's heels clicking along the wooden floor of the entrance hall in Daisy Cottage Nursing Home, signalling her return. Her employer was absenting herself more and more during recent months, and now with Jane missing also, it was hard at times to cope with some of the young care workers. She had to admit that there was an age gap, albeit only a handful of years, but her experiences at university and in the workplace as well as the trials of motherhood, set her apart from the rest of the staff. At times she found it difficult to sympathise with their problems, and now this latest revelation coming closer from home about her brother Simon was adding to her feeling of separation.

Leaving home at the age of eighteen to go to university, and then living in Hull had begun the process of division, although she had always preferred her own company for as long as she could remember. Rachel had seldom confided in her. She was always regarded as the little sister, and she realised now that her slide from grace by becoming pregnant after a so called one-night stand, with no memory of the father, and then losing her job, could be regarded as a protest from a little girl trying to cope in an adult world.

She had tried to be sympathetic when her sister's marriage ended in a divorce, and played the role of aunt to the twins over the years with ever-increasing difficulty as they awkwardly embraced each stage of their development. She was ashamed to admit that she was relieved, albeit in a self-centred kind of way, to see that their advancement into puberty was putting a great strain not only on Rachel but on everyone in the family, and had greeted her sister with well meant sympathy when that lady had arrived during Daisy's absence.

However, Rachel's condemnation of their brother Simon and the fact that it seemed she herself was the last to be told, restored the feelings she had once had of not really belonging in this close-knit family, especially since her father had died. She could not with all conscience criticise her brother for his lapse. She had hardly been an angel herself, she thought. And as for Rachel, with a failed marriage behind her and a loveless one ahead of her for the rest of her days, she guessed that given half a chance.... She sighed. What could she say? What should she say?

'Mum is going to have a word, or so she says,' Rachel had continued. 'But will she? You know what she is like over her sons, and now Leigh. Look what a problem he has caused with that poor misshapen child. It has all lead to this. Marie has taken on the role of Grandmother even though the real one is that creature Molly, and condemns the family for not being Catholic. She should have stayed in Ireland. But it doesn't excuse Simon, all the same. Surely he should be over all that nonsense by now. Justin is dedicated to his work and trying to be a good father to the twins.'

Emma had nodded. Rachel's husband still reminded her of Mr Collins in *Pride and Prejudice*. She could not imagine that sexual activities had ever played a part in his prosaic life. Good for Simon, she thought. Marie, her sister and her brother-in-law should all be put in a big bag and shaken up.

She smiled sweetly at Rachel. 'Mum will sort it. You'll see. She has always sorted everything. Do you want a cup of coffee?'

'No thank you. I've got an auction to organise. I didn't think you would come up with any suggestions. Your Poppy will be straining at the leash soon. Let's hope she hasn't inherited any family traits. Still, you probably won't know the extent of that, will you?' Rachel's mouth curled into a sneer.

Emma had watched her walking towards the office door and sighed. She did not like this version of her sister. The old version of a battered wife had given her some family support, but this self-satisfied so called 'vicar's lady' image was a poor substitute for the sister she had known through her childhood and teenage years. She had experienced a moment of sneaking sympathy as she noticed a slight touch of weariness in her sister's gait, but then the shrug of the shoulders appearing to express futility and contempt, and the final jibe hardened her heart, strengthening her sympathy for her brother.

Meanwhile, if the gentleman in question had known to what extent his family and acquaintances were involved in his affairs of the heart, he would, at first, have been mortified and then extremely angry. However, in spite of the conversation between himself and his mother, the old adage that love is blind still applied, although he had to admit now to feeling nervous about his future. His body still ached for physical contact with Maxine, comparing her with Marie, who had never taken his emotions to such heights.

He busied himself for the remainder of the day, avoiding any further contact with Maxine and continuing to work in the failing light of the late summer evening long after his employees had left. In spite of his lingering feelings of defiance, he could not look Hannah in the eye, and, after declining supper, he went to bed declaring that he had a headache and was not to be disturbed.

11

Crooked Dreams

Elphine was in a state of great excitement. Jane had taken her down to the village store, and bought her a drawing book together with a pencil, a rubber and a packet of pencil crayons. The little girl had longed for such possessions for some time but had been denied them after she scribbled on her bedroom walls with a black biro. Her grandmother Marie had been very cross with her, and from that day any kind of writing implement had been kept carefully out of the child's reach. Jane was not flouting this rule. Indeed she had no knowledge of it, and in consequence Elphine had no qualms in accepting the gift. She could not wait to walk back from the village street, and ran ahead along the driveway waving her treasures in the air and calling out to anyone, friend or stranger alike. Not one of them could possibly know how this purchase would influence the child's development.

Unbeknown to this extended Clayton family, the past was coming back to haunt them in the form of a certain Zacchaeus Pound. Everyone in the family, apart from Emma's daughter young Poppy, and of course Elphine, was familiar with the name. For the twins, Karl and Kirstie, it reminded them of the part they played in the revealing of the truth of her adoptive status to their cousin Alice. This spiteful disclosure led to the nine-year-old child running away in tears and falling into the clutches of Zacchaeus Pound, who recognised her from a few years previous when he was dismissed for dishonesty from his job at the garden centre. His attempts to profit from the abduction failed when Leigh had one of his special dreams and the police were alerted. Zacchaeus made his escape and evaded future arrest because Alice deliberately gave the police misleading information about his van, and claimed that she could not remember anything about his physical appearance. She was afraid of his mother's retribution from beyond the grave, and both her parents and grandparents were anxious to comfort her over the trauma of her discovery regarding the details of her adoption. In any case he had not molested the child, and she had experienced a sneaking sympathy for him when he told her that he also was adopted.

However, in spite of his brush with the police twelve years ago, Zacchaeus Pound was still intent on revenge. His mother constantly plagued him in his dreams with demands of retribution, and in his mind he regarded his dishonest practices during his employment with the Claytons all those years earlier in a new light. After all, he reasoned, he had only been getting back what they owed him for all of his hard work. Peanuts, he thought bitterly. That's what they paid me. Peanuts! His mother supported his convictions like an avenging angel from beyond the veil, her dark eyes and sallow complexion imprinted on his memory from her past tyranny. Now, after years of casual labour, living in squats and frequenting soup kitchens, he had returned to Norbrooke.

During the years of his absence, he had changed from a reasonably vigorous man into an old bewhiskered vagrant; down at heel, raggedy and unwashed. He had changed his name unofficially to Tom Smith, a surname accepted by travellers who frequently crossed his path, taking pity on him and occasionally giving him food and shelter.

Now, from the shadows of the willow trees, he stared along the driveway into the garden centre, observing the new buildings and signs of prosperity. He watched as Jane turned in through the gates accompanied by a crippled little girl, who, in spite of her infirmity, skipped and jumped along clutching a packet in her hand. He noted how they turned to the left into the pathway leading to the house.

'Another little Clayton, I bet,' he muttered.

In that same instance, Hannah was looking along the drive from the kitchen window. She felt very responsible for the safety of the child, and yet she had the utmost faith in Jane. In spite of her concern for Simon and her decision to confront him, she was aware of a lightening of the atmosphere since the departure of her daughter-in-law. It seemed that now that the Mooncat stayed on the windowsill all of the time, instead of being banished to the cupboard during the day, there was a sense of security. Elphine settled down at night, and there had been no tantrums during the last two days.

She watched Jane with the child turning onto the house path, and was reminded of the love of Auntie Ella all those years ago during the wartime. There was something about their kind of people, she thought; eternal youth; simplicity. Whatever it was it ought to be bottled. This was a favourite expression of hers and she smiled in recall, imagining it escaping like some kind of fairy tale genie.

Jane constantly decried her own urban ways, apologising for her ignorance of species of flora and fauna of the countryside, yet her homespun philosophy was her charm. Hannah had often wondered about her circumstances before coming to work at the nursing home. From occasional comments she gleaned that life throughout Jane's childhood had not been easy for her parents, but the 'whys and the wherefores' were never explained. Was she an only child? Did she have close relatives? Were her parents still around? It was obvious that she loved children, and the residents at Daisy Cottage Nursing Home constantly sang her praises. It was plain to see that her husband, Clive Spryfoot adored her. His name had evoked amusement when he first came onto the scene, and yet it suited his brand of energy, made more intense by the bright ways of his little Jane as he called her.

Now, as temporary child minder and general aid, Jane looked to Hannah for guidance with a natural respect for one whom she considered to be wiser than herself. It was this respect that endeared her to the older generation, and her child like sense of fun captivating the young members of this family.

Elphine's laughter and excited calls of 'Great-grandma' heralded their return, and Hannah pushed aside her anxieties for her son, rejoicing in the happiness of this sunny afternoon at Willow Cottage – with no awareness, of course, of the return of Zacchaeus Pound.

It seemed to Hannah that the remaining days of the week followed each other quickly, and she commented to Jane that time was flying by and that it would be Christmas again before they knew it. She mentally labelled these kinds of days as 'padding days' when nothing remarkable was entered into her diary, and 'got up, had meals and went to bed' summed them up. Jane nodded, scarcely listening. She was tired. For her it had been a busy week; the responsibility of household chores and coping with the mood swings of a handicapped child were beginning to erode her enthusiasm. Clive was not feeling well, and although he was very capable of looking after himself after years of being single, he now took badly to preparing his own meals. Hannah had invited him to move in with his wife, but he had declined on the grounds that he needed to be up early in order to stock up his van at the suppliers, and he would disturb the whole household. Jane knew that really he liked to settle down at night with his own choice of television viewing, the sports channels being a favourite. She sighed as she reached for the tea towel. It was difficult to please everybody.

By two o'clock, household chores completed until Elphine's teatime and preparations for family supper, Jane sank down into the old upholstered kitchen chair. Her tired muscles relaxed in the comforting heat radiating from the solid fuel range.

Hannah had arranged to meet up with Daisy. 'Be about an hour,' she called through the hatch.

Elphine was busily drawing an image of the Mooncat. Since the purchase of the art materials, she had astounded everyone with her ability to sketch. Fractious behaviour was now limited to those times of adult demands to put away her pencils and crayons particularly at bedtime. As her screams echoed around the house, it seemed to everyone else that Jane had somehow opened a hornet's nest as Simon put it, and that Marie had been right after all to discourage scribbling. Jane protested that the child was not scribbling and that she had amazing talent. However, on this particular afternoon she had little energy to enthuse, and the sound of Elphine's chattering slowly merged into the world of her dreams as she sank into a deep sleep.

Now the child, with no one to impress, looked about for inspiration. 'What should I draw?' she asked the Mooncat. 'I know. I'll draw my rabbits.' She knew that leaving the house without Jane was forbidden, but the idea of going to the shed on the far side of the garden on her own created a huge surge of excitement. She scrambled from the chair clutching her drawing pad and packet of pencil crayons, and, putting her finger to her lips, warned the old dog Bobbie to keep quiet. He gave a feeble wag of his tail and sighed. He had spent an hour in the garden with the young apprentice, and his old bones needed a long rest. The multi-coloured clip rug, evidence of Hannah's enthusiasm to emulate Auntie Ella's 'make do and mend' aspirations, was spread across in front of the range and was a favourite place for dogs, cats and children alike.

Elphine looked across towards the garden centre area before turning right and heading towards the small orchard and the old chicken huts in the far corner of the private garden. One of the huts was unused, the keeping of chickens long since becoming an unwelcome chore in the busy life of the Clayton family. The other hut had become the home of two black and white rabbits, Patch and Dab, so named by Simon with reference to their markings. Patch had an area of white on his back, whilst Dab sported a white nose. On most days, weather permitting, Elphine was taken to the shed, but usually the young gardener lad, Josh, did the cleaning out and general chores. Elphine had never been in the other hut. She liked old places and the smell of decay. As she approached this abandoned area, she was curious to witness the antiquity without adult intervention. The door opened unwillingly it seemed to the child, her imagination colouring the operation. What was in there? Why did they not allow her to go in? She reeled back in fright, almost losing her balance. An old man was sitting on a packing box in the corner. He was smoking a pipe, and reading a newspaper. He looked up and took his pipe out of his mouth.

'Well, well,' he said. 'And who are you?'

'Elphine. Who are you?'

'You can call me Uncle Tom.' Zacchaeus Pound put down his paper on the muddy floor and beckoned to the child to come and sit on the packing case with him.

'So what's your second name then? Is it Clayton?'

Elphine nodded. 'My daddy is Leigh and my mummy is Alice, but they are away at college and I live with my grandma and my granddad and my great-grandmother and my Aunt Jane.' She proudly reeled off the names, wanting to impress this old man with her knowledge. 'Are you the crooked man with a crooked cat, and is this your crooked house?'

Zacc, as he was known before he changed his name to Tom Smith, grinned broadly, exposing an uneven array of crooked yellow teeth. 'Well how clever of you,' he said. 'Of course I am the crooked man, and you must be the crooked little girl. I have heard about you and how clever you are. How good it is to see you.' He rubbed his hand down his trousers and then held it out to grasp her tiny fingers.

Elphine hesitated, drawing her hand away from him, but then grinned, exposing her evenly spaced white teeth. Her reddish, golden curls framed her lopsided little face. Her expression reminded Zacc of her mother Alice. That episode in his life often came back to haunt him in his dreams or in times of reverie. He had not meant to harm the child, but the fear of his mother with her threats from beyond the grave still made him restless for revenge. Again he speculated as to whether this was his second chance. He could entice Elphine away now, but he had heard her screams coming from the house and guessed that she would react more violently than her mother had done. He sighed, already weary of his plans. He needed some food in his belly. That was it, he thought. Perhaps if he could persuade this child to get him something from the refrigerator, it would satisfy his mother. Those Claytons always ate well. He remembered the smell of baking wafting through the kitchen window in the days when he worked in the gardens, and he moistened his lips in anticipation of a tasty sausage roll.

'I'm hungry, duck,' he said. 'Could you be a little sweetheart and nip back to the house and bring me something? A sausage roll would do, or anything that's going. Don't tell nobody whatever you do. Your folks will send me packing and I want to stay in my little house.'

Elphine nodded. 'Won't be long,' she whispered.

She skirted around the back of the house, dodging behind the greenhouse and stumbling with the unevenness of the ground and the impairment of her legs. Her breath was coming in short bursts as she reached the old back kitchen door. She had seen Jane storing some cold ham in the big refrigerator, and taking a plastic box from the cupboard, she transferred in to it a few slices from the pile, adding tomatoes and lettuce from the salad drawer. She made her way slowly back, pain now joining the fatigue, and at last arrived breathlessly back at the door of the hut. She struggled to push open the door and found to her disappointment that the old man had gone.

The exertion was telling badly on her little misshapen legs. She was trembling with anxiety and fatigue. Clutching the box of food she turned to go, remembering to pick up her pad and crayons. It was too late now to draw the rabbits. Aunt Jane would be awake and looking for her.

Indeed Aunt Jane was very wide-awake, and frantically searching for the missing child. Initially, she had expected to find her in the living room, known as the great hall because of its lofty beamed ceiling and gallery. Elphine loved to sit up in the gallery on a big floor cushion splendidly embroidered in cross-stitch, depicting an elephant surrounded by traditional Indian motifs. However, in this instance, there was no sign of the little girl. Jane called her name, as she hurried around the house. The back kitchen was deserted, but Jane's sharp eyes noticed that the pantry door was ajar. For a moment she was relieved, expecting to find the child hiding behind this door, but the empty space disappointed her and her anxiety increased. Surely she had not wandered off outside.

Elphine heard her calling as she rounded the end of the big greenhouse. She sank down onto a section of the trunk of an old plum tree lying along the ground. She could feel the warmth of the wood through her cotton dress, and momentarily she relaxed, opening her drawing book, and beginning to sketch the shape of a rusting bucket lying abandoned and tipped sideways at the end of the tree trunk. Part of it was disappearing from sight into a mass of stinging nettles.

As Jane's calls now indicated that she was closer at hand, Elphine responded with child-like guile. 'I'm here, Aunt Jane, on the tree trunk. I'm drawing a picture for you. I thought you were tired.'

She smiled nervously as the familiar shape of her present carer rounded the corner of the greenhouse. She was an openhearted child in spite of her occasional tantrums, and such deceit did not come naturally to her. Suddenly, she remembered the plastic box containing the food for the old man was lying at her feet, and she pushed it under the tree trunk amongst an abundance of chickweed where it would seem to be destined to stay for the duration of the presence of the rotting wood.

Jane clicked her tongue with impatience as she drew near, her concern now changing to irritability.

'That was very naughty of you to go off on your own,' she reproved. 'There are lots of strangers around and you know that it is not allowed. You will get me into trouble with your great-grandma, and goodness knows what your grandma would say if she knew.'

'Sorry.' Elphine screwed up her eyes, trying to produce tears of contrition.' I didn't go far. Do you like my picture? I am doing it for you.'

Jane reached out and pulled the child to her feet. 'Beautiful,' she said, giving a quick glance at the few lines on the paper. 'Come on. I think we both need a drink and a biscuit. I have got some nice ham and salad for tea.'

Elphine resisted the urge to look back towards the chicken huts. She could visualise the 'crooked man' and could not wait to draw his face in her book. She remembered how his eyes did not match and how irregular his teeth were. She decided not to show anyone her pictures from now on. There were lots of faces she saw in her dreams that she intended to draw; her secret friends, and she wanted this Uncle Tom to be a part of it all.

Maxine had witnessed the little girl's deceit from the far side of the apple trees. Elphine had to be eliminated somehow from her plans for becoming mistress of Willow Cottage and the garden centre. Still, it was almost a certainty that if Marie left, the child would go with her. Alice and Leigh, in spite of their holier than thou attitude, had no place for a handicapped child in their lives. She raked up the weeds and grass cuttings into a pile, and forked them into the wheelbarrow ready to be taken to the compost heap near to the chicken huts. She had noticed that the fence was broken behind the sheds, and reminded herself to tell Simon when he was back from the wholesalers. He had seemed a little off hand this morning, she thought. Oh well, I'll soon sort that. She twisted her mouth into a pouting smile, her lipstick glistening in a sudden burst of sunlight.

Simon drove back along the narrow lane along the south of the village. He glanced at the sheaf of paperwork on the seat beside him. That should be the last of it now until after Christmas, he said to himself. This millennium business was worrying him. He had come late to computers, preferring proven traditional ways. The kids were quite dismissive of the scaremongering, maintaining that with all the money and technology at their fingertips, the financiers would sort it out. Simon had always been a so-called belt and braces kind of man, much to the amusement of his students. He gave a twisted grin. 'Oh well,' he muttered. It would soon be the hour of reckoning, and he had all of his bank statements neatly filed.

His thoughts turned to Maxine. He had tried to avoid her before he went out. Rachel was becoming a pain in the backside. It would have to be her who saw them in the greenhouse. Emma would have lectured him, but she would not have told their mother. He lurched around a sharp bend, the back wheels bouncing in the rutted verge, causing a pheasant to utter harsh warning cries and run into the shelter of the hedge. He dropped down into third gear. This was a bad stretch of road and he turned his attention away from his illicit relationship, instead concentrating on avoiding large potholes.

He was relieved to find that Hannah had not returned. Jane, her face wreathed in smiles, had a calming effect on his jangled nerves.

'Is she being a good girl?' he asked, nodding in the direction of Elphine, who was concentrating on colouring in the shape of the bucket and the nettles in her previous hasty sketch. Elphine felt the colour rising in her cheeks and lowered her eyes. She had just had a sudden impulse to bring a corner of the plastic box containing the ham and salad into sight in her drawing, being mentally aware of its presence amongst the weeds, but then thought better of it. It may prompt investigation and exposure of her guilt.

Jane also wished to avoid any criticism of her neglect, and enthused about the quietness and good behaviour of her charge. 'We are having a light meal tonight if that's all right with you. Ham salad.' She turned as Elphine cleared her throat, and narrowed her eyes in a warning look.

'That will be fine with a few spuds thrown in.' Simon grinned. 'Anyway. Work's calling. I'll get changed into my scruffs and press on with clearing the long greenhouse. We are filling it with Christmas stock. Chrysanths and poinsettias mostly. Perhaps winter cyclamen. I clinched a good deal with the wholesalers. They'll make a brilliant show, don't you think?'

Jane nodded, rather surprised that he was asking for her approval in his future plans. He often confided in her husband Clive, respecting his knowledge of the vegetable trade, but he rarely sought out her approval. She listened to his tread on the stairs and instinctively knew that all was not as it should be. She followed him, turning at the end of the hall into the old back kitchen. Hannah would soon be back anticipating a meal to be in the throes of preparation. Apparently they would expect jacket potatoes baked in the oven, and the salad needed washing and chopping. She opened the refrigerator door, reaching for the salad container, and noticed how the bag containing the boiled ham was pulled out of shape exposing the ends of the slices. She remembered how the pantry door was ajar when she was searching for Elphine, and immediately suspected Josh the young lad who had recently been employed to help with the clearing of the summer stock in preparation for the Christmas season. 'I bet his hands were filthy,' she muttered, as she returned to the front kitchen. Oh well, she thought, with memories of her childhood spent in back street poverty, we must all have our peck of dirt before we die.

The sound of a car in the driveway heralded the return of Hannah. Elphine closed her drawing book and gathered up her pencils. She had been cupping her hand around the drawing she was making of the old man, knowing that Jane was too busy to try to see beyond it, but guessing that her great-grandmother would be curious. She was in no mood to be cross-examined. Her guilt was still nagging away in back of her mind. She kept visualising Bobby sniffing around under the fallen tree trunk, and dragging out the plastic box into public view. The picture was so clear in her head that she knew it was going to happen. It was too late now, but perhaps the opportunity would arise tomorrow for her to retrieve it and put it in the dustbin. However, as she tossed restlessly in her bed an hour later, she knew that this was the beginning of an unstoppable train of events.

Hannah watched her son walking towards his car. He had been the major topic of conversation with Daisy that afternoon. She knew that he was lying when he said quietly that he was going for a pint and a game of darts at the local public house. It was not unusual for him to do this, but earlier she had had cause to swerve to avoid Maxine hurrying along the drive, her head bent and looking to be in a state of agitation. Obviously someone had upset her and Hannah hoped that the culprit was Simon.

There was a small but noisy group gathered at the bar and at first Simon had difficulty in locating Maxine sitting at the far end of the room in a recessed corner along the side of the inglenook fireplace. Generally, it was not a favourite seating place with little legroom and a small table barely big enough to hold two glasses. They had used it once before when they were avoiding attention, but now it seemed to Simon that Maxine was inviting intimacy. He carefully drew the chair back well away from the table to distance his legs from hers and leant forward to place his half-pint of beer on the table next to her glass of white wine.

'We'll drink this and then go,' he muttered. 'I will drop you off at the college.'

'Can you make up the team tonight, Simon? We're one short,' the local darts enthusiast called across from the other recess where a practice game was going on in readiness for the weekly match. Simon got up, pushing his chair noisily across the floor. Maxine heard him say that he was taking the student back to college. 'Kept her late, bless her. It's the least I can do according to my mother. You would think I had been gallivanting all day instead of battling with wholesalers. Still, soon be Christmas! What time are you starting? Ten minutes? Sorry, I won't make it. Perhaps next time, although I am hoping we get rushed off our feet with the millennium to follow.'

He returned to the table but did not sit down. Instead, he stood drinking the remainder of his half pint in several gulps and waited for Maxine to empty her glass.

Neither of them spoke until he steered the car along the college driveway. Then, they both began to speak, breaking off again at the sound of each other's voices. Simon could feel the dampness of perspiration on his forehead. He was aware of her knee close to his hand as he pulled on the handbrake, and avoided eye contact with her even though he sensed her steady gaze and unevenness of her breath. His breath was quickening too, both with anxiety and the terrible urge to embrace her.

'Oh for God's sake, Max!' He turned to speak, but then quickly resumed his former posture, staring ahead along the driveway towards the main college block.

'You've been got at then?' Maxine's voice broke the silence. 'Is it your mother or has Marie been on the phone?'

'Rachel saw us in the greenhouse. She told Mum. I expect the whole family knows now, except Marie.'

'Why don't people keep their noses out? That Rachel's a fine one to criticize. One marriage down and another one heading for a breakdown.'

'Where did you hear that? Anyway, she's not bad. Emma has not said anything. It can't work.' Simon turned to face Maxine. 'What would Marie do and where would my mother go?'

'Marie could take that child with her. I don't suppose the parents would care. Everybody could have a bit of peace. She would drive me mad with her screaming. That's all Marie wants, isn't it? She certainly doesn't care about you, and your mother will soon be ready to move into Daisy Cottage.'

'Don't say such horrible things. My sisters and my mother have shares in the business, you know.'

'Really! So you are well and truly stitched up, aren't you?'

'I think you had better go. I could arrange for you to finish your work at college rather than coming over to us, and I will give you a good report. It can't work, Max, can it? It was fun but doomed from the start. You made me feel young again and brought out the rebel in me and I am sorry that I took advantage of you. Can we be adult about it and put it all behind us?'

'I suppose so. It has been no big deal for me. I think I felt sorry for you with that dreadful wife of yours, but that's your problem. I can take my pick. I'll finish my course if you don't mind. I don't want to ruin my career or my reputation with awkward questions. I'll see you tomorrow.'

Simon watched her walking along the drive. He was stunned by her spiteful words, but what did I expect, he asked himself? God, what an idiot he had been. It was obvious now that she was hoping to get her hands on some money. She had backed off immediately when she realised that it was a family affair. She had one more week of her job experience at the garden centre. He drove off slowly, feeling relieved and anxious at the same time. He would make sure that she was kept well occupied and out of his way. Hopefully Marie would stay with her sister until the end of the month. He shook his head. 'Wow,' he muttered. He realised that he had narrowly missed ruining his life, and all for the sake of a bit of excitement. His anger against his sister and mother now became bruised humility. He was particularly sad that he had caused his mother to worry. Rachel had done her bit in that department, he thought with regret rather than rancour. His thoughts turned towards his wife. Poor Marie did not deserve this. It was not her fault that she could not conceive or that she had been brought up in a strict Catholic faith. He knew of her religious convictions when he married her.

Maxine had disappeared from sight now and he switched on the ignition, revving the engine as he moved forward into a three-point turn and then sped away back towards the college gates.

Hannah heard the sound of his engine and the scraping of the garage gates over the rough cement. He had not been long and that was a good sign. Of course she had not believed his professed intention of playing darts, and had spent the last hour agonising over his possible actions. Daisy had been sympathetic, yet dismissive. Apparently, her attitude favoured non-interference in marital affairs although Hannah recalled that it was only a few months ago when her friend was full of condemnation for her daughter-in-law's brief lapse of fidelity. And what about her affairs of the heart? Was her latest obsession, this new bloke, married, she had wanted to ask, but then the telephone rang and Daisy became embroiled in a long conversation with the social services. Hannah had excused herself and had briefly joined her daughter Emma, who was having a coffee break before tackling a pile of papers requiring filing. It would seem that the subject of Simon's irresponsible behaviour was not on her agenda. Hannah was not even sure if Rachel had told her of the episode in the greenhouse. Yet she would be surprised if they had not communicated. This was a close family when it came to matters of personal joy or grief.

Later, she tried not to stare at Simon when he joined them in the living room. Jane remarked innocently that it must have been a quick game of darts. He grunted, and fiddled with the remote control.

' It looks like the usual load of rubbish on the box,' he said after flicking through the channels. 'I think I'll have a bath and an early night.'

Jane looked anxiously after him, commenting as the door closed behind him that he did not look well, and that perhaps he was missing

Marie. 'I must seem like a poor substitute. Marie gives a lot of time to the business, as well as running household matters.'

Hannah assured her that she was doing a marvellous job, and had had a very calming effect on Elphine. She herself was not anticipating the return of Marie with any pleasure, and had no idea how Simon was feeling.

Elphine, as if contradicting Hannah's earlier claims of Jane's calming influence, had a solid hour of night terrors, and in consequence the whole family struggled to face a new day with any enthusiasm.

Hannah was dismayed to see Maxine walking down the driveway at eight o'clock. She had hoped that the whole episode was over, but apparently not if the student's jaunty wave in her direction was anything to go by. Simon was still avoiding eye contact. She thought that he looked very tired, and now longed to give him a hug whereas last night she could have slapped him. He ate a slice of toast and gulped down his coffee before saying that he was spending his time in his office sorting out the entire latest stock intake, and Mike could cope with any queries.

Hannah found Mike in the gift section together with Maxine who pointedly ignored her. Hannah responded by giving the young woman a long hard stare, before turning to Mike and relaying her son's message.

'I think he is worried about the stock with all this talk of computers crashing, and this end-of-the-world scenario predicted. What do you think, Mike? I don't understand all this technology.'

'Me neither. We were better off with cash in our pockets and pencil and paper.'

They both ignored the small noise on their left, recognising it as derisive. They were becoming as practised in the art of ignoring youthful comments as the younger ones were in the habit of making them. Hannah walked over to the area where Josh was erecting shelving in readiness for the incoming Christmas stock, turning her back on Maxine and complimenting the lad on his proficiency.

She joked, 'You deserve an extra biscuit with your coffee.' However, the humour was not reflected in her voice, and she turned away and walked quickly towards the door without a backward glance, although she could sense the insolence in Maxine's steady stare. Her anger mounted as she walked back along the path leading to the cottage. It had taken great control not to assault the girl physically. Hannah fumed inwardly. How dare the wretched creature behave with such arrogance? She had to speak to Simon again. This whole situation was intolerable.

She made a cup of coffee and went through to the office. Simon was sitting back in his chair with his eyes shut as she peeped around the door.

'We need to talk. Drink this and please put me in the picture. It is obvious by her manner this morning that matters have come to a head.'

Simon took the proffered cup of coffee. Hannah noticed the slight tremble in his hand and any anger she felt towards him for his lack of judgement was replaced with compassion.

'Sorry Mum,' he said. 'She is almost blackmailing me now. I told her that it had to end. Not that we were so involved with each other, you know, Mum. It was just a crazy impulse that made me feel so good about myself at first, but now I can't believe how I could be so stupid. Anyway, she insists on completing her job experience and I am keeping out of her way. Don't challenge her, will you? She has threatened to tell Marie if we make a fuss. She knows about Rachel seeing us together, and that Rachel has spoken to you. I just don't know what she is capable of.'

'I won't interfere unless she threatens this family, and then she will regret it.' Hannah stared out of the window. This was one of her favourite views, and this room, now a small private office, used to be the so called music room, where she spent many happy hours as a small child playing the piano or rearranging the books on the shelves in the chimney recess. The books, old with heavy binding and ornate gilded lettering, had long since all gone with the change of ownership after Aunt Kate died. That woman Margot Sergeant, uncle Harry's sister had a lot to answer for, she thought, her face suddenly coming to mind, and bearing a resemblance to this latest serpent in the nest. She wondered, as she had done many times, whether Margot was still alive. She was a lot younger than her brother and profited well from her trouble making. Still, money was certainly not everything, although it was good to have the comforts of Willow Cottage. Fate it seemed had allocated it to her and no little tart was going to spoil it for everyone.

'I'll leave you to it then. Don't worry. She will soon be out of our hair. Is it the end of the week she goes?'

Simon nodded. 'I have told her I will give her a good report. To be fair, she does deserve it. She has got a good future, and it was as much my fault as hers. It's just all this business with Marie and the child. I think we need a break.'

Hannah could not settle to any household chores. Jane had everything under control, and suddenly she felt old and redundant. She had noticed earlier, as she stared through the office window, that the rose garden had a neglected air. This side of the cottage with its flagged steps and seclusion was a suntrap and a favourite place for family gatherings. It had been little used during the past summer months and was crying out for attention. The sun was shining now, drawing attention to some large sow thistles and a patch of nettles amongst the roses. Some drastic pruning was needed, and she made her way along the side of the house armed with a pair of secateurs and a plastic bag. Immediately, nettles stung her bare hands and she cursed herself for her neglect. She knew that she did not have an impregnable pair of gardening gloves, and laughed to herself in remembrance of Uncle Harry's story of the village chimney sweep who always had his chimney on fire each year. She was as bad; part owner of a garden centre with shelves full of gardening aids. Now was the time to use her prerogative and take a pair of gloves from off the shelf. She wandered around to the back of the sunken field, approaching the new building along a narrow path. A window was open and she could clearly hear a single voice. She recognised it as Maxine's, and stopped to listen. She was using her mobile phone in the small storage unit.

'I need to stay until the end of the week for my assessment. I know, but I don't have to speak to anyone. Will you just listen Pete! He doesn't even own this place. It is shared between the sisters and that cow of a mother. No! Quite honestly I think he is struggling. I would be lucky if I could get a hundred out of him. I could just settle for a glowing report, or I could get my own back somehow. See you later.'

Hannah heard her making kisses into the air, and then the sound of the door closing. She took in a deep breath. Little madam, she thought. So that was her game. What a scheming minx and what a foolish son! She walked slowly back to the cottage, gloves forgotten, and her enthusiasm for gardening decidedly on hold.

12

Ancestors Anonymous

Marie was back. Both Hannah and Simon were relieved that there had been a clear weekend between her homecoming and the completion of Maxine's studies in her job experience. The picture of them meeting face to face, and the risk of Maxine at the least dropping hints or at the worst having a major confrontation with the family, had kept Hannah awake night after night. She did not protest at the sight of the empty space on the windowsill less than an hour after Marie had arrived. However, Elphine did. She began to scream, clinging to Jane, and shouting 'Go away' at the top of her voice.

'Take her for a walk Jane. Marie dear, you look tired. Why don't we have some afternoon tea and you can tell me all about your sister. I do hope she will be able to cope without you. Simon has missed you. Well, we all have. Jane is very good though. You will notice a difference in Elphine. She is so clever at drawing. Jane bought her a pad and some crayons.'

Marie did not comment. Instead she asked why Simon had sent Mike to meet her at the station.

'He's gone to the wholesaler's. He's putting in an order for Christmas trees, and wanted to see them in the plantation before he decided on the quantity. We are so limited for space. I really worry about the safety of all this stock, but he wants to get everything sorted before the New Year.'

'Oh, this millennium thing! I'll be glad when it is January. Christmas is bad enough with all the commercialism. People have forgotten what it is all about.'

It seemed that the world around them was clearly remembering that it was Christmas, and that it was shortly to be a new millennium. In spite of, or perhaps because of, the threats of worldwide chaos with crashing computers, people were spending a lot of money. It was as though there was no tomorrow, Hannah thought.

Everyone in the family was put on a work rota. Daisy released Emma from her office duties each afternoon, and Rachel and the twins served behind the counter. Jane, now relieved of childcare duties, restacked shelves during the evening, and Hannah positioned herself at varying locations amongst the shoppers, with an eye to discouraging shoplifting. Each evening, after the gates had closed at six-thirty, became a time for the residents of Willow Cottage to slump in front of the television with a meal on a tray.

No one paid much attention to Elphine, apart from Marie, but even she did not seem to be interested in the child's scribble as she called it, and Elphine in her turn did not show her grandmother or anyone else for that matter, the increasing gallery of faces on the back pages of her drawing pad. She was now able to access her friends of the night as she called them, without the daytime contact with the Mooncat. She knew that her great-grandmother brought him out of the cupboard each night, and night terrors were becoming a rarity. She looked forward to the children who visited her in her dreams; the little fair-haired girl called Lucy, and the boy called Nigel. She did not know who the old lady with the cats was, but the Mooncat did. He was often there, sitting on her windowsill with lots of cats around him. A kind lady cuddled her in her best dreams and a man and woman with a big black dog sometimes wagged their fingers at her and told her to be good. She could recall them at any time by looking at her drawings. The crooked man looked out at her, his whiskers bristling and his crooked teeth shaded yellow. His ill matched eyes frightened her and she wished that she had not coloured them in.

❄

The busy days masked the tension in the household. Marie seemed burdened with yet more responsibilities now that she communicated with her sister on a regular basis, taking it in turns to share the telephone calls. It seemed that she had little time to contemplate the state of her marriage

Hannah watched and listened, desperate to keep the status quo, yet wanting them all to be happy. Was compromise good, she asked herself? Perhaps it was the only way for Simon and Marie's marriage to survive. So much hinged on it. The relationships in this family were so intertwined.

A stranger in the village brought tensions to the surface. Apparently, according to Rachel, she had recently moved into the Manor, a large stone built house in the centre of the village. In times gone by it had been traditionally the home of the second son of the landed gentry. The Hall always housed the eldest son, and very often the vicarage provided accommodation for a younger son, or a close relation. The family line dating back to the eleventh century had died out before the First World War, and it became first the turn of the so-called nouveau riche to maintain these grand houses and in recent times people who had climbed the ladder of success in modern businesses. Now the Thorntons had arrived and were trying to establish themselves in village life.

The church presented a sphere of influence for Sarah Thornton. Apparently, she had a degree in psychology, and ambitions to set up a private school in the stable block for young children with learning difficulties.

Her husband, it seemed, was indifferent to his wife's aspirations. Ownership of the grand house afforded access to the hunting set and to golf club membership. His wife's little games were not part of his big plans.

It was obvious to everyone that Rachel was flattered by the attentions of Sarah Thornton. She told Hannah how she had invited her to the monthly coffee morning when members of the ladies' church group met to discuss future charity events and fundraising for the repair of the church roof. Sarah had promised monetary support from the generous allowance made to her by her husband, and hinted on more to follow when she had set up her private school. To her disappointment no one appeared to be curious, and Rachel had felt obliged to enquire.

'I found myself talking about Elphine and her need for guidance, not only in education but also in the embrace of the Church of England. I realised later with some misgivings I must admit, that she is not the kind of woman to be put off. She rang me to arrange a meeting with you and I have agreed, but would really prefer it if Marie isn't around. Could you bring Elphine out for a ride and meet up here?' Rachel paused for a breath.

Hannah was also hesitating.

'Rachel,' she said. 'This is none of our business, and it is not up to Marie either. It can only be discussed with Leigh and Alice. But if you want my opinion, the child is too young to be labelled. She is a bright happy little soul most of the time, and should not become piggy in the middle. I know that you don't see eye to eye with Marie over the baptism, but in my opinion it is the choice of the individual and until Elphine is old enough to have an opinion, I think we should leave things to her direct family.'

'But Mother, we are not a Catholic family. Leigh and Alice were educated in a C of E school, weren't they?'

'Don't forget that Molly is Catholic and she is Alice's biological mother.'

'And gave her away. What does that tell you about her beliefs?'

Hannah sighed. 'Look Rachel. Leave me out of all this. If you want my advice you will steer clear of this woman. It is pretty obvious that she is using you to get herself noticed, and I don't think that she is qualified to dabble in special educational needs. I am sure that the church funding can struggle on without her.'

There was no reply from her daughter. The sound of the phone being slammed into place jarred in Hannah's ear.

The following days brought nothing more significant than the common task. Alice and Leigh were coming home at the end of the week, and Marie concentrated on giving their room a thorough cleaning, hardly necessary in Hannah's opinion, when it would soon be impossible to find a clear space in there. She had long since given up trying to understand the younger generation. It seemed that life was too short to worry about order. As far as she was concerned the problem lay in materialism. It had become a 'must have' society, with technology presenting an endless stream of gadgets. In spite of concerns to preserve the environment, paper was piling up on shelves and in cupboards. Hannah was amazed at the resources in the classroom, once recounting to an amused Alice of how children struggled to write with stubs of pencils, and exercise books lasted for a term. Yet the constant cry was that schools were under-funded. She pointed this out to her apparently disinterested daughter-in-law, and then got off her high horse and agreed to take Elphine for a walk down to the village shop. The child was bored, and Marie was obviously intent on cleaning every window in the house.

Elphine was excited by the prospect. She wanted more paper and pencils, and a pencil sharpener. Poppy had sharpened her pencils when she had spent the previous Saturday at Willow Cottage; a day away from her mother Emma, who was in the throes of a stomach upset. Elphine had enthused on the contents of Poppy's pencil case, particularly coveting the pencil sharpener. Usually, she had to rely on Simon to sharpen her pencils with his penknife when he was not too busy or too tired, but if a favourite colour became blunted, she had to resort to picking splinters of wood away with her nails to reveal the pigment.

Hannah, with her 'make do and mend' philosophy well entrenched on this particular morning, saw no reason to encourage this kind of material gluttony. 'You must use up what you have got first,' she advised. 'Perhaps Santa will bring you some more.'

Elphine began to scream, and threw herself down on the shop floor, narrowly missing a box containing rolls of Christmas wrapping paper. The owner of the shop sighed and shook her head as Hannah struggled to bring the child to her feet.

'They need a good slap these young 'uns',' she muttered to the lady she was serving.

'Not at all,' the lady replied. 'Some guidance perhaps.'

The same lady was waiting outside as Hannah emerged with the now triumphant Elphine grasping a pencil sharpener firmly in her hand. 'You must be Rachel's mother,' she said. 'She is so proud of you. You used to teach I understand. I would value your advice. Would you join me in a morning coffee?' She nodded in the direction of the imposing wrought iron gates at the entrance to The Manor on the other side of the village street. 'I am Sarah Thornton, by the way.'

Hannah was feeling both embarrassed and irritated by the shopkeeper's comments, and was seduced by the invitation and Rachel's apparent regard for her. The thought of returning directly to Willow Cottage, and the obsessive behaviour of her daughter-in-law, propelled her into an uncharacteristic decision. Under normal circumstances she was not a 'coffee morning' kind of person.

With her guard lowered, and the child skipping along beside her, she crossed the street, curious to see beyond the Manor gates. Surprisingly, considering that she had lived for many years in this village, both as a child and an adult, she had never been in the grounds of the Manor, let alone the house itself. The previous tenants had welcomed only visitors of their level in society, keeping the gates tightly shut against curious villagers. The tradesmen's entrance was through a narrow lane at the back of the house and afforded limited views of the gardens. Dense shrubberies and mature trees bordered the front driveway, and it was along this shaded rather rutted track that the three females made their way to the front door. Hannah had seen photographs of this house in parish records, and was familiar with the style of architecture. It was built of Ancaster stone, locally quarried in Lincolnshire and famous nationwide, and was typical of Georgian renovation with its symmetry and tall, sash windows. However, there were fascinating glimpses of earlier Elizabethan influences in one section to the left of the main door, and Hannah could hardly wait to go inside this impressive building.

The marble columns of the wide portico invited Elphine to run her fingers up the smooth surface, her eyes noting the striation of a variety of mineral deposits.

'It's marble,' her grandmother explained.

Elphine nodded. She knew what marbles were, but wondered how they could all be fastened together in these tall columns. However, such mysteries were left unsolved as they stepped into the large entrance hall. One wall was hung with several large portraits; people peering through the dimly lit space, revealing by their clothes an age long gone. Sarah gave what could only be described as a sheepish grin. 'Those are previous tenants', she explained, 'but nothing to do with us. 'They came with the house at a price. Of course any valuable ones were auctioned. We never saw them, but apparently they fetched a good price. I don't think anybody wanted these dismal daubs, but my husband fancied them as part of the décor.'

Her laughter froze in her throat. Elphine had made a gasping noise and was staring towards a small alcove on the right. 'There's another crooked man,' she whispered. 'He's just come out of that picture.'

The two women followed the direction of her gaze seeing only a table housing a large earthenware vase in the alcove.

Sarah shivered. 'That's the one that gives me the creeps,' she said. 'He's got very strange eyes.'

Hannah stared into the shadows. She knew that the child had a vivid imagination, yet there was an atmosphere about the place, and for a moment her memory returned her to The Mermaid Inn and the portrait of Selina Constable. How could she doubt the child when she had witnessed a similar event?

'Is he still there?' Her voice was hoarse with fear, and her hair prickled on her arms.

Elphine was looking at the portrait. 'No,' she whispered. 'He has gone back into the picture.' She shrugged her shoulders and walked towards the door. Again, Hannah's thoughts were back in the past. She remembered how Leigh at the age of eight had reacted to visiting the bombsite where her mother and grandparents had died. He had suddenly fainted and fallen to the ground, but recovered quickly and continued the conversation as though nothing had happened. Elphine was certainly Leigh's child, not that it was ever doubted. She had the mark of the Flynns with the red in her hair, inherited from Grandma Flynn's line in Ireland; a characteristic of Celtic blood leaving its mark on her father yet according to Uncle Patrick not apparently on anyone else in the family.

The coffee and cakes were welcome, but both adults were still feeling uneasy and Sarah jumped at the slightest sound, looking behind her to the gloomy entrance hall. Elphine nibbled at a biscuit, and fidgeted on the large leather pouffe.

'Does she like dolls?' Sarah asked. 'I have some in the stable block. Well it is not a stable now. It has been converted into workspace for my new venture. I have quite a collection of toys. Did Rachel tell you of my plans to set up a class?'

'She mentioned a school for children with learning difficulties, but I think I misunderstood her. There are tight regulations regarding the care of the young, particularly the less fortunate ones. Are you planning on running a playgroup with the church? I do believe a lady in the village already runs one. She would be glad of some help and some extra resources.'

'No, not a playgroup!' Sarah shook her head and wrinkled up her nose. 'I do have a degree with experience in nursing, and it would be a sort of career move. I could organise and lead such a venture but I know I would have to employ a qualified teacher and that is where you could come in. We could sort out a monetary agreement regarding Elphine's needs. Tit for tat so to speak. What do you think?'

They had reached the stable block now where there was not a hint of its previous usage. Hannah had to admit that it was well restored. Sarah had made a great effort to decorate the walls with colourful posters, and large trays of toys and puzzles were placed on tables along the length of the far wall. Elphine ran over to a blackboard and easel and picked up a stick of chalk.

'Can I draw?' she asked. Without waiting for a reply, she began to sketch, the chalk lines quickly showing the outlines of a face, and moving down to illustrate the chest and shoulders.

The two women watched in silence as the child roughly replicated the character depicted in the oil painting. Again the hair stood up on Hannah's arms, and she stepped forward shaking her head and reaching out to remove the chalk from Elphine's grasp.

'You have your answer, Mrs Thornton It was flattering of you to think that I could return to teaching after years of retirement, but rather than help Elphine to live a normal life, I think she would find the atmosphere very disturbing as indeed I do. Besides, she is Alice and Leigh's child and usually her grandmother is in charge. Rachel means well but is becoming a little obsessive. Thanks for the coffee and for showing me around. I expect we will bump into each other again sometime.'

Hannah had difficulty in persuading Elphine to put down the chalk. The drawing was recognisable now as a portrayal of the old man. It was amazing and more detailed than the oil painting itself. The child's description puzzled her. What did she mean by 'another crooked man'? Her mind appeared to be halfway between fact and fantasy.

'I would be obliged if you do not mention this to anyone particularly Rachel. I don't want her interfering with Marie's plans for this child. We have enough worries at the moment.'

Her tone of voice and hard stare reminded Sarah Thornton of days in the classroom, and she quickly agreed that it would remain a secret between them, knowing, however, that she could hold her husband's attention later with a ghost story. He longed for ghosts, a commodity not obtainable with a chequebook. She turned to go, resisting the urge to turn and look once more at the chalk drawing. She shivered and glanced at Hannah, but her companion appeared to have forgotten about it; rather surprising she thought, after her insistence that no one should know.

Hannah remembered it as she reached the village street, and reproached herself for the second time in a few minutes for being so easily persuaded to go against her inclinations. She reasoned that like her daughter she had been impressed by wealth and position. She had not met the husband. For all she knew they could have been lucky and come up on the pools, or inherited a large lump sum. But then that did not make them bad people. She was being a snob again. Oh well! It was too late to go back. She seemed to be a decent woman with good intentions and surely would not want to be reminded of the strange events or prosper in any way by keeping Elphine's drawing. No doubt she had rubbed it out by now.

13

A Portfolio of Souls

Emma had been sick again. Daisy rang the day after Hannah had lain awake from the early hours agonising over her stupidity in exposing little Elphine to public gaze. Marie would be furious if she knew, and confrontation with Rachel could lead to disclosures of Simon's infidelity. Now here was Daisy worrying about Emma.

'I don't like the look of her,' she said. 'She insists on working. You know what she is like. Do you think you could come over and talk some sense into her. I am struggling with two carers down. Poppy has gone to school. Clive took her in his van, but I really can't spare Jane.'

Hannah told her to calm down, and promised to drive over within the next half an hour. Of course Daisy did make a meal of things just lately, she thought. But there again Emma was never ill.

Daisy was involved in issues with the social services as usual, and Jane, now the senior carer on the daytime shift was instructing a new carer on all matters of hygiene. She gave a cheery wave and asked after the family.

'They're all fine thanks Jane,' Hannah replied. If only that was true, she thought. She found Emma looking tired and pale sorting papers into three piles ready for filing.

'You ought to be in bed young lady. Can I do that for you? Have you managed to eat?' She studied her daughter. If it were not so unlikely she would diagnose pregnancy.

'Mum! Don't worry. I have got a bug. Poppy was sick the other day. It's going round. I am not going to explode or implode if it comes to that.'

Hannah's brain instantly recalled those words from the past. 'Explode and implode'. It was a joke in the family during the late months of pregnancy.

'You're pregnant, aren't you?'

Emma looked up both startled and dismayed by her mother's perceptiveness, and tears began to stream down her cheeks.

'How do you do it? Sorry, I'm not really upset. It's just that you caught me offguard. Actually I couldn't be happier.' Emma rummaged with her fingers up the sleeve of her cardigan seeking a tissue and dabbed at her eyes.

'Really. So this was planned then?' Hannah frowned. This was the last thing that would have entered her head. Emma did not feature on the family crisis list this month. 'Can I ask who the father is, or is that a difficult question?'

'It is a bit awkward at the moment. I would rather not discuss it here. Can I come over at the weekend, and escape with you somewhere for half an hour? And don't worry about me, Mother. I went all peaky with Poppy, didn't I?'

'But that was twelve years ago, and you were in your twenties.'

Emma grimaced. 'Mother, I am only thirty-five. Lots of women have children in their thirties, especially if they want to concentrate on a career. It's all about balancing work and motherhood these days. Childcare is so expensive, and don't tell me that you stayed at home. Times have changed and I am pretty good at being a single mum, you know.'

'Oh! So there is no man on the scene again. Or should I say no man staying on the scene?'

'Be patient with me. And please keep this to yourself. Rachel is aggravated enough with Simon, without adding me to her list of sinners'.

Hannah wanted to tell her about the visit to the Manor and the repercussions she feared would follow. On reflection, she now had no doubts in her mind that Sarah Thornton would gossip about Elphine's strange encounter, and that the blackboard would not be wiped clean. However, she decided that this was not the right time to burden Emma with other people's problems. Instead, she reminded her daughter to take care of herself, and not to be such a martyr. 'Daisy can manage,' she said. 'She has got that Graham bloke for support. Apparently he is wonderful. I can't really comment as I have never met him.'

'I think you will find he is called Greg.' Emma pushed the pile of papers to one side rather impatiently, her mother thought.

'Oh well! I knew it began with a 'G'. Come on. You've done enough. I'll leave you to pack up and just do as Daisy tells you. She doesn't know, does she?' Hannah was remembering all the secrecy when Alice was pregnant. She still harboured a grievance about Daisy knowing before she did.

Emma assured her that she was the first to know, and reminded her to keep it a secret until the weekend after the 'heart to heart'.

Alice and Leigh were home for the weekend and did their best not to antagonise Marie. They had noticed the tension in the atmosphere not long after they had arrived, and assumed that it was still about Marie's conflicting religious beliefs. Although they both experienced reservations about established church dogma, they were concerned about a breakdown in the family relationships. Alice commented to her grandmother on how her father hardly opened his mouth these days except to eat, and even the act of eating with the family appeared to be a strain.

Hannah talked about the worries of finance and how much pressure there was on small businesses. 'He is pinning all his hopes on the Christmas sales,' she explained. 'And I shall be glad when the New Year has arrived.' This explanation did not satisfy them, and later Alice spent an hour with her mother having what she described as a 'cosy chat' in the front kitchen. The solid fuel range had been stoked up and dampened down on the previous evening, and by the following afternoon the stored heat was conducive to sleeping rather than animated chatter. Elphine had gone for a walk around the village with her father, and Marie glanced frequently along the driveway.

'Mum! She will be fine. I wish you could relax and tell me what's wrong. You and Dad are hardly speaking. Have you had a row? Is it over your religious beliefs or what?'

Marie shrugged. She wanted to talk about the failure of her marriage. Molly Petch coming back into their lives was the last nail in the coffin, she thought. It was not something she could discuss with her adopted daughter. Where would Alice's loyalties lie? It was different for Simon. There was not a real father waiting in the wings to reclaim his daughter's affection. She shrugged again. 'Overwork,' she said. 'We should never have come here. There is no escape from it.'

She had no wish to disclose her real grievances. In fact she could not bring her grievances out into the open at all. She was remembering how Rachel had approached her on the previous day with the details of the proposed establishing of a special needs school at the Manor house, and when she herself, already spoiling for a fight with her sister-in-law over comments concerning her religious beliefs, told her that Elphine was going to stay at home, Rachel's parting words spoken with apparent vindictiveness had left in their wake new suspicions of her husband's infidelity. 'I see that little tramp Maxine has gone. I expect Simon will miss her,' she said.

Marie had not given Rachel the opportunity to elaborate on her comment, but the words had bounced around in her head ever since, keeping her away from restful sleep and increasing her fits of irritability.

If only she could share her suspicions with Alice. If only she could put her arms around her daughter. But she was at least fifth in line to a claim on her affections, she decided.

Alice sighed. She felt no closer to the truth and looked along the drive to see if Leigh was on his way back with Elphine.

In fact Leigh was discovering a new side to his daughter. He was amazed by the sudden development in her language skills. It seemed that she had moved from stammering baby talk and repetition to an almost adult level. However, physically, she was still disadvantaged and would always be so. She had begun to struggle, her legs moving awkwardly along the uneven surface. Leigh hoisted her up and carried her on his back, pretending to be a horse, but her jumps and 'gee ups' had quickly reduced him to exhaustion. 'You are getting a bit too big for that,' he explained as he lowered her down onto the carved tree trunk.

'I like this tree trunk,' the child said. 'It has faces in it. Are all these people dead?'

'I think they are just pretend ones, like in a story.'

'My faces are dead ones. I see them in my dreams and then I draw them.'

'I haven't seen those. Can I have a look sometime or are they secret?' Leigh was not surprised. He could still accept psychic ability as though it were an everyday accomplishment. However, he was being cautious, bearing in mind that Elphine was regarded as an infant not yet reaching school age, and it was obvious that she bore characteristics of autism, even though such a condition, with all of its manifestations, was sometimes difficult to diagnose. For the average child, the awareness of a limited material life span and a continuance of life after death was seldom the norm. He was curious to know what his young daughter understood, yet afraid to overstep the mark.

'Of course you can see them, but don't tell Grandma. She doesn't like me drawing and I don't let her look at the back of my book.'

'Can Mummy see them?'

'Yes, Mummy can see them, but no one else.'

She jumped up from the tree trunk and pulled at Leigh's hands. 'Come on Daddy, you lazy bones. My bum is going to sleep.' She giggled. 'Great-grandma says that's rude, but everybody says that, don't they?'

'It was rude when Great-grandma was a little girl. Your Great-granddad Jack was put in a cupboard for saying that word. Can you imagine?'

'I haven't drawn him yet. I talk to him though. Do you?'

Leigh shook his head. It seemed these days that all the spaces in his mind were taken up with medical terminology and drug categories.

Those wonderful special dreams as Grandma called them were a thing of the past. He had not communicated with his sister Lucy since he was a child, and somehow the Mooncat, now banished to the cupboard, no longer appeared to have magical qualities, its big yellow eyes staring ahead into apparent emptiness. And then there was that episode with the ouija board he thought. It had alarmed both he and Alice, and as if by mutual agreement they did not talk about such things these days. What would Alice think of her daughter's ability not only to communicate with the spirit world, but also apparently to draw their likenesses? He could hardly wait to see Elphine's drawing book, and yet he had a feeling of uneasiness, suddenly regarding the whole thing as witchcraft. What if Elphine was in touch with his mother? What if her face was looking out of the pages of his daughter's book?

When they reached the gates of Willow Cottage they could see Emma's little orange car parked in the gravelled area in front of the house.

'It's Great Auntie Emma and Marigold!' Elphine shouted excitedly, her thin little legs moving awkwardly, and her hand pulling away from her father's grasp. 'I hope Poppy is with her.'

Leigh grabbed at the back of her anorak, as she lunged forward. At the same time he had a sense of disappointment, knowing that he would be expected to share in the reunion with his aunt, and that Marie would be in charge. Perhaps Elphine's psychic artwork would have to wait.

Meanwhile, Hannah was wondering how she was going to isolate her daughter Emma from this family gathering. She had found it difficult not to think about her daughter's pregnancy. Her head was so full of anxieties, each one seeming to increase as time passed by. Where did it all end, she wondered? At what point was she going to switch her mind off? Perhaps it must wait until that final act, and then was that really the end of the journey? She knew that there had been enough evidence in her experience to point to involvement beyond the grave, but what kind of involvement? She felt a certain level of helplessness now. Circumstances were moving out of her control, yet she was still not prepared to be a passive bystander.

She stared at Emma, not really taking in any details of her appearance. Emma reacted, brushing her hair away from her face and turning to acknowledge Elphine who was jumping up and down with excitement.

'Calm down, child!' Marie snapped. 'Poppy is not here.'

Leigh jumped to Elphine's defence. 'Shall we go and find your Mummy?' he suggested. In spite of his earlier reservations, he was longing to see his little daughter's drawings, and this would seem like an opportune moment when Marie, distracted by wider family issues, was helping to organise afternoon tea and cakes.

Alice was upstairs in their bedroom folding clothes and hanging up others in the large double fronted wardrobe.

'Hello you two,' she said. 'Did you have a good walk?' She raised her eyebrows and nodded her head in the direction of the staircase leading down to the hall. Leigh recognised the sign language, knowing that she was implying a deliberate escape strategy, and including him in it. He grinned.

'Actually,' he said, 'we've got something to show you. It's Elphine's secret so we had better be quick.'

Elphine led the way into the bedroom that she shared with her grandmother, and retrieved her drawing book from under a pile of doll's clothes on a shelf in her toy cupboard. She glanced nervously over her shoulder towards the open door, and pressed the book against her stomach in an attempt to conceal it.

'Lets go into our room,' Leigh said. Elphine ran ahead of them, and sank down on her parents' bed, still clutching her precious book.

Now, with Alice and Leigh sitting on either side, and the door securely closed, she turned the pages revealing line drawings of the cat and the dog, various objects in the house including the Mooncat, her grandmother Marie, her great-grandmother Hannah, and finally her grandfather Simon.

'The dream people are in the back,' she said in a casual manner as though that was quite acceptable.

'Gosh! You are so clever, Elphine. I didn't know you could draw so well. Look at that one, Alice. It's amazing.'

Elphine giggled and turned the pages over quickly now to expose the drawings of her so-called dream people. Leigh turned and looked at Alice anticipating a surprised reaction. He was not sure how she would react after vowing to leave affairs of the occult behind. She did not look at him, concentrating her gaze on the turning pages, and biting at the bottom of her lip. For a moment she stopped breathing, and then drew in a long gasping breath as each picture came to light. Leigh recognised his sister Lucy and the little boy Nigel immediately. His sister apparently liked to show off her ballet skills as she had done in the past, being depicted in a frothy ballet skirt and pointing one toe forward. He knew that Nigel had died in childhood and was the son of Harry and Kate Churchill. He could recall their likenesses in his grandmother's photograph album, and here they were with Winston, their black Labrador dog. The old lady on the next page could only be old Mrs Knight, the guardian of the Moon Cat. It seemed that all of her cats were with her, the whole space being taken up with a variety of breeds and colours. His daughter may have seen photographs of the Churchill couple, although he doubted she would have taken much notice, and only his grandmother would recognise the drawing of the old cat lady. Elphine could have no idea what Lucy looked like just before she died.

He briefly relaxed as the last picture came into view. It was of an old man with long grey whiskers, with no sign of his parents.

Alice gasped. 'I know who that is! It's the eyes, look. One is brown and one is green. I have never forgotten what he looked like even though he did not have a beard then.'

'Who are you talking about. I've never seen him have I?'

'No, you didn't. I bet Grandma would recognise him. It's Zacc Pound. You know! The horrible old man who locked me in his house all night. Well thank goodness he is dead.'

Elphine saw her father give a quick shake of his head, pursing his lips into a silent shush. She closed the pages and stood up. She did not wish to discuss 'the crooked man' with anyone. Her contact with him must remain a secret to avoid questions about the missing ham and her wanderings in the garden. She heard her mother tell her father not to say anything about the drawings. Apparently they were all afraid of the crooked man. The hair stood up on her arms.

Downstairs, Hannah suddenly realised that at last she was on her own with Emma. She could see Marie through the kitchen window, deep in conversation with Simon over some seemingly urgent matter. She briefly let her thoughts dwell on his recent relationship with the student, and then pushed them aside, turning her attention instead to her daughter.

'So, what's the big mystery? I have been worried sick about you. I hope you know what you are letting yourself in for.' Hannah paused for a breath.

'Right Mum. I have been wanting another child for a very long time. I have always felt that Poppy should have a brother or a sister, and the years have gone by so quickly. I am happy in our relationship, but an only child can end up lonely, and she doesn't really relate to Karl and Kirstie. I know what you are going to say. There will be a big gap and Poppy will not relate to a sibling any more than she relates to the twins or Leigh and Alice, but it will be a link somehow with Elphine. At the moment she is the baby of the family. I'm sure that she would feel quite special to be regarded as a young lady with responsibilities towards a younger child.'

'Yes, but where does the father come into this? You talk about being happy as a single mother. Can I ask who the father is, or is that a secret?' Hannah leant forward, dropping her voice into almost a whisper.

'You don't know him. He joined the readers' group a few months ago, and we have been meeting up ever since. He comes to the nursing home to bring Daisy entries for the monthly news-sheet. You know she is the secretary, and it all has to be kept up to date with book lists and booking speakers and monthly reviews. He tries to get the business side over quite quickly, which isn't easy because Daisy plies him with tea and cakes.'

'Is this that Graham she talks about then?'

'No Mum! There isn't a Graham! It's Greg. Look.' Emma reached for her bag and foraged down amongst an assortment of possessions, pulling out a hairbrush, a tape measure, and a bunch of keys attached to a fluffy teddy key ring, before extricating her purse. She opened it to reveal a section designed to hold her 'plastics' as she called her various cards, and an open space for banknotes. She drew out a small square and handed it to her mother. Hannah turned it over to reveal a photograph; the face of a man, probably in his middle age. It was difficult to judge, as he had a moustache and beard both succumbing to differing shades of grey. His lips were closed over his teeth, but his eyes denoted a sense of humour, laughter lines crinkling at the corners.

'The strange thing is Mum, I know that he was the man I described in that story I wrote about you. Do you remember? I had seen him several times in my dreams and somehow put you and him together. You will like him I know. He is a widower, and still struggling with the trauma of his late wife's sudden illness. I don't think he is ready for a serious commitment.'

How serious a commitment was pregnancy Hannah wondered. Suddenly she was recalling that day after Rachel's second marriage. Sally had wagged her finger at her, and said that Emma was throwing the runes and she should watch out for a bearded man on the horizon. They had laughed at the idea as they linked arms and walked to Sally's car.

'One wedding is enough,' she remembered saying. 'Anyway it is your turn to get a mate. I've done it and got all these descendants to prove it.'

She gave a little shiver. 'Someone's just walked over your grave.' That was another voice from the past. The expression had always puzzled her as a child. How could it make sense unless one was dead already?

'A penny for your thoughts Mum,' Emma was clicking her fingers in front of her mother's face. 'So, what do you think then? You will like him. He has such a sense of humour.'

'I don't doubt your judgement. It all depends on his commitment and his loyalties. Do you know anything about his past? And what about Daisy?'

'What about her?'

'She talks about him every time I see her. She thinks he has fallen for her.'

'For goodness sake! He is only in his fifties, and how old is Daisy? Way past retirement like you, isn't she?'

Hannah nodded. 'Late sixties I think. He would certainly be a toy boy as they say. It always seems acceptable for a man to be older than a woman but a bit of a joke the other way. Anyway, when do I get to meet him?'

Emma was relieved to see a twinkle in her eye, not realising that her mother's sudden lightening of spirit came from knowing something not yet known by her friend and that it was her turn to gloat now.

However, the intimacy between mother and daughter resumed its normal proportions by the end of the afternoon. Emma, determined to make her news public in spite of her lack of surety of a secure future, announced the forthcoming event to the family. She was prepared for the inevitable 'what ifs', but her single status became a weapon against the world, being answerable to no one. She knew that her major critic would be Marie with no blood connection and therefore no family loyalty. Primarily her ability to conceive would be envied by her sister-in law, perhaps masked by her religious standards of morality.

The other members of the family gathering on that December day kept their opinions to themselves. Simon believed that as a mere man, his views on procreation would be dismissed by his female relations, and Leigh and Alice were in no position to make any judgement, having conceived a child themselves outside of marriage with apparently no plans for a legal relationship to follow.

Both Hannah and Emma knew that as a mutual friend, and in Emma's case employer, Daisy Buckerfield was to be the main antagonist, in spite of Emma's protests. Now that it was no longer a secret, it would not be long before it became known outside of the family; pregnancy being a condition of course that could not be concealed.

14

Loyalty to Daisy

Hannah's initial smugness at learning of the coming event ahead of her friend quickly changed to anxiety. She was not given to that kind of 'one upmanship' as one might call it, and recalled her friend's apparent pleasure in the company of this new man in her life, albeit as a committee member of the group. It was not going to be easy to shatter Daisy's hopes for a romantic relationship with Greg, she thought, but she automatically took on the cloak of matriarch of the family already planning her next meeting with her friend and rehearsing in her mind the best words to use to explain the situation, thus providing Daisy with some kind of escape route from future embarrassment, whilst protecting her daughter from any repercussions.

It was with some misgiving that she rang her friend later in the day to arrange to meet for coffee at their favourite inn, in a neighbouring village close to the junction leading to Daisy Cottage Nursing Home. Daisy at first protested that she had other more pressing engagements and that they had only recently met for coffee, but then allowing curiosity to sway her, she agreed.

The sign displayed above the door, of a gold crown entwined with a white rose, identified the hostelry as The Rose and Crown, and Hannah carefully steered her car into the confined space allotted to parking, at the rear of the building. It was immediately obvious that Daisy had not yet arrived. Her expensive, top of the range, bright red sports car would be apparent in a much larger car park than this. She decided to stay in the car and wait, taking the chance to re-read an early Christmas card, the first one in fact, from a cousin-once-removed in America, who was again inviting her to stay in the new year. It did not seem long since she had been reading an almost identical message, but of course it was written on the card delivered twelve months previous. How quickly time was moving on, and yet each month had been significant for its events.

Her mind had become so caught up in recall that she did not witness her friend's arrival through the entrance into the car park, and jumped violently at the raucous sound of Daisy's car horn. Her heartbeat accelerated, quickening the pattern of her breathing. She waved, and pushing the card into her bag struggled to open the car door and get out. 'For goodness sake,' she admonished herself, raising her hand again as she approached her friend.

Daisy's appearance as usual was appropriate for any occasion. Her brown jacket and beige bootleg slacks looked tailor made, yet casual enough for a midday appointment. Her hair shone under the grip of a layer of lacquer and her make-up softened the hard lines around her mouth and eyes. Hannah felt naked in her own deficiencies. A polo-necked jumper and jeans could not compete with such elegance, and she wished that she could be on a more level playing field, cursing herself for her indifference to all the trappings seemingly required by most people at such an everyday kind of venue.

Now, her confidence was undermined in every way. She knew that this was going to be very difficult. Did she have to tell Daisy just yet? Would it be best to wait? Emma might have a miscarriage. She frowned and dismissed such a notion, concentrating instead on expressing her pleasure at meeting up once more, and on such a lovely sunny day for the time of the year.

They found a table at the far end of the small lounge, taking comfort from the sight of the flickering flames of a log fire burning in the grate half way along the wall, without feeling the excess of heat.

'Well?' Daisy looked expectantly at her friend. 'This had better be important. Some of us have a job to go to.'

'Oh, I'm sorry, Daisy. You ought to have said. Look, I don't want to hold you up. We could leave this for another time. It's not urgent.'

'Oh for goodness sake, Hannah! Come on! What's the big secret? I need my shot of caffeine, secret or no secret.'

Hannah watched the expression of lively curiosity on her friend's face change into astonishment followed by frowning disapproval, as she briefly described the relationship between her daughter Emma and Greg.

'I'm—s—sorry, Daisy,' she stammered. 'I really had no idea. I just seem to sense pregnancy with my girls, particularly Emma. But it is a bombshell for me as well. I have only just found out. Greg sounds like a decent bloke. Perhaps we all read too much into things. Perhaps we shouldn't complicate our lives at our age.'

She stopped talking and waited for a response, but Daisy was standing up and pushing her chair noisily across the floor.

'Well, I've got work to do, so I must leave you to have a coffee on your own. No doubt Emma will inform me of her intentions job wise.'

Hannah watched her walking out, noticing for the first time the slight deformity in the top of her spine, a warning of bone loss, and the unevenness of her gait. Her initial feelings of irritation at her friend's reaction quickly changed to those of sympathy. They both seemed to be on a downward spiral. She offered to pay for both coffees, excusing the departure of her friend to the landlord's wife. 'She suddenly felt unwell,' she explained.

The lady nodded and accepted the payment. 'You look like you could drink both cups,' she said. 'Take your time. Everybody seems to be in an almighty rush today.'

Hannah did not take her advice, gulping down the strong coffee and shuddering at the bitterness on the back of her tongue. Daisy's cup went untouched and minutes later Hannah was back sitting in her car. She wanted to escape from the whole sorry episode, yet found herself looking across the tarmac into a neighbouring field where water from a recent shower had gathered on the surface indicating a band of clay in this predominately sand and gravel terrain. She stared dispassionately at this yellow stickiness, too upset to switch on the engine and drive home. She had known Daisy for such a long time, and thought of her as a 'sister come lately' along with Sally Blenkin, the bosom friend of her youth. This close companionship of contemporaries gave her strength to cope with the daily issues of modern family life especially since Jack had died. It was always comforting to return to the familiar topics and occupations of their own generation through both conversations and activities in spite of the occasional differing of opinions.

Now she visualised recent events piercing through this buffer, and in her mind's eye could see the small boy who tried to keep the dyke from bursting by putting his finger in the hole. The illustration in an old book came readily to mind. She had read the story many times to primary school children, and she saw herself trying to keep back the flood of family complications threatening her daily life.

Of course, she reasoned, there had always been problems. That was life after all. Yet this one seemed to have escaped the boundaries, crossing over the generations and testing her sense of loyalty.

Back at Willow Cottage she decided to ring Emma and warn her that Daisy could be on the warpath. After a resumé of the brief conversation between her and her friend, she paused for breath awaiting her daughter's reaction.

Emma was expressing her concern, begging her mother not to say another word and to leave it to her.

'This is my problem, Mum,' she said. 'Well, not really a problem, and I know you are trying to help, but I don't want you to fall out with Daisy. You are such good friends.'

Hannah could hear the impatience mixed in with the concern, and reproached herself for getting involved. Why had she not listened to that warning little voice in her head? It was just that she could not help feeling responsible for the actions of her children. As she had told herself many times since Jack died, it was time to switch off and step back. But then would not that be regarded as indifference?

She replaced the receiver and sank down heavily onto the settee. She felt old and tired. All that she wanted to do was to go over to the nursing home and put her arms around her friend. She knew from life experience that this rift could widen beyond a point of reparation.

'It's no good, Emma,' she declared, staring at the television screen. This single positive statement triggered a burst of energy into her legs, and she sprang to her feet, hurrying towards the front entrance and out to her car parked on the gravelled forecourt.

There were no hold-ups on the road, tractors having made their links between farms and fields at an earlier time, and ten minutes later she approached the gates where the boldly decorated sign displayed the words 'Daisy Cottage Nursing Home'. She brought the car to a halt and stared at it, wondering whether to drive in to the grounds. She had passed this sign many times since that first encounter when she was making arrangements for Ella their old housekeeper to have nursing care, accepting the bright white and yellow daisies on the deep blue background without that initial criticism. But now, with rain clouds gathering and blotting out the sunshine everything had taken on a shabby air. The blue background paint was beginning to peel quite badly and weeds were growing unchecked around the pillars either side of the gates. Ivy straggled along the bricks, tendrils reaching forward towards the road.

She thought of her friend's efforts to fight back against advancing age, witnessing on recent shopping trips the large amounts of money she spent on cosmetics that claimed to banish wrinkles and maintain a youthful complexion, and was reminded of her own concern over the neglected area around the entrance to Willow Cottage Garden Centre. Funds were being strained by an increasing cost of living. Health and safety issues were a big concern for Daisy, and insurance against every possible disaster was becoming very expensive. Perhaps it was the apparent wealth of this gentleman that attracted her rather than a romantic relationship.

She could see Daisy's bright red car parked in her private space at the side of the building, and she drove around pulling up along side of it. Daisy's office window looked out onto this space, and Hannah concentrated on walking to the side entrance, hopefully avoiding accusing stares and praying that her friend had calmed down.

Meanwhile, Daisy watched her friend struggling out of her car, knowing from her frown that her back muscles were protesting at the sudden change of posture. She regretted her actions at the Rose and Crown. After all, it was not Hannah's fault. She knew that her earlier anger was really directed towards herself. How could she be so naïve as to believe that Greg could be anything more than a friend with shared interests beyond the workplace? She had guessed already that Emma was aware of this morning's episode by the way she had avoided eye contact. Now, she wanted to hug her and congratulate her on her good news. She listened for footsteps along the corridor, anticipating her friend Hannah's face flushed with embarrassment, apologies tumbling from her lips in that familiar stammering way.

She stood up to open the door at the same time as Hannah raised her hand to knock, and they spontaneously embraced. The relief shone out from their faces. They were back in their own domain, comfortable and secure in their familiar grasp of life.

15

The Millennium Bug

'Christmas is coming. The goose is getting fat. Please put a penny in the old man's hat. If you haven't got a penny, a ha'penny will do. If you haven't got a ha'penny well God bless you!'

Elphine clapped her hands and laughed. She was sitting with Jane on a big cushion on the floor of the gallery, turning the pages of her favourite book. The lights on the Christmas tree twinkled, and the flickering flames in the inglenook cast strange shadows around the walls of the 'Great Hall'.

'What is a ha'penny?'

Jane smiled, noticing how the changing light emphasised the irregular features of the child, and put out her hand in a gesture of affection. 'It's an old coin,' she replied. 'Really it should be half penny, but it was always called a ha'penny. That was much easier to say.'

'That wasn't much to give a poor old man, was it?' Elphine wriggled on the cushion. She was suddenly visualising the old man in the chicken hut. What did her mother say? Zacc somebody. She still thought of him as the crooked man. That poem about the crooked man was on a later page and she did not want to reach it. She still felt guilty about her wanderings in the garden and taking the food from the back kitchen. Now she visualised the plastic box containing the ham and salad, which she had pushed out of sight amongst the nettles under the felled apple tree as Jane was rounding the corner.

'I think we had better see if your grandma wants any help.' Jane struggled to her feet and groaned. 'I feel like an old woman today,' she joked.

'No you don't, Auntie Jane. You will never be an old woman.'

Jane felt an overwhelming surge of love for this dear little child, followed by pangs of regret that she had never been blessed with a child of her own. The news of the future arrival of another little Clayton had pleased her, but like Hannah she was aware of all the undercurrents stirring under the surface of this close family. Spending the greater part of her adult life as a single woman had sharpened her awareness of the complexities of other people's lives, and there was very little that she did not know of these people around her. Not only did they confide in her, they did not try to hide their emotions either, allowing their reactions to register on their faces. Simon's indiscretions with the student had escaped her notice initially, but she had picked up on Daisy's infatuation from the very beginning, and her tenderness of heart was strained between her employer, Emma and Hannah. In spite of her empathy with Marie over her inability to conceive, she was uneasy with her strict code of childcare, and Rachel's newly found zeal seemed to threaten this little child's welfare. Her own neglect of the child when she fell asleep and woke to find Elphine missing still gave her palpitations as she envisaged all the possible outcomes.

But, as the nursery rhyme said, Christmas was coming. The garden itself was enjoying its winter hibernation; the trees bare of leaves, and tender shrubs and plants basking in the insulated surroundings of the long greenhouse. The work force was employed in the relatively new 'gifts and tools shed' sited in the sunken field to the left of the main centre. In Hannah's opinion, the title of 'shed' belied the splendour and atmosphere of the place. The shelves were stacked with an assortment of gifts suitable for the season, and the high quality tools promised a return to the joys of days spent in the garden. It seemed that everyone was intent on making this a special Christmas; the last one in the old century. Of course, the daily reminder of a world crisis in the banking system because of a possible computer crash, blighted some people's enthusiasm, but on the whole there was a kind of 'don't care' philosophy. 'What the hell...' people were heard to say.

Simon reported record sales after locking himself away in his office for a couple of hours on Christmas Eve. Everyone relaxed in an atmosphere of tinsel, the anticipation of a well earned rest, and the bonus of special meals and treats.

Elphine could not wait to go to bed. The adults, joined by cousin Poppy, described how the elves were working hard to help Santa, and they were so caught up in the excitement that they found themselves half believing the fantasy. In recent years Elphine had not understood what Christmas was all about, and Poppy had outgrown her childish expectations. So, this year everyone enthused on Christmas Eve for the sake of the small child in their midst. Even Marie, with her strict code of Christian beliefs did not muddy the joy of the legend in the presence of her granddaughter.

On Christmas morning Elphine was so appreciative of the pillowcase full of delicious treasures; the favourites being the doll with its sets of clothes; the pencil box with an assortment of coloured pencils and felt tipped pens; the amazing pencil sharpener in the shape of a parrot; a thick drawing pad; beads and bangles, and a fancy hair band.

Her joy knew no bounds when she had to close her eyes and be lead to the Christmas tree in the great hall. She squinted through her lashes at two large items draped with wrapping paper.

'Mummy's and Daddy's first,' her grandfather advised.

He helped her to remove the paper and sticky tape to reveal a doll's pram. Alice and Leigh had decided that such a toy would not only prepare Elphine for the arrival of a new baby in the family, but would give her limbs added stability, replacing the baby walker which she now regarded with some disdain.

Elphine put the doll she had found in the Christmas sack into the pram and began to push it away from the tree.

'One more to go,' Simon called. 'This one is from Grandma and me.'

Hannah looked across to where Marie was standing in the open doorway. Please Elphine, she inwardly prayed, please love this present as much as the pram.

She need not have worried. Elphine was entranced with the dolls' house. It had been made by a local carpenter, and based on Willow Cottage.

'It's my crooked house,' the child exclaimed, jumping up and down with excitement.

'Great-grandma bought all the furniture for it and she and Grandma have made all sorts of bits and pieces. What a lucky little girl you are with such lovely presents. I think everyone deserves one of your special hugs.' Simon relaxed, his face wreathed in smiles as he held out his arms to embrace his grandchild, his hands guiding her to Marie. Hannah stepped forward to catch her from stumbling over a cardboard box left with wrappings on the floor. She was not desperate for recognition, but understood Simon's concern. The atmosphere between him and Marie was still apparent to everyone.

She later noticed that, after all the initial excitement, Elphine chose to return her attentions to the pencil case and to press her fingers around the intriguing shape of the pencil sharpener. This obvious appreciation for tools of creativity above all else gladdened her heart. It would seem that traditional skills could still compete in a world of so called press button technology.

Later, in the privacy of her room where her family had insisted she remain until all the clearing up was done, she sat on the edge of the bed feeling a little uncomfortable, the turkey alongside all of the traditional vegetables and seasonings now weighing heavily on her stomach. She admitted to herself that the Christmas pudding had been a step too far, but knowing that it was Marie's speciality she had not liked to refuse.

She studied the collection of fossils in a cardboard box beside her on the bed alongside of a new jumper and collection of 'smellies', as the bath time potions were known. No one ever knew what to buy her these days with her rather conservative choice of clothes. She had a passion for fossils, regarded by the family she suspected as an eccentric interest, but nevertheless had provided them with a choice of a combined Christmas gift. She loved to run her fingers around the shapes of ammonites, and feel the texture of crinoids and fish released from the grip of aeons of lime deposits. The dinosaur teeth and bones gave her such an awareness and incredulity of the passage of time and her role in it, heightening her sense of importance in this great scheme of things, rather than diminishing it as some would maintain. She traced her index finger over the irregular surface of one fossil labelled quite graphically 'dinosaur poo'. Everyone who touched it wrinkled up the nose, automatically anticipating odour. She pictured a time millions of years ago when a creature went through its regular business of emptying its bowels, never knowing that the results of his labour would one day sit in a plastic tray with an attached label. What would human beings leave behind, she wondered?

She carefully transferred her presents onto the chest of drawers and stretched out on the bed. Within minutes Jack had entered into her dream world so clearly that she had no desire to return to reality, and Emma's voice calling her name from the foot of the kitchen stairs became part of that dream state. A gentle shaking of her shoulder brought her back to the pressures of Christmas Day. She jumped up, protesting that she must have dozed off for a few minutes. It was Jane who brought a welcome cup of tea, and told her that, together with Daisy and Sally, the rest of the family would soon be here.

Hannah took gulps of tea in between teaming up her new jumper with some black trousers, and avoiding the usual choice of fluffy winter socks, selecting instead a pair of knee length, black nylon socks. She could not cope with tights, hating the feeling of being encased from the waist downwards.

Soon Willow Cottage was vibrating with the sound of voices from all directions. Sally was the first to arrive allowing for her and Hannah to catch up on the latest family gossip in the privacy of Hannah's room. Emma and Poppy in 'Marigold' were followed down the drive by Daisy in her sporty red car, and Justin with Rachel in the front and the twins Karl and Kirstie in the back seat appeared ten minutes later in a long black car described by Sally in a whispered comment as somewhat funereal.

As usual, they formed into groups, the younger ones congregating up in the gallery. The ladies from each generation headed for the kitchen, comfortable to be away from youthful chatter and relaxed away from the men.

Simon at first found himself in the company of his brother-in-law Justin, and they stood on either side of the inglenook each with a glass of wine, making what could only be described as polite conversation. Simon missed his father and brother at times like this, feeling outnumbered by the opposite sex. He always found it difficult to talk to Leigh. The generation gap seemed to get in the way. But right now he was wondering how much his sister had revealed to her husband of his infidelity. Justin, his mind definitely on the problems of sex, was satisfying his feelings of inadequacy both in his marriage and in communicating with his wife's family, with a silent condemnation of his brother-in-law's actions. They talked of climate change, and the millennium bug, both with little knowledge of either, using recall of television programmes, and were relieved to be joined by Clive Spryfoot, and to discuss the latest sports news. But that soon began to pall, and the sound of the bell ringing out in the entrance hall was a welcome distraction.

Here a large table had been extended and laden with a buffet selection of savouries and sweets. The young set clattered down from the gallery, Poppy helping Elphine to negotiate the steep wooden steps. Hannah, Sally and Daisy were glad to follow each other around the table filling their plates with tasty morsels, and then retiring to the great hall and the comfort of the settee and armchairs. Marie, Rachel, Emma, now with the help of the late arrival Jane, continued to make sure that everyone was eating well and took it in turns to replenish cups or glasses.

Slowly as the fire burnt down and both old and young began to tire of the traditional games, the conversation drifted into the plans for a firework display on New Year's Eve. It had never been the custom to have fireworks on New Year's Eve, and since the children had grown up even November 5th was not remembered at Willow Cottage. However, this year as Simon explained to Sally, they had really pushed the boat out with a big outlay on fireworks, and it was a pity she could not be there. She explained that she had an invitation to a big do, as she described it and apparently Daisy had other plans too. Hannah sighed at the prospect of a possibly cold night ahead and another round of making merry. She did not like the loneliness of New Year's Eve. But here it was looming up, heralding a new century without Jack by her side. And what about this Millennium Bug, she thought. The papers were full of it.

❄

'That's your lot, folks!' Simon rubbed his hands together. 'I'm ready for a large brandy. I don't know about all of you.'

It was ten o'clock, but seemed more like midnight as smoke from neighbouring bonfires and sulphurous fireworks hung in the damp air. The finale had been spectacular. A single firework costing a small fortune in Hannah's estimation had lit up the sky in a series of bursts of coloured lights, accompanied by gasps of astonishment and appreciation from the spectators. It appeared like a huge umbrella of light, and Leigh later described it as akin to an alien spacecraft.

A normal supper was accepted as the celebratory feast, and they watched a television programme following the course of the millennium celebrations around the world, with spectacular firework displays in the capital cities. Simon listened for news of crashing computer systems, and was reassured by the chimes of Big Ben and the pictures of revellers in Trafalgar Square.

It was approaching one o'clock in the morning, and unable to sleep, he got out of bed and crossed to the window with its view of the garden centre and the sunken field. As his eyes adjusted to the darkness, he became aware of a red glow and then the sight of yellow flames leaping into the air. Had someone lit a bonfire in a neighbouring field at this time of night? Had the huge rocket landed and caused a fire? He ran down the stairs calling to Marie and Leigh to join him. Hannah heard the commotion and pushed her arms into her dressing gown sleeves, almost falling down the stairs in her panic as she ran through to the side door.

It was obvious now that the gift and tools shed was on fire. Leigh was ringing the fire brigade, and Simon was running along the path towards the blaze. The time that passed by between raising the alarm and the actual presence of fire fighters seemed, to the anxious family, like hours rather than minutes, yet the fire seemed to be extinguished very quickly once the team employed the use of hoses. Two police cars had joined the fire engine in the driveway, cordoning off a wide area around the smouldering remains of the building.

When all of the family had been accounted for, and the police were satisfied that there were no casualties on the site, they left, promising to return in the morning to investigate the cause of the fire. It was hinted that the likely culprit was a firework. Apparently, the fire brigade had been on call all night and the services of the local police force were being stretched to their limits, with drunken revellers causing mayhem in the city. But then insurance was mentioned, and Simon had the uneasy feeling that he was already under suspicion. After the emergency teams had left, he walked cautiously around the perimeter directing a beam of light from his torch across the charred remains of his stock. He sighed. This was not the curse of the Millennium Bug. He suspected arson. He suspected Maxine with her threats of revenge.

Hannah, watching that lone figure from her bedroom window, was remembering Maxine's conversation with her boyfriend when she said that she would get her own back somehow. This scheming girl would know that Simon's guilt and fear of exposure would silence any suspicions he may have concerning her part in it. She drew the curtain across and struggled into bed, her limbs aching with stress and fatigue. It could still be that rocket, she thought, remembering how it lit up the sky in bursts of explosions before falling back to earth.

16

Arson

A policeman arrived early on the scene the next day accompanied by a man and a dog, apparently from the forensic department.

'Normal procedure sir,' the young policeman said to Simon, who was trying to focus his mind on waking up after long hours of sleeplessness, his mind plagued with money worries, Maxine and Maria. Finally, he had succumbed to sleep at well past six o'clock aware of the smell of smoke in his hair, and the moon shining brightly in the winter sky.

Now, only a few hours later, he stood in the sunken field, away from the tapes surrounding the scene of the fire, watching the methodical search made by two men and a dog. He hoped that they would discover the burnt out remains of a firework. Would arson invalidate his insurance? He had been in the act of reading the small print when he had heard the sound of the police car tyres in the gravel, and had hastily returned the insurance documents to the desk drawer.

The young policeman had joined the dog handler, and Simon watched the two of them deep in conversation, the first one pointing and leading the way to an area of grass beyond the blackened wall of the building. The dog was straining ahead of them, nose to the ground. Simon saw them stop and begin to pull up clumps of grass, carefully pushing them into a large plastic bag.

Minutes later, the policeman rejoined Simon and requested his presence at the station for further investigation.

Hannah and Marie, watching through the kitchen window, were horrified to see Simon getting into the police car. He gave them a wave and called, 'Don't worry. I'll be back soon.'

'Don't worry!' Marie exclaimed. 'I haven't had a wink of sleep. You don't think they think he's done it, do you?'

'I'm sure they don't. It all has to be officially logged as an incident for insurance. You know, given a number and all that officialdom. He looked quite cheerful.'

'He's good at looking cheerful.'

Hannah could not agree, remembering Simon's state of unhappiness over the last few months. It seemed like an age since he was his normal cheerful self. Perhaps he could claim on the insurance. He certainly paid a high premium. But no, she told herself trying to quell her suspicions, Simon was too honest and hardworking to try to defraud the insurance company. But then he had cheated on his wife. She grunted out loud and shook her head.

Marie turned away from the window staring expectantly at her mother-in-law.

'Nothing,' Hannah said. 'Just tired like you. I'll start on breakfast. I expect the young ones will emerge soon.'

It was Marie's turn to grunt.

The grandfather clock sounded the hours. Elphine counted on her fingers. 'Eleven,' she shouted. She was very intent on mastering the telling of time, turning the metal hands on the toy clock that Hannah had bought for the Christmas stocking. It was always such a thrill when a child could work out the seemingly complex business of telling time, Hannah thought, remembering not only her family's sense of achievement but going back even further to her own childhood before the war. How little milestones stick in the memory, she mused, and yet one struggled to recall comparatively huge events. It was as though the painful memories buried themselves deep in the subconscious, occasionally attempting to emerge, but then hastily being suppressed by a level of will power capable of negating the past. Hannah bit her lip. Time seemed to be sweeping her away from her good memories. Jack darling, her inner voice sighed.

The familiar sound of Simon's car engine alerted Bobbie, who, raising his head, gave a small bark of acknowledgement before sinking back down again into sleep. Marie turned away from the boiling kettle and stepped across to the kitchen window. The sound of Elphine counting the hours became an irritation, and Hannah clicked her tongue against the roof of her mouth and shook her head. 'Not now dear,' she said.

An air of silent expectancy met Simon as he entered through the side door. He did not speak at first, taking off his anorak and sitting down heavily into the old fireside armchair.

'Well?' Marie broke the silence.

'They think it is arson. There is evidence of a trail of petrol leading across the field.'

Hannah thought of Maxine and her boyfriend. She stared at her son, wanting to ask him if it was possible.

Marie sighed. 'So where does this leave you then? Can we claim insurance?'

'Is it coffee time? God my mouth is dry! Those places would make a saint feel guilty! I have no idea, Marie. It is all in the hands of the police now, and we are not allowed onto the scene of the crime until they have finished their investigations. The only advantage for us, if you can call it that, is that we have an incident number for a possible insurance claim. I am going to have to check the policy and inform them without any further delay. They are not really satisfied yet.' He nodded his head in the direction of the burnt-out building.

Hannah took her coffee outside and watched the young police officer following a line across the field indicated by the pointing finger of his colleague. He appeared to be heading in the direction of the private part of the garden. She alerted Simon, who was in his office once more studying the insurance policy. He went outside and watched as both of the policemen seemed to be following a trail across the muddy, partly dug-over vegetable patch. They were taking photographs of something along the way, and had now reached the old chicken huts. He heard the sound of a door scraping along the rough earth, and then a loud shout of 'Oh my God! Get an ambulance, Neil.'

He was not prepared to remain an onlooker any longer, in spite of police instructions. This was not the scene of the crime, and it was his garden after all, he reasoned. He ran along the normal pathway towards the chicken huts.

The young policeman held out a restraining arm. 'Sorry sir,' he said. 'I'm afraid you can't go in. We've found a body. We have to have official confirmation of death.'

'Is it the culprit? Is it a woman?' Simon stammered. 'I mean is it a man or a woman?'

'Sorry sir. You really must go back to the house.' The policeman returned his attention to his phone. 'An old man by the look of his hands. Difficult to tell with the burns. Perhaps a vagrant. Yes, the trail led here. Definitely the same shoe imprints. Yes sir. All photographic evidence we need. Thank you sir.'

Simon turned back to the house. Not Maxine then, but an old tramp. Had she paid someone to do her dirty work for her? He sank down onto the plum tree trunk, where Elphine had sat during that earlier week when she had hidden the evidence of her theft of the food from the pantry. He could not be seen by anyone back at the house, and he put his head in his hands in a gesture of despair. How stupid he had been, he thought. She could go on punishing him forever if she so wished. The sound of the approaching ambulance, followed by another police car, brought his attention back from those foolish moments of passion to the present tragedy. He returned to the vicinity of the chicken huts and watched as the shrouded body was carried on a stretcher across the vegetable patch and up to the gateway. The silence following the engine sounds of a car and the ambulance seemed to him to be even more threatening, and he turned to walk back to the cottage and to his family.

Hannah and Marie were waiting in the kitchen for Simon's return. They had watched him disappear from sight in the direction of the orchard, their minds straining towards a possible explanation.

He came into view again and they noted the frown accentuated between his brows and the apparent tiredness in his footsteps.

'They've found a body,' he announced, as he entered the kitchen. 'An old man. Probably a tramp,' he added. He avoided meeting Hannah's gaze, directing his words to his wife.

'They wouldn't let me go near of course. Did you see the ambulance at the gate? He has to be confirmed dead, and they will be examining everything now. But from what I could gather from the young copper's telephone communication with the station, the body is badly burned, so he could be the arsonist.'

'But what if it was an old tramp sheltering in the building and then having to escape, and dragging himself to the chicken hut? Why should an old tramp risk his life setting the gift shed on fire?' Marie's hand shook as she poured water onto the instant coffee granules in his cup.

Hannah made no comment. It certainly did not make sense, she thought, unless it led back to the vindictive student. Her thoughts were running along the same track as her son's. Maxine could have bribed a down and out. She suddenly put her fingers to her lips and pointed towards the kitchen door. Elphine had been settled into her bedroom to play with the doll's house, but now by the sound of it she had come down the stairs.

In fact the child had arrived on the other side of the door in time to hear her grandmother's last comments. She immediately thought of the old man she had encountered in the chicken hut. The crooked man! She shivered. What if they found out how naughty she had been? What if he told them about her going to fetch him food? She would pretend that she did not know him, even if he said that she did. But then she had shown her parents the drawing. She turned to run back up the stairs with the intention of ripping out the page, but the door was opening and her great-grandmother was reaching out towards her to help her down the steep steps.

'Did you want something, darling?' Hannah asked. 'Or are you tired of playing on your own?'

Elphine nodded in response to the second question, and sat down at the table, cupping her chin in her hands and closing her eyes.

This posture was so normal to the child with her changing moods and little sulks that the adults disregarded her, concentrating instead

169

on the business of drinking coffee, and half heartedly discussing the latest weather forecast.

Simon had not sat down. He made vague responses to news of the so-called millennium bug, casting anxious glances along the drive. The ambulance and one police car had gone but the two young officers were still looking for evidence. Was the culprit an old tramp? Had he survived? Was it anything to do with Maxine? All of these questions buzzed around in his head with a myriad of possible answers it seemed. He ran his fingers impatiently through his hair and sighed.

Hannah watched her son, noticing how hunched his shoulders were becoming and how deep the frown line showed between his eyes. She shook her head in silent disbelief. What a terrible beginning to a new millennium! It was not the expected world disaster, but on such a personal level it seemed to hit harder.

Now a policeman was making his way along the muddy track that lay between the orchard and the house. Simon stretched his head forward, peering above the net half-curtain through the murky light that inevitably seemed to follow celebratory fireworks. Remnants of smoke from the blazing shed still lingered in both sight and smell. He could make out that the policeman was waving in recognition as he drew closer, and Simon muttered something unintelligible and pushing his feet into his Wellingtons went out through the side door.

Hannah and Marie followed him out of the kitchen and stood in the porch, sheltering from the sudden outset of a heavy shower of rain. Elphine raised her head and held her breath in an effort to hear the adult conversation. She heard the two ladies repeat the word 'dead' and was relieved that the crooked man could no longer threaten her with his tale of her disobedience.

It seemed that the policeman required Simon to return to the station to re-establish the times of the previous evening's activities, and then to go to the hospital morgue to see whether he recognised the old man and could shed any light on reasons for the act of arson. Hannah offered to accompany her son, declaring that she may have known the old man in the past if he came from these parts.

'I'll drive over,' she said, 'and I can bring you home. You will be OK, won't you, Marie? Alice and Leigh are on the move.'

Elphine chose this exodus of her grandfather and great-grandmother to pretend to use the facilities of the downstairs cloakroom, locking the door carefully behind her and pressing her ear against the door.

'They seem to think it was the old man who caused the fire. They've taken the body away and your dad and grandma have gone to see if they can recognise him. What a start to the year! Why ever should he want to set the place on fire unless he was trying to keep warm?' she heard her grandmother shout to her parents upstairs. The next sounds she heard, as she continued to press her ear against the door, were of their footsteps on the landing and then on the stairs. She waited until the click of the latch indicated the closing of the kitchen door, and then carefully turned the key and tip-toed out. She must find her drawing book and destroy the drawing of the crooked man before anyone saw it. She remembered how her mother had shown relief at his picture appearing at the back of her book amongst all her dream people, and how her father had shaken his head.

She ran across to the shelves in the corner of the bedroom she shared with her grandmother, and lifted up a box of crayons and a pile of comics. The drawing book was not there. She knew that she had put it back after showing it to her parents. The dolls' clothes were not there either. She always covered it up with them.

'Sorry Elphine. We needed to look at your book.' Her mother's voice coming from the open bedroom door startled the child, and she spun around, almost falling as her ankle twisted against the leg of the dressing table.

'Don't tell Grandma, please. I went to the shed to draw the rabbits and he was in the old one. He was hungry and I got some ham from the pantry, but then he had gone, and Aunt Jane came to find me and she was very cross with me and she said not to tell Grandma because she would be cross, but I drew him in my book because he said he was the crooked man and I wanted to draw his crooked teeth and his crooked eyes. One was brown and one was blue.'

'Oh darling. Calm down. No one is cross with you.' She turned to speak to Leigh who had followed her back up the stairs. 'This explains everything. It was Zacc Pound still trying to get his revenge. Fancy after all these years! Thank God he didn't harm Elphine.'

'Don't scare her, Alice. I think we ought to ring the station and explain.' Leigh was searching in his pocket for his phone. Minutes later he learnt that Hannah had identified the body at the morgue as that of their previous employee Zacc Pound. Like Alice, she had never forgotten his strange eyes and had recoiled in horror at their fixed stare as the sheet was drawn back and the shock of seeing him again in the flesh rather than in recurring bad dreams weakened her legs, causing her to stagger to one side.

Now Hannah listened to the policeman talking on the phone as she sipped the hot sweet tea from a thick heavy mug. 'That was your grandson, Mrs Clayton. Apparently his daughter had seen Zacc Pound in the shed. It seems that he was taking shelter in there, and she felt sorry for him. Do you remember the Zacc Pound abduction case, sir?' An older man had come into the room, and Simon and Hannah recognised him as the officer who had lead the search for the nine-year-old Alice.

'I certainly do. It always annoyed me that we never caught up with him. Well, he's got his comeuppance, although he's had a tough life by the look of him. Still, one less criminal on the loose.'

'You won't need Alice or little Elphine for your report, will you? Will there be an inquest?'

Hannah was getting the strength back into her legs and her brain was responding to the return of her physical energy. She waited for a reply, but her son spoke instead.

'Is that all then, sir? Can I begin to clear up the site and assess the damage and financial loss?' Simon was looking anxiously towards the door in anticipation of a release from this part of the nightmare.

'I would advise you to contact your insurance company now and don't touch a thing. We have made a preliminary report and you have an incident number to quote. Leave it all to the experts, is always our advice. We have all the photographic evidence, and he left a good trail of footprints and petrol leaking onto his clothes. There will have to be an inquest.' He turned to Hannah. 'We will let you know if any of the family are required to attend.'

Simon offered to drive but Hannah shook her head. 'I would rather if you don't mind. It will keep my mind occupied. I expect you need a coffee or probably something stronger. I don't suppose you got much sleep. Still, at least we know who did it and with a police report and everything, it should speed things up with the insurance.'

'I wouldn't be too sure about that, but as you say we do know who did it.'

They both knew whose name was in his thoughts and it was not Zacc Pound. Hannah still could not dismiss the possibility that the old man had been paid to commit the crime. She needed to speak to Elphine, but how could she approach the child without causing more fear? She drove back along the winding road through the villages between Lincoln and Norbrooke, scarcely noticing the darkening sky and the first pattering of rain on the windscreen. Simon had closed his eyes, the wipers now acting like a kind of metronome, the rhythmic ticking steadying his brain into a near sleep state.

The cessation of the motion of the windscreen wiper at the same time as the sound of the tyres on gravel brought him out of his semi-conscious state, and he peered through the misting windscreen at the number of cars parked on the gravel. He recognised Emma's orange Fiat and Rachel's hatchback parked alongside each other, and Clive's large van pulled over to one side. Bad news travels fast, he thought.

Alice walked out to meet them, pursing her lips in a warning gesture and slightly shaking her head. Hannah grabbed her son's arm, seemingly for support, aware of Marie's anxious face at the window.

'We haven't told Marie about Elphine's involvement in this. Jane will get it in the neck for letting her wander off. I just said that the police recognised him, and that it was Zacc Pound come back after all these years to get his revenge. Surely they won't question a four-year-old.'

Hannah was relieved to find on entering the kitchen that Marie had decided to remove Elphine from the adult gathering. Emma and Rachel had escaped into the great hall to bask in the warmth of the blazing fire, leaving Justin standing awkwardly in front of the kitchen range.

'What a bad start to the year,' Justin said in what Simon thought was an accusing tone of voice. 'Let's hope the insurance will cover it.'

'It's a blessing that no one was in the building. At the end of the day people matter, not things.'

'So was it the old tramp then? No one seems to know.'

'Yes. He was perhaps trying to keep warm. He was probably in a bad way. I don't expect we will ever know.' Simon sat down heavily in the fireside chair. The last person he wanted to discuss family affairs with was his brother-in-law.

Emma was having similar thoughts regarding her sister. Rachel had expressed fears of lost capital in the business, and Emma, being typical of Emma, was making light of the whole thing. Inwardly she was fuming at such lack of sensitivity. None of the family had come to any physical harm. The fact that she owned part of the business and could suffer a loss was the last thing on her mind. It was a relief that apparently the student was not involved. She wanted to point this out, but decided that this could aggravate matters. Instead, she enquired about the twins, both still intent on following a career in physical training, and then wished she had talked about herself instead.

Rachel launched into a heated criticism of the education system, and of the head teacher's emphatic belief that they would not qualify for a place in their chosen colleges. Emma obligingly shook her head in a gesture of disbelief, although her memory reminded her of her mother's recent comments about Kirstie's 'laddish' ways, and Karl's recent disgraceful behaviour in the local public house. She wanted to tell her sister that it would all pass, but Rachel's bitterness apparently knew no bounds, transferring her attention to Simon's past indiscretions.

'Justin thinks it could be connected with that student. Honestly, I couldn't believe my eyes when I saw them in the greenhouse. I just hope Marie doesn't find out.'

'Why should she? None of us are going to say anything, are we, Rachel?'

'Of course not! How are you by the way?' She pointed towards her sister's stomach. 'I expect you were worried about family reactions. I don't think Mother was too pleased.'

Emma gave her sister a long stare. 'Actually,' she said, 'she's very happy for me. She thinks it will be good for Poppy to have a sibling, and Elphine will have to share the attention, which will do her good. You got it over in one go having twins didn't you?'

Rachel shrugged and walked over to the window. Hannah sensed the tension as she walked into the room.

'Well thank goodness we are in a new year!' she exclaimed. 'Surely things can only get better.'

17

Misplaced Hormones, Middle Age and Mixed Messages

The next bombshell as Hannah described it, exploded in the late spring of that same year. Rachel had come on her monthly visit a week early. Hannah watched her struggling to get out of her hatchback and noticed a general decline not only in her agility, but also in her appearance. She was not given to wearing fashionable clothes, but always managed to look smartly dressed and made regular visits to the village hairdresser to have her curly brown hair cut into a neat bob.

Admittedly it was a wet and windy day but somehow her whole being had a jaded look, her mother thought. She cast her mind back to the days when Stephen, Rachel's ex husband had treated her so badly. Surely history was not repeating itself. Justin was a bit of an odd bod in her opinion, but she would not class him as violent.

She opened the side door and called out, 'It's kitchen company. I have just put the kettle on.'

Rachel avoided eye contact as she met her mother at the door and stepped past her, picking her way over the sausage-shaped draught excluder and heading towards the guard around the range.

'Move that washing, dear. I'm sure it is all dry by now. Marie likes

Elphine's clothes to be toasted! Have you got a cold coming? Would you like some milky coffee instead of tea?'

Hannah knew that she was trying to bridge a gap to put Rachel at her ease. Words covered up her embarrassment, and she did not expect an answer.

None was forthcoming, and for a few minutes only the rattle of teacups and the drumming sound of the kettle coming to the boil broke the silence.

'Tea will do,' Rachel suddenly replied. 'I haven't got a cold. I have just had a terrible shock.'

Hannah poured the boiling water onto the tea in the teapot and stirred the brew vigorously, at the same time casting her mind in various directions searching for a hint of a clue. She was agitated with a burning curiosity and with concern, but yet she wanted to retreat into the peace of her own sanctuary. All this happened in the same moment and she chided herself for her selfish attitude. However, after one quick sip of her tea, her daughter invited her to share her secret.

'It's Kirstie,' she said.

'Not pregnant!' Hannah gasped.

'No. It's worse than that. She's gay. You know, a Lesbian.'

Rachel said the word as though it was written in italics, Hannah thought. She searched for a response, suddenly recalling how she herself had wondered if she could be a Lesbian at the teacher training college when she had what she now realised was a teenage crush on another student. At the time she had no idea what a Lesbian was, and to be honest, she still had little idea of what was involved in such a relationship.

She used her recall to make light of it. 'I believe it is quite common for girls to have these emotional relationships. Don't worry, She'll grow out of it.'

'I don't think so, Mother. She has arranged to move into a flat with this student, and doesn't want us anywhere near her.'

'Does Justin know about this?'

'Yes. He is being really nasty. I assume it is totally against his beliefs. He used to say how sweet Kirstie was, but now he claims to have never liked her and says that she is a born liar and a waste of space.'

'Really! He had better not say that to me. What about Karl then? Doesn't he like him either?'

'They have never got on. It's the male thing, isn't it? Karl feels that he was here first and Justin has no right to boss him about. I feel sometimes that he is getting more and more like his dad. Oh Mum, I have made such a mess of my life, haven't I? Emma can do no wrong even though she is expecting another baby, and in spite of being an idiot Simon is protected by everyone. I am trying to keep on track being a good wife and mother, yet everything and everyone seems to go against me. I used to get on with Marie. She always seemed to be struggling to keep herself from drowning in family issues, but she has wrapped herself up in her Catholicism.'

Hannah wanted to point out that Marie had a right to her religious beliefs, but knew that this would not help. Rachel did not need confrontation. It was obvious that she was greatly in need of sympathy. Tea and sympathy – would that be enough, she wondered?

The emotional dam was broken and Rachel began to expose all of her grievances in a low voice casting quick glances towards the kitchen door.

'There's no one else here,' Hannah reassured her. 'It's all just between me and you. I knew that you have not been happy just lately. Teen age can be such a trial, but it's your marriage isn't it?'

'It's everything really. I felt that I had a role to play, you know, and it was all wonderful at first. I enjoyed organising functions and raising money for the church, but then that woman arrived and started telling everybody what to do. It has split the congregation in half. She thinks she is lady of the manor, and talks about our family and describes Elphine as a strange little child, even hinting at witchcraft.'

'Oh! You mean that Sarah woman. What's her name?'

'Thornton. She is certainly a thorn in my side. What made you take Elphine in her house? It was all around the village about her seeing a ghost and drawing a picture.'

'I asked her not to talk about it, but of course she had to. Not a good sign for someone who wants to set up a special school. She was probably piqued because I didn't go along with her idea. I was just curious, I suppose. It was a house I had never been in, strangely enough, after all these years.'

'Well, she has a big enough following. People get so caught up with social climbing. Stephen's family were the same, weren't they?'

Hannah nodded. Rachel's first husband always managed to make her feel inferior, especially when she was in dungarees and Wellingtons cleaning out the chicken sheds.

'This is the last straw with Kirstie. I really can't take anymore.'

'Oh dear! Look, let's have another cup of tea and try and sort this out. You have been doing so splendidly. I have had no end of people commenting to me on how organised you are and how much more they have enjoyed being part of all the events. That husband of yours doesn't appreciate you. Anyway, we are all different even though we are related. Simon loves nature and the land like his dad, and Emma is very good at academic things. I feel that she is wasted at the moment but then I am not God, am I? You were always the practical one in the family.' She stared across to the window, not seeing the beginnings of raindrops running down the glass. Her thoughts were suddenly with Mark, that precious son who would never give her any more heartache except in remembrance.

The sound of voices made Rachel reach hastily for a tissue from the inside of her handbag. She dabbed at her eyes and then blew her nose, looking towards the door leading out to the side of the cottage. Elphine's shrill laugh and Marie's 'Hurry up' immediately identified them. Rachel stood up and retrieved her coat from the back of the chair. 'I'd better go,' she said. 'Don't say anything, Mum, will you?'

Hannah shook her head, and reached forward to guide her daughter's arm into the sleeve.

'Just in time for a cup of tea,' she enthused as Marie and the child came in through the door. 'You look cold, Elphie. Your nose is bright pink. You've just made it, I think, before it rains in earnest. Are you sure you won't have another drink, Rachel?'

Rachel shook her head. 'Excuse my rush, Marie. I've got so much to do. I hope you are keeping well. I'll be in touch, Mum.'

Hannah watched her daughter getting back into her car and felt concern for her as she had done when she arrived. Now she understood the reason for her apparent lack of well-being.

The sound of the car engine faded, and Marie busied herself with emptying the plastic carrier bag and stacking groceries in the corner cupboard. Hannah gave the tea a stir and poured milk into Marie's cup. Elphine was still looking out of the window, and suddenly she began to wave.

'Is that your granddad? I think he smells tea?' Hannah leant forward to look for her son.

'No. It's Uncle Justin. He has just missed Auntie Rachel. Shall I go and tell him?'

'I can't see him. His car's not there. He wouldn't have walked.'

Marie leant forward peering through the late afternoon light.

'There's nobody there, Elphine. Stop telling fibs.'

Hannah looked anxiously at the little girl who had begun to cry and shake her head. 'Can you still see him?' she asked.

Elphine nodded. 'Almost,' she said. 'Oh no, he has gone now.'

'So perhaps we can get on with preparing supper. Elphine, fetch me some potatoes from the cellar and be careful of the steps. Don't worry. She is managing them very well, and she needs to get more confidence.' Marie had turned towards Hannah and had not changed the tone of her voice from addressing the child.

Hannah knew that the apparent appearance of Justin had frightened Marie. It frightened me, for goodness sake, she thought. It was obvious that it was not make-believe, even for Marie. After all, she spent more time with Elphine than anyone else. Poor woman. She was really going through a testing time. It was obvious that she worshipped her little granddaughter, yet her faith would not condone what she declared to be the work of the devil. Elphine appeared to have forgotten about the whole experience and once again Hannah was reminded of the time in Hull when Leigh as a small child had recovered so quickly after his psychic reaction to the bombsite where her mother and grandparents had died in the blitz.

Ten minutes later, there was no longer a mystery. The phone rang in the hall. A distraught Rachel told her mother that the police were at the rectory with bad news. There had been a traffic accident, and Justin was dead.

✳

Hannah told no one of that incident in the kitchen, and she was sure that Marie would not do so either. Elphine still appeared to have dismissed it from her mind, although apparently she was aware that her uncle had died. It all must appear to be perfectly natural to her, which of course it is, Hannah thought.

The church was full to overflowing ten days later, and Sarah Thornton had already tried to put herself in charge of affairs, maintaining that the grieving widow needed to concentrate on her family arrangements and the choice of hymns. The Archdeacon officiated, and the whole procedure went like clockwork according to the aforesaid Sarah. The church warden, a man well past his prime and seeming to some people in the congregation to have been in the village for ever, gave the eulogy, praising the beloved Justin Day for his dedication to the many duties of his living, shared as it was between three parishes, and for his wisdom and compassion in his daily life.

Hannah could feel no grief and struggled with any sense of compassion for the untimely ending of his life. Over the years that he and Rachel were married, there had never been a word or gesture of affection from him to his mother-in-law. She had tried to include him in family gatherings, but the title of son-in-law always eluded her on the occasions when she had had to introduce him to friends and colleagues. She found herself describing him as Rachel's husband, or even on one occasion as Rachel's second husband.

She bowed her head as the pallbearers passed along the aisle, and the sob choking in her throat was for Jack. Her dear husband was cremated, whereas this was a burial. She found burials so hard to cope with. She had only experienced one in her lifetime. Sometimes, she thought that it would be reassuring to put flowers on her son's grave, but did not do so. Jack never accepted Mark's death and even though they had not discussed his own funeral arrangements, she knew that he would have chosen cremation. Suddenly the very fragility of existence led her thoughts to her own life. She must make it quite clear that burial was not for her, although she would like her ashes to be mixed in the soil with Jack's ashes. She had created a little site and planted a rose tree for remembrance. It was called 'Sweet Dreams' and had been amongst those delivered to the garden centre nearly a year after his death, prompting her to transfer his ashes from the funeral urn into the soil.

The wake was held at the rectory. Rachel had employed caterers and a long trestle table erected along the length of the dining room was covered in a variety of savouries and sweets. Three stalwart ladies were in charge of beverages. Over the years, they were in attendance at every church event and always drew comment, appearing to be as timeless as the church itself. Indeed, a function without their sedate presence was unimaginable. It was always the same ones, Hannah thought, and no doubt their husbands had carried the collection of folding tables and chairs from the village hall and erected them earlier.

Hannah picked out a sandwich and a savoury pastry, and looked across for her daughter. Simon, Marie, Leigh and Alice were sitting together at a table tucked away in the corner of the room. Emma, Poppy and Daisy shared another table close by. Poppy was holding the attention of the two adults with her chatter, in between chewing vigorously. Hannah had to smile. The solemnity of the occasion had obviously not taken away her appetite. Emma had decided that Poppy was old enough to cope with not only the concept of death, but also the lengthy procedure. However, nothing had been discussed in the presence of Elphine. It was judged by the family that she was too young to understand, and Jane had volunteered to remain at Willow Cottage and look after her. Hannah had agreed that it was no place for a young child, although secretly she had speculated on the level of sensitivity and understanding of children, particularly in the case of this little one.

Rachel, together with Karl and Kirstie, had been standing for almost half an hour accepting the condolences of those who had not spoken at the graveside. She welcomed her mother's advice to get something to eat and find a spare table and chairs. The twins made an instant beeline for the refreshments, piling up their plates.

'Here we are my dear,' Hannah said. 'You look completely done in. Is everyone going to clear up for you? They are all very kind, aren't they?'

'Yes Mum. Daphne Chappell organised it all. Well, with help from Danny, her husband. They are such good friends to me, and put so much effort into everything. Needless to say, that Sarah has been pushing herself in. I wonder how she thinks we all managed before she arrived. I reckon some of them have sussed her out. She will soon find that she is not lady of the manor. In fact lady doesn't come into it.'

'So how do you stand regarding the rectory? They won't expect you to move out straight away, will they?' Hannah had 'tied cottages' in mind. During preceding centuries the squire provided accommodation on the estate for agricultural labourers for the duration of their working lives. Once they could no longer work through ill health or old age they were obliged to find other accommodation, and younger or more vigorous men would be housed.

Rachel laughed. 'Don't worry, Mother. They won't throw us out on the street. It will probably take about six months before they appoint somebody, and in any case I will be looking for somewhere smaller as soon as I get everything sorted. I can't afford to heat a place this size.'

Hannah nodded, noticing how the laughter dispelled the anxiety from her daughter's face, and how young she suddenly looked.

The move was sooner than they had all expected, although the church authorities were not renowned for speedy organisation with so much paper work being shuffled about. When the opportunity arose to rent a delightful detached house on the edge of the village, Rachel did not hesitate. Renting, it seemed, was the best option whilst the twins still required accommodation during weekends and vacations. These days, with high student expenses, it was becoming the norm for young people to stay in the family nest well into adulthood. The so-called empty nest syndrome had gone into reverse on many a wish list, being replaced with a longing for a tidy peaceful space with all the chicks flown.

Rachel was looking forward to being in charge of her own space. Justin had always decided on décor and had delegated the rooms in accordance with his needs. The library housed his books only, and the study, his papers. The kitchen was always of little concern to him, but the sitting room with its large heavily upholstered furniture was never to be changed. An ancient television crouched in the corner opposite to the door leading into the hallway, and he had closely monitored the programmes. After the funeral was over and life returned to a kind of normality, the twins spent most of their time viewing programmes forbidden in the past, regardless of Rachel's preferences. In truth, she did not care. She felt free, wanting to escape from the oppressive atmosphere of the old building. In the evenings she took the radio upstairs to her bedroom, and listened into the early hours of the morning, increasing the volume to smother the sounds of mice scampering under the floorboards. She often fell asleep with the sound of voices penetrating into her dreams and leaving her awareness half in and half out of reality.

The available house to let was unfurnished, and as the rectory furniture was part of the fixtures and fittings she would need to buy something to sit on, eat off and sleep on, as she told the twins. She blessed her wisdom in keeping her own money from the sale of her house secure in her own bank account. Justin had no assets to speak of, apart from a life insurance, always living in church premises after his return to England.

At first, living at the rectory had all seemed rather grand. She could understand Sarah Thornton's attitude, being new to such splendour in the old Manor House, but soon the disadvantages outweighed the grandeur; the chimney in the sitting room belching out smoke on windy nights and depositing soot into the numerous nooks and crannies; the old cooking range, impossible to clean; the steep staircase; the draughty cold bedrooms decorated in dreary creams and pinks, and the antiquated bathroom, a godsend to the mice who used the holes around the pipes to access the living space between the floor boards and the ceilings beneath. Admittedly, Willow Cottage had what one could call its downside to old-fashioned charms, but there was always a sense of well-being, Rachel thought. The sun shone through the windows, and the fires burnt bright. But then the kitchen was a thorn in the side of Marie, she remembered, suddenly sympathising with her sister-in-law.

She decided to ask Marie to accompany her and help her with her choice of furniture. Simon deserved to pay for his indiscretions, she thought. It was about time he gave his wife some consideration. The kitchen section in the big store was close to the lounge and dining furniture sections. She herself would have no need of appliances or units. They were all part of the modern kitchen in the rented house, but Marie would certainly be enlivened with kitchen layouts and brochures.

Emma was invited along. She was intent on buying a new sofa for her living room, and creating a nursery in the tiny bedroom at the rear of her nursing home unit. As they wandered along amongst the different displays, the three women found that both their desires and their frustrations drew them more closely together in the wake of Justin Day, late of this parish.

Simon thought of the kitchen brochures spread out on the kitchen table, and sighed. He was still struggling with the paperwork involved in the insurance claim after the millennium fire. 'Nothing seems to be straightforward these days,' he complained to Hannah, who was delivering his morning coffee. He went on to explain how everything had to be written in triplicate as well as recorded on disc. Apparently goods stored, goods sold and goods displayed with relevant codes and prices, plus invoices relating to the cost of the building constituted a small part of the information required.

'You know what I'm like at book-keeping Mum. Marie's the one with office training but now she doesn't want to know. It's all Elphine or her new kitchen these days. Did she tell you that she wants us to abandon the front kitchen and convert the old back kitchen with fancy wall cupboards and units and miles of worktops? Oh then there's the island in the middle. Has she mentioned an island to you? Oh for God's sake! This bloody machine!'

Hannah shook her head. It's not just me then, she thought as

185

the computer went into some kind of denial and closed down the programme.

She waited in silence for him to restore it, and to finalise the figures.

She was not really happy with her daughter-in-law's big plans. She often wondered if Simon's affair with the student had really escaped Marie's attention. She did seem to have a cold edge to her these days, and Simon did not argue. Admittedly, Marie had been encouraged by Emma and Rachel to stand her ground about the kitchen, and she was pleased to see them all on better terms these days, but poor Simon was becoming outnumbered.

'I can see her point,' she replied. 'The old back kitchen is much bigger and would certainly lend itself to a modern layout. You know, we always said that there was a bricked in doorway in the Glory Hole. We could unbrick it and walk from the front kitchen to the back without going up the steps and through the back hallway. It wouldn't take much doing. It would be a start, and then the rest could be done slowly without a major hassle. That would give you time to get your insurance claim sorted. We could get Leigh and Karl on the job during the Easter holidays.'

Simon grunted. Hannah recognised the grunt. It was the same one Jack used to make when she had suggested in the past that Simon and Mark could help. What was it about men and their young male relatives?

However, it seemed that her fears of Marie exacting some kind of revenge were unfounded. She seemed happy to merely speculate about her kitchen. She made a large number of measurements preferring feet and inches, and complaining bitterly about the complexity of the metric system. Her plans did not seem to match up, and she constantly changed her mind about the colour scheme and style of cupboards. Simon was relieved to indulge her in her fancies and organise the rebuilding and stocking of the gift and tools centre after a generous pay-out by the insurance company restored his faith in human nature, and the worthiness of the yearly premiums. The centre was even more splendid than it had been before with toilet facilities and a small refreshment room.

Soon the weather brightened, and the garden centre itself became alive with a large input of plants and a bustling influx of customers. Simon was back with the life he loved, putting behind him his infidelity, the millennium bug and the arson attack. Good times were ahead, and Marie would get her kitchen, he promised, once the springtime rush was over.

Kirstie did not look well. The dark shadows under her eyes indicated lack of sleep, and Hannah studied her granddaughter as she waited for a reply to her question about the family move. It was an unexpected visit. Kirstie always seemed to have difficulties in relationships made more evident in her teenage years, Hannah thought, her own emotions mixed with guilt and compassion. This sudden need to confide had alerted her to possibly deeper issues. Rachel had not mentioned the proposed flat sharing with another girl since Justin's death. Could that be what this visit was all about?

She did not have to wait long for an answer, and Kirstie's explanation did begin with her intentions to find a place of her own.

'Did Mum tell you that I wanted to move out? I expect she did and that I had decided to be a lesbian.' Kirstie studied her grandmother's face for any change in expression, moving on quickly when she saw no look of incredulity. 'She did, didn't she? Well I don't really want to move out and I am not really a bit gay. I thought I might be because I have always liked boys' things better than girls'. I always envied Karl getting train sets and cars. I remember once burying a doll you gave me in the garden.'

Hannah could not help but smile, and reached forward to pat her granddaughter on the knee. 'Bless you,' she said. 'I know exactly how you felt. I was a tomboy, climbing trees and tearing around on my bike. Lots of girls are like that. You have amazing abilities. I'm sure you will settle down when you start on your course. Does your mother know that you do not want to move out then?'

'No. I am finding it hard to talk to her. We were kind of allies you know until she married Justin. I used to listen to my father shouting and creep down the stairs after he had gone out. I was terrified he was going to kill her. I saw her once coming out of the shower, and she had a huge bruise on the top of her arm where he had grabbed hold of her. I don't think anyone knew how violent he was, and at first she seemed to be so happy after the divorce and it was just the three of us, but then she married Justin. He used to ignore her or say things to make her feel inadequate. In a way it was as bad for her as physical violence. She wouldn't discuss it with me if I said anything and seemed to spend all of her time trying to prove that she was holier than him, if you know what I mean. She was pretending to be happy.'

Hannah nodded. She recalled her past concern over those people destined to be victims and of how she had wondered whether Rachel's second marriage would result in happiness. Her daughter's critical attitude towards her family, and her increasing obsession with religious ethics had certainly not been indicative of contentment.

'I can't speak to her, Grandma, even now, but I must tell someone and I hope that you will understand. I needed to escape because he was making my life a misery.'

Hannah had been watching Kirstie's hands clenching and unclenching in her lap. She looked up quickly, her mind alert to what was coming. She knew without any further explanation.

'He didn't actually, did he?' She asked.

It was Kirstie's turn to be shocked. 'He tried,' she stammered. 'I was fifteen. I remember, the exact time because I had just had a party, and Mum had insisted that I wore a party frock like the other girls, and I had been in a sulk all day. I was quite flattered in a way when he came into my bedroom and told me how much he sympathised but how pretty I looked. The next thing he had pushed me backwards onto the bed and then was on top of me and I couldn't breathe.' She stopped and turned her face away from Hannah's gaze. 'You are the only person I have ever told. I managed to get away and ran out of the room. I was really scared. It has been in my head ever since. But then it didn't stop there. There were all the times when he tried to hold my hand or slipped his hand under my school skirt. I used to run up the stairs and put jeans on as soon as I got home. Mum constantly nagged me to be a young lady, but I had no desire to be that. I wanted to be as ugly as possible. Then I had the idea to be gay. Surely that would make a difference I thought. Anyway, things caught up with him and I am so glad that he is out of my life. I don't think I will ever want a relationship.'

She began to cry, and Hannah reached for a tissue wanting to comfort, yet knowing that talking about her own experience would not help. As she waited for Kirstie to calm down, she cast her mind back to that night when she awoke to find her foster father Tom Porter lying across her, his breath rank with the smell of brandy. The details, it seemed, had long since been obliterated in her memory. Indeed she did not want to remember, but the scene in the barn and picture of the demented Elsie pushing her husband to his death in the fire could not be blotted out. Kirstie would not be able to relate to the memories of an old woman. The fact that she was confiding in her grandmother indicated a youthful attitude that old people knew nothing about sex. No doubt she would recoil at the idea of her ever having had sex even though she had given birth four times. Now, to hear that she actually understand lust personally and was sympathising would not help. This was Kirstie's time – her agony from beginning to end.

'Do you think I should tell my mum?'

'No, there's really no point in doing that. It would not undo it now, and it would add to the bitter memories. In fact strange as it may seem, your mother could blame you for his lack of affection. It could take away her sense of guilt at her failure to please him, but then you would be the guilty one if you see what I mean.'

'I never encouraged him, Grandma!'

'I know you didn't, but guilt plays bad tricks on people's minds. No. Don't tell your mother. You have told me and I promise you I will never tell another living soul.'

Kirstie began to cry again and Hannah did not try to stop her. Instead, she stood up and walked to the window. She felt waves of bitterness sweeping over her. She had welcomed two strangers into her world, each destined to harm her family, and she had done nothing to protect her dear Rachel. Kirstie's next words established the feelings of guilt.

Her granddaughter blew her nose and dabbed at her eyes now swollen with crying.

'You know, Grandma, I have always felt that nobody loves me. With Mum it was always what Karl was doing, and you always seemed to love Alice more than me. I know it was very spiteful of me to tell her that she was adopted. I really didn't understand. I was so little. But I knew that it would upset her and I wanted you to love me more than her.'

'Oh darling. Of course we all love you. We are all different. You must shine at what makes you happy and not try to be like anybody else. All my family are different. Mark was so outgoing and Simon loves to be connected to nature. Emma was always the academic one and your mum was practical, more of a homemaker it seemed, but we never know. You have such ability with your physical strengths. I wish I could run and jump. It takes me all my time to touch my toes these days!'

Hannah knew that she could easily touch her toes. In fact she was determined not to allow her muscles to seize up, but her sole intention was to reassure Kirstie as she had reassured Rachel. It appeared to have worked in some small measure. Kirstie smiled and dabbed at her eyes.

'I am determined to get qualified in physical training and one day have a centre for physical fitness. Karl wants to do this as well. We still tend to think alike you know. So, as they say two heads are better than one.'

'There are lots of heads in the family full of ideas to help. Get back on good terms with your mother. You will be at university soon, and as they say the world is your oyster.'

After Kirstie had said goodbye and given her grandmother a quick hug, Hannah watched her peddling her racing bicycle along the drive to the gates of the garden centre and out onto the village road. She seemed to be full of vigour now, her mind cleared of guilt. The burden was passed on, she thought wryly. She herself had carried her burden until that weekend in London when she had spent time with Sally. It was time spent on reminiscing and she remembered the relief of talking to her friend about Tom Porter, but could not now recall the exact conversation. One would think I would never forget every detail of that unburdening. Poor Elsie Porter, pregnant at fifteen with her father's child and then an abortion leaving her sterile, she thought. No wonder she had become hysterical when she realised that her drunken husband had abused their little evacuee. She had never told Jack what led to Tom's death. It would have scarred his mind as well. Perhaps Sally would remember. Perhaps Kirstie too would slowly forget the enormity of the situation, now that she had shared it, and the perpetrator of the crime was dead. But she knew that the bitterness would still be there if she lived to be a hundred, and if her mother knew of her late husband's depravity, she would not only loathe his memory but could blame her daughter for what would seem like a betrayal.

18

The Man in the Moon

The next few months were, as Hannah described it to Daisy, like a major reshuffle. Since the beginning of this millennium, so called events had come thick and fast, and everyone had moved along in some way. A stronger relationship was developing between Rachel and Marie. With a kind of mutual understanding, they had put aside their religious differences and concentrated on shared interests. Elphine, with her increasing independence, did not demand so much time from her grandmother, and was allowed to accompany her grandfather in the garden centre when he was doing routine jobs. Leigh had one more year beyond this one to qualify for his medical degree, and Alice was enjoying her first appointment in a secondary school in Newcastle teaching English. Karl and Kirstie had stayed on for another year in the sixth form and were both working hard now to get good grades after bad results in the previous year. The longer days of springtime with promise of high sales led to an intensive labour schedule. More staff was taken on and everyone seemed to be prospering.

Hannah was absenting herself more and more from the business. Now that Marie and Simon were back on good terms with each other, and Marie was offering her skills in the bookkeeping department, she was more than happy to leave them to it. Daisy also was preparing for retirement with Emma at the helm. Pregnancy seemed to suit Emma. She glowed with health and showed off her bump as she called it with no sense of embarrassment.

'How times have changed,' Hannah commented, nodding in the direction of a retreating Emma, as they sat on a bench in the private garden at Daisy Cottage enjoying the warmth of the early summer sunshine and the sight and the scents of the newly mowed lawns. 'There is no attempt to conceal it is there? In fact, it seems that they all want it to be blatantly apparent. My grandmother would have had a fit.'

'Well you are going back a long time, my dear. I expect your grandmother would have a fit to see us exposing our arms at our time of life, never mind our legs.' She stretched out her legs, admiring her new sandals and silently inviting Hannah to comment. Hannah obliged, recognising the significance of her friend's movements. The same little charade, she thought, snags of criticism catching in her mind. Even so, she obliged.

'New sandals?'

'Yes. Do you like them? I have every colour under the sun, but no green ones. It is not often you see this shade of green and it exactly matches my blouse.'

Hannah nodded, and then said, 'I've had a letter from Molly Petch. She wants to see Alice and Elphine and apparently Uncle Patrick wants to see me. It is ages since we saw them. I know we keep in touch but Molly says Patrick is really looking his age now and will never make a long journey. I wonder how Elphine will react to another grandmother. She will not remember seeing Molly. She was only two years old, and it was such a fleeting reunion for them all.'

Daisy crossed her feet and sighed. 'I don't remember that. Where did they meet then?'

'On some film location down south. It was a bit of a secret at the time. She has the statutory pair of grandmothers, hasn't she? But they are both on the same side. I hope Marie can be civilised about it. It is hard for her to accept Molly as Alice's mother so what the grandmother status does it's hard to say. Poor Molly. She must long

193

to see her own flesh and blood, although apparently she has met someone who she describes as 'super duper'.'

'She decided to follow a career instead of looking after her child. We could all have done that.'

Hannah gave her friend a sharp look. She was given just lately to making rather vinegary comments, she thought. She was sure it was all about her feelings for Greg and being pushed out of the equation. But he was far too young for her, for goodness sake!

'Anyway, I'm going to get it organised before Emma goes into action. I know she has Greg to support her. It was different with Poppy. She really needed the support of her family then, but I still feel that I should be there for her. You never know with men. They can run a mile at the sight and sound of a newborn baby, and as for nappies! Jack was the world's worst.'

The school term finished on Friday 20th July and Emma's baby was due on Sunday 12th August. A few days in between would be the ideal time to spend in Ireland Hannah explained to Alice during a telephone conversation with her granddaughter. She had not broached the subject with Marie, knowing that she would object to Elphine going on such a long journey. It was up to Alice to make the arrangements. In spite of her absence, she was still the child's mother, and in spite of Molly's absence, that lady was still the child's grandmother. In any case, she thought, she herself wanted to see her uncle. According to Molly he was looking very frail. She was not sure of his age, but he must be heading for ninety. Her own father would be well over that she reckoned, and although he was the eldest and Patrick the youngest, there was not a huge gap. This could be her last chance of seeing him. Rebecca Lickis had talked of the Irish connection and more dots to join. 'Time will tell,' Hannah remembered her saying. Well this was as good a time as any.

Marie of course did her best to exclude Elphine from being part of the proposed journey, but Alice insisted that it was the right thing to do. 'This would be a huge adventure for her,' she said, and in any case they all agreed, apart from Marie, that Molly was entitled to see her granddaughter.

Alice had recently passed her driving test and Simon had indulged her in the gift of a second-hand car. She was to fund the running costs, although he had paid the first year's insurance. She happily took to the roads, driving backwards and forwards from Manchester for weekend breaks, and allowing Leigh the occasional lesson. Every spare half an hour was spent in lavishing love and care on her treasured possession. She named it Jason after the legendry great adventurer, and aimed to explore the whole of the British Isles. Hannah admired her for her confidence. She herself had relied on Jack to drive on long journeys, and now, in her retirement, found motorway driving quite a challenge.

It was decided by Alice that they would drive to the airport in the early hours of Saturday, ready to catch the first flight to Belfast. She took charge of all the organising and Hannah was happy to enjoy her personal preparations, relaxing in happy anticipation of an adventure shared with her granddaughter and great-granddaughter, and the future pleasure of once more spending time with her uncle.

Elphine was like a cat on a hot tin roof according to Simon. The child was intrigued by the expression and repeated it so many times that Alice told her to be quiet and try to get to sleep.

The alarm clock woke them at four-thirty and an hour later they were in the car. Elphine was secured in the rear seat, wrapped up in a blanket with two cushions pushed around to give support to her legs. Very soon it became obvious to the adults that she was asleep, and they felt free to discuss family issues.

Alice was finding it hard to come to terms with the attitude of her cousin Kirstie, having gleaned from Karl that she was planning to leave home and move in with a fellow student. He had hinted at the nature of the relationship, and Alice now seized on the opportunity to see what her grandmother knew.

Hannah was loath to disclose details of her conversation with her daughter and more recently with Kirstie, but she was not happy to know that this was affecting the unity of the family, especially as Kirstie's sexuality was no longer in question and she intended to stay in the bosom of her family so to speak. Alice was continuing to criticise, talking of Justin's untimely death and the loss of stability in their lives. 'What on earth is Auntie Rachel going to do now that she is no longer committed to the church?' she asked.

Hannah was silent, choosing her words carefully before she spoke and glancing back at the sleeping child.

'I think you ought to know something before you criticise Kirstie,' she said. 'Justin did have a hidden side to his character, and sadly imposed this on his stepdaughter if you know what I mean.'

'Oh, really! What, he abused her? Is that what you are saying? Oh my God! Poor Kirstie! No wonder she wanted to leave home. I think I would declare myself to be gay. So she's not really then?'

'No apparently not. We all know she is a bit of a tomboy, but then I was the same. It doesn't mean that you have to spend all your time with dolls just because you are female. I loved to be up in trees. An old willow tree, long since gone, used to be my hideaway.'

'I know. I remember you talking about it. So poor Kirstie. I'll have to get together with her when we come back.'

'Well don't say that I have told you. I promised not to tell anybody. Of course Rachel does not know. At least I don't think so. So please don't tell Leigh, will you?'

Alice shook her head, and sank back into silence. It was not easy to talk to Leigh these days.

'He's very single-minded,' she suddenly said.

'Who is?'

'Leigh. The past still haunts him you know. Did he ever tell you about the ouija board? That really scared him. We both thought that we were getting too caught up in it all and then along comes Elphine.'

Hannah glanced back at the sleeping child.

'Is she still asleep?'

Hannah nodded, although she thought she saw a slight flicker of the eyelids and remembered how she herself used to pretend to be asleep and listen in to adult conversation.

'Do you think Kirstie can get back to any normality with her mother?'

'She has offloaded it on to me! It reminds me of the old man of the sea who sat on someone's shoulders and the only way to get him off was to persuade someone else to take on the burden.'

'Oh you poor Grandma! I hate to think of you burdened down. Everyone tells you their problems.'

'It's all right. I am keeping my head above the waves, but it's like ripples in a pool. The only difference now is that there are so many pools making ripples and not just mine. I used to think that life was like a jigsaw puzzle, each piece a part of a big picture, but now there are lots of pictures.'

Once again her thoughts were back with Jack. Whatever would he have thought of this modern generation? He was angry about the violent abuse from Steve, Rachel's first husband, so what would he have thought of Justin?

It was daylight now, and more traffic was building up as people headed towards their places of employment. A fine drizzle clouded the windscreen, and windscreen wipers broke the silence with their rhythmic action. Elphine made a moaning sound and Hannah turned to reassure her.

'Soon be there, darling. Do you want a drink?'

Elphine struggled to sit up. Her legs cramped very easily, the muscles twisting against the irregular bones. The placement of a calliper had been necessary after the last hospital visit, and an operation to try to straighten the right leg was to be carried out in the near future. Alice had arranged for a wheelchair to be available at the airport, and Molly had acquired a pushchair for the times when the child could not cope with long walks.

The car was securely parked in the arranged parking area, and, after what seemed like an interminable length of time spent in queues for passport and luggage checks, they boarded the plane. Elphine sat by the window next to her mother, and Hannah occupied the seat nearest to the gangway. They spent the whole of the flight time caught up in the incredulity of the child. It was worth it just for that, Hannah thought, remembering how the first flight she had experienced had amazed and at the same time frightened her. Elphine stared and stared, not even turning her head away from the window to speak, as if one split second away from the view would be a huge loss.

Molly was waiting with an old but very robust pushchair. It had a footrest and a hood, and was capable of being folded flat. It reminded Hannah of one she had when her children were small, and was probably of the same vintage.

Molly looked a lot older than Hannah remembered. Her hair was longer, but showing signs of damage from peroxide. Yet she was still only thirty-eight years old, Hannah reminded herself. The car had also seen better days. The smell of cigarette smoke clung to the upholstery, and old tissues and parking slips were stuffed into the trays at the base of the doors. The cottage reflected the same habits. It was much as Hannah remembered it; cold and sparsely furnished. She wished that she could invite Molly to share her life with them, drawing her into the comforts of Willow Cottage, but knew that that was impossible.

It was the same arrangement as before when she and Alice had first spent some time with Molly, only this time a 'put you up' had been erected next to Alice's bed. The other bedroom, apparently Molly's, had been made ready for Hannah, with clean white sheets and a freshly laundered towel laid across the foot of the single bed. The air was stale with tobacco, and Hannah was reminded of the small bedroom at Eastfield Cottage in those early days of evacuation. She had remembered to bring hot water bottles this time even though it was July, and put them to one side as she unpacked her case, hanging her blouse on a hook on the door and placing a spare pair of jeans and a jumper on a chair in the corner.

Molly and Alice were deep in conversation when she went down and joined them in the living room. The ashes from a previous fire were spilling over from the grate onto the hearth. Elphine was drawing patterns in them with a poker, and listening to the adult conversation.

Molly, in spite of her protestations about being the real grandmother had taken little notice of the child apart from the initial greeting, and now Hannah was acutely aware of how the mother and daughter side by side closely resembled each other not only in looks, but also in a lack of affinity with Elphine. Both had given birth at a time when they were not prepared for the responsibility of motherhood. Now, Molly and Alice were like sisters, and as such had a lot in common, but what would the relationship have been like when Alice was a child. Possibly like the relationship now between Alice and Elphine. A kind of no man's land, Hannah thought. Marie, for all of her strict ways, was the stabilising force in the child's life.

It was with mixed feelings that she tidied her appearance in readiness for her visit to her old uncle. The initial excitement had waned, being swamped by sadness for Molly and for the obvious disappointment experienced by the little girl. She was determined to create some good memories for both of them and for Alice who was caught up amongst such a tangle of emotions.

Elphine was happy to be pushed along the narrow road to the large house where Uncle Patrick now lived alone.

'He has a daily help now,' Molly explained. 'Mrs Feeney's death upset him terribly. She was with him for a don't know how many years. As long as I can remember.'

'He never said,' Hannah answered. 'Mind you, he hasn't replied to my last three letters. I feel terrible about not ringing, but when I did it always seemed to be at a bad time.'

'I have tried to persuade him to have a mobile phone or at least a cordless one in case of emergency but he won't hear of it, and old Mrs Feeney thought they were the work of the devil. Here we are. Do you remember it?'

'I remember the leprechaun,' Alice said, pointing at the stone ornament at the side of the steps leading to the front door. 'Look Elphine! That's an Irish kind of pixie. This one is made of stone of course, but they are known as the little people, and they play all kinds of tricks or do good deeds and bring good luck.'

'That is why your Uncle Patrick has one outside his front door. To bring him luck. You had better say hello.' Molly waved her hand and Elphine copied her gesture, wriggling her fingers and grinning widely.

Molly reached forward and rattled the letterbox, and then produced a key from out of her pocket. 'He can't make it to the door now,' she explained. 'I hope he is awake. Stamp your feet a bit on the way in so that we don't make him jump.'

Hannah sighed. She had a feeling that this was going to be something of an aborted mission, but then she reminded herself once more of Rebecca Lickis and her prophecy of more dots to be joined. They all wiped their feet vigorously on the inside mat and Molly noisily cleared her throat.

'Can we come in?' she shouted, putting her head on one side in a comical gesture making Elphine giggle nervously.

'Come in.'

Hannah recognised her old uncle's deep voice and was relieved at the normality of the tone. He was sitting in the chair by the fireplace just as she had left him several years earlier it seemed, only now she could see evidence of the passage of time etched into the contours of his face. He looked incredibly old and frail, and she experienced a surge of compassion mixed with guilt. The last occasion when they had physically met was at Rachel's wedding, and now that was well and truly water under the bridge she thought.

She walked quickly towards him; arms outstretched, her words leaving her mouth in her customary nervous gabble at times when she would describe herself as at a loss for words. She awkwardly embraced him, aware of the hardness of his shoulders through the chequered fleecy shirt. His hands briefly squeezed hers before he sank back into the comfort of his high-backed chair.

'You remember Alice of course, and this is her daughter, Elphine your great-great-great niece. What a lot of greats, Elphine!'

Elphine repeated it several times until amusement became impatience as the adults each tried to change the subject resulting in a tangle of words and then silence.

Molly pulled at Elphine's hand.

'Come on.' she said. 'I have a treat lined up for you. There is a park just down the road with all sorts of rides, and we can get a bag of chips each and sit on a park seat near to a lake and feed the ducks. How about that then?'

'Is Mummy coming?'

'Of course, but not Great-grandma. She is going to have some peace and quiet with her Uncle Patrick.'

A silence followed in their wake and Hannah was reminded once again of the last lines of her favourite poem of childhood, 'The Listeners', which tells how the silence surged softly backward when the plunging hoofs were gone. It was a private reminder these days. She knew that she had repeated that line many times to her family and they had acknowledged it many times, but recently she had noticed that her reminiscences were barely given listening space, and she realised that like it or not the ageing process had her in its clutches.

She waited for the final click of the front door before she turned her attention back to her uncle.

'So Uncle Patrick, Molly told me that you have something important to tell me.'

'Where do I begin? I suppose I could say that you are not who you think you are if that makes sense. I suppose I could say that I am your half uncle and leave it at that, but you have a right to know.'

Hannah had sat down on the sofa and leant back, but now she pulled herself forward her whole being suddenly alert.

'Your father Martin was my half-brother. He had a different father hence the red hair and artistic kind of temperament. His father was a passionate Catholic, who got caught up in religious issues. By all accounts he was a talented artist and he wooed my mother with pages of poetry. I still have it all secure in a box and will give it to you before you leave. Well as you know, our family is Protestant on both sides. My mother disgraced the family at the age of sixteen by becoming pregnant and betraying the faith. Apparently she was literally kicked out by her father and was forced to work in a spit and sawdust public house where she was little more than a skivvy. She continued to share her life for a while with her lover Michael Cafferty, but then one dreadful night in a drunken brawl he was mortally wounded. She must have been desperate. She told me before she died that she worshipped the ground he walked on. Luckily, or some may think unluckily for her, my father was attracted to her, and to give him credit where it is due he married her and gave her son his name. It was not long after the birth that she was pregnant again, and nine months later my brother Anthony was born. He was obviously a Flynn, whereas Martin bore no resemblance to anyone other than his real father. For as long as I could remember during our childhood years my father treated Martin with great cruelty.

There was quite a gap between me and Paul, and I did get the best of things I suppose as my father prospered, but poor Martin was always in trouble, his red hair a constant reminder of who he was. What I told you about the village girl and how he was accused of fathering her child was true, and he did disappear one night. I remember that my mother cried for days and my father vowed that he would kill Martin if ever he returned. Even when the truth was known about the village girl and Martin's name was cleared, he still said 'Like father, like son', and made my mother's life a misery. We couldn't wait to leave home. I look back now and think how we deserted our dear mother, but times were hard and we needed to survive. None of us knew the truth of everything until I came over before my mother died and she told me the whole story. My father had died during the previous year leaving everything to the three of us including this house, and mother was obliged to pay us the rent. Of course we banked it for her. Still she had no one to fear anymore. It made me happy to think that she had kept in contact with Martin when you told me of the book she sent to you. So many divisions, mainly religious you know, and so much stacked up against women. It seems to have gone the other way now. Young Molly had ambition didn't she? She had such heartache over abandoning her child but it all seems to have worked out.'

Hannah noticed that he was beginning to slur his words, and leant forward to pat him on the knee. 'Would you like a cup of tea or something?' she asked. Inwardly her mind was racing. It was all like something out of a novel. Her grandfather was an artist and a poet. No doubt he was psychic; his gene pool still manifesting in Elphine. Her father had always told her that his mother was a bit of a witch. She could visualise the attraction between her and her first and only love Michael Cafferty. Hannah repeated the name several times as she waited for the kettle to boil. She should have been Hannah Cafferty. How strange life was. Suddenly a new character enters the plot from the wings yet his name has always been so significant.

She carefully balanced the tray of tea and biscuits as she walked across the kitchen floor and through into the living room beyond. Patrick's head was bowed in sleep. She slowly sipped her tea and watched the rhythmic rise and fall of his chest. Life was ticking away from him and she knew how relieved he must be to honour his mother's name.

Hannah was aware of the box secreted away at the bottom of her duffle bag under a collection of items she considered necessary for a long journey. She had resisted all temptation to examine the contents when she had returned to Molly's house. She needed to be in total isolation where she could examine past evidence with no interruptions from the present. As she sat in the aeroplane waiting for lift off, the sounds of excited chatter from all about her faded into an unintelligible hum. An hysterical shriek from Elphine caught her attention momentarily but then her mind focussed back again on the old box with its secrets of the past, and she was, unusually for her, unaware of the aircraft clearing the runway and lifting into the air.

Elphine had her face almost pressed against the glass. Alice was reading a magazine; turning the pages quickly in the attempt it seemed to find something of interest. She gave a deep sigh and her grandmother patted her on the knee.

'Soon be home,' she reassured.

'Oh I don't mind this bit. It's all the messing about at the other end I hate. I hope they have got the wheelchair organised. I don't know how Molly survives, do you?'

The sudden change of subject caught Hannah off her guard. She shook her head. 'Smoking doesn't help and up until all hours. Did she mention her boyfriend?'

'He's called Sean and he is on the stage.' That was Elphine's voice.

'Did she tell you that Elphine or are you telling fibs? I don't remember her mentioning his name.' Alice looked at Hannah and raised her eyebrows.

'He told me. '

'But we didn't meet him, did we?' Alice frowned. 'Who do you mean?'

'He's the man in the moon. The man in the moon came down too soon and asked the way to Norwich. Where's Norwich? Can I have some crisps? I'm starving.'

Alice sighed again and returned to the magazine. Hannah signalled for service and bought crisps and fruit juice. Elphine ate her crisps noisily and gulped down the juice with all the normality of a five-year-old.

Alice's fears concerning the organising of a wheelchair were justified. Apparently there was not a single one available; hard to believe in an airport of this size.

'This is disgraceful!' Alice stabbed her finger along a line of writing on the travel document. 'Look! We had this organised for the return. How can the rules have changed over the weekend? Do you expect this child to walk from one end to the other and then along to the car park?'

Hannah watched as her granddaughter became more and more frustrated and demanding. She was undoubtedly living up to her schoolteacher image these days, she thought, remembering how quiet she had been during most of her life. Regretfully that dreamy child had disappeared into the past, she decided.

Alice had certainly made her point and a porter with a motorised luggage carrier was ordered to transport the suitcases and the child to the exit and beyond to the car park. Hannah was worried. How far did their insurance cover such arrangements? Alice lifted the child on to the luggage space next to the cases and walked along holding Elphine's hand, without a backward glance to her grandmother still clutching her duffle bag and struggling to keep up. Hannah was tired. This is the last time I am flying anywhere she thought, but then a picture of Patrick's weary countenance flashed across her mind, and she sighed. How soon would she be paying him her last respects? One door closes and another one opens. Emma's son was waiting in the wings. Exits and entrances. Who would occupy or leave the stage first, she wondered? She would not have to wait long to find out.

The last stage of the journey was completed almost in silence. Elphine fell asleep as soon as the car engine became a steady hum, and Hannah found herself drifting in and out of strange little dreams triggered by traffic sounds and the experiences of the weekend.

Soon after their arrival back at Willow Cottage Alice disappeared into the privacy of the downstairs cloakroom together with her mobile phone. Hannah heard the name Molly and then Sean, and guessed that she was talking to Leigh. She glanced across at Marie. It was so hard for her to play a kind of second fiddle, she thought. Yet she was like a mother to the child, declaring that Elphine should never have gone, and a cup of warm sweet tea and an early night were what she needed.

However, Hannah's concern for her daughter-in-law was suddenly replaced with concern for her daughter Emma. Simon called from the hall that Daisy was on the phone with news of early contractions and an ambulance on the way.

'I've told her that we'll get over to the hospital. I guess you want to be there for her,' Simon said, wagging a finger at his mother. 'I think you should have an early night after all of your gadding about but I know you will not agree.'

'Emma will want somebody there, but what about Greg? Surely he has been told.'

'Apparently he is away on business, Zurich I think. No one thought it would be this early. I'm sure he will get back as soon as he can.' Simon as usual felt outnumbered with Leigh away for the weekend and leapt to the defence of a man he scarcely knew. Both he and Marie were united in their opinion that Emma had made a big mistake. However, he knew how concerned his mother was and this was not the right time to sit in judgement.

Marie insisted that everyone had a drink and a biscuit before doing anything else, but Hannah was already putting her coat back on, and, still clutching the duffle bag, she stood waiting for Simon to find his car keys.

Emma's son was born two hours later, seven pound two ounces in weight seeming to indicate that all was well. However, because he was three weeks premature he was put into the special baby unit under constant observation and viewed through a glass screen. Hannah with memories of the trauma of Elphine's birth was loath to leave her daughter's side, but by eleven o'clock she was forced to admit that she could not stay awake for much longer. The box and its contents would have to remain in the duffle bag until the morning.

❄

No news was good news, and everyone slept well after the adventures and dramas. Hannah awoke with a strange sense of uneasiness and listened for any sounds beyond the little staircase door. She put on her dressing gown and ran her fingers through her hair. She could not rationalise her feelings. Was it Emma or the baby? Was it Uncle Patrick? Something was happening somewhere. She could hear the sound of water gurgling through the pipes and guessed that Simon and Marie were getting up. Early morning sunlight shone through the yellow curtains flooding the kitchen in colour. She drew them back and was surprised to meet the face of the Mooncat. She always pointed his eyes in the direction of the willow trees when she put him on the windowsill at night. Her arms prickled under her dressing gown sleeves.

Of course, she suddenly thought. It was excitement over the box still waiting to be opened. How could she forget about it?

'Morning, Mum. Are you OK? You look tired. Rest for you today, I think. I hope you are not chasing off to that hospital.' Simon shook cornflakes into a dish and took a bottle of milk out of the refrigerator.

'Leave some for everybody else. That's all we've got.' Marie had followed him into the kitchen and it was obvious that she was not in a good frame of mind.

Mark mouthed 'Elphine' behind her back and Hannah guessed that the child had talked about Grandma Molly since waking up.

'Shall I see if Elphine needs any help, Marie? I expect she is tired after her busy weekend.'

'She's mardy. I know that much. Still Alice knows best.'

Hannah sighed and looked at Simon. 'I'll go and get her dressed.'

Simon nodded. 'I'll go down into the village and see if I can get some more milk.'

Elphine looked very tired. She was drawing in her sketchpad, and hastily closed it as Hannah went into the bedroom.

'Come on, young lady. You'll be in trouble if you are late for breakfast. There will be plenty of time to draw later. You will have to share them with me sometime. Your daddy tells me you are getting very clever.'

'I don't want Grandma to see them. She wouldn't like me drawing my dream people.'

'I promise I will keep it a secret. Who are your dream people?'

Elphine held the book tightly closed. 'Just people,' she replied.

'Are you coming down?' Marie's voice broke into their conversation. Elphine pushed the book under the quilt and jumped to her feet.

'Can I borrow it? I will take great care of it. Look, I'll wrap it up in some clothes for the wash, and hide it in the Glory Hole.'

They parted company at the bottom of the stairs, Elphine carefully making her way to the front kitchen steps and her great-grandmother turning to the door leading to the old back kitchen which housed the laundry facilities. The so-called Glory Hole was an ideal place to hide the book. This walk-in cupboard housed all kinds of things from the past, periodically having a spring clean when most things were returned albeit with more sense of order. Hannah's diaries were in here together with the family photograph album, and she carefully slotted the sketchpad between them.

The Mooncat had been put back in the cupboard. This was quite normal these days. It was the first thing Marie did when she came downstairs, but Hannah could still picture him when she had drawn back the curtains, his big yellow eyes staring into the kitchen. She felt the hair rising on her arms, and a prickling on her scalp. Marie was carefully pouring boiling water into the teapot, and Hannah opened the stairs door and went up to her bedroom. The duffle bag was where she had left it at the foot of the bed. Now she had three exciting quests; two kinds of Holy Grails, and a new life to observe when Emma came home with her son. Her spirits rose, taking her beyond fatigue. She could not imagine ever taking a back seat.

19

The Magic Box

It was agreed that Simon and Marie were to visit Emma in hospital. Baby Gary was still under observation in the special baby unit and apparently Emma was depressed. Simon was surprised at his wife's willingness to share in the excitement of a new life, and his spirits lifted. Perhaps they had both weathered the storms. However, Marie, it seemed, was full of sympathy for Emma. She identified with depression, and somehow such a strong sense of ownership of this condition gave her an edge on the situation. For her the arrival of a child was incidental.

Alice decided to take Elphine to see Poppy who was helping Jane at Daisy Cottage. She often entertained the residents with her piano playing and sing songs as they called them. Elphine loved Poppy. They were a generation apart, yet there was only a space of seven years between them, a gap that would surely close with the advancing years. Elphine loved to sit at the piano and pretend that she was an accomplished musician. Poppy had taught her to play 'Twinkle Twinkle Little Star,' with the right hand, and she wanted to learn 'Ba Ba Blacksheep'.

Hannah felt the wave of silence following their exit with both relief and excitement. At last she could explore the past. She sat on the bed and drew the duffle bag towards her. The box itself intrigued her with its ornately decorated lid. She fancied that it was part of the Arabian Nights scenario; treasure from Ali Baba and the forty thieves. The fabric covering it was threadbare in parts, but the jewelled embellishments and shimmering gold and silver weave still showed the remnants of a mythical scene. She carefully removed the elastic band somewhat perished by the passage of time, and opened the lid. The contents, released from the pressure of the lid, now rose higher than the top and began to spill out.

Hannah resisted the impulse to tip them out onto the bed. They could be in chronological order she thought, but then if that was the case should she begin from the bottom and work her way up? She put her hand over the top and carefully transferred the contents over onto her other hand. She placed each item one by one along the patterned border of the duvet cover as though she was playing Patience with a pack of cards, identifying each one on the way as perhaps a letter or a sketch or water colour. Two black and white photographs, reduced to a misty grey with age and confinement within the box, appeared near to the bottom of the pile. Hannah stared at the completed line along the duvet. She was drawn to the photographs, but decided to view each little document in turn.

The first one was a letter, folded and refolded as though it had been made as small as possible in order to conceal it. The resulting creases marred the written words and Hannah guessed at My Darling Katherine. The signature was Michael, followed by Your Eternal Love. Her eyes scanned the page. She felt a sense of guilt, and patted her hand down against the creases in the paper. This was so private. The next five folded papers revealed small water colour paintings and pencil sketches of wild flowers and landscape. Each one was signed Michael Cafferty. Hannah marvelled at their detail and thought of Elphine, his great-great-great-granddaughter. The photographs came next. The figure of a young woman, presumably her grandmother Katherine, was shown standing against a wooden carved chair. She looked elegant and Hannah guessed that she was dressed in her best clothes for what would have been a special occasion. It was a typical studio photograph of the late nineteenth century. She could see a marked resemblance to herself as a young woman. She felt a surge of elation. The war years had robbed many people of a record of their ancestry, but she had felt doubly robbed with not even a memory of spoken history. She ran her index finger along the contours of the face. 'Hello Grandma,' she said.

The next photograph was of a young man. She could see a likeness to Leigh immediately, and the shape of the face reminded her of her father. She had problems recalling it and would need to refresh her memory by looking at the old photograph again of him in his younger days. She turned the photograph over and written on the back was the name Michael Cafferty. This was in fine copperplate writing, and she guessed that Kathleen had written it. She turned the photograph over again and studied it more carefully. He was a handsome man. Uncle Patrick had described his hair as red. She imagined it to be the same colour as Leigh's. The colour of marmalade Elphine often teased.

A few pages fastened together with a paper clip were closely covered in lines of writing, with words crossed out here and there. Hannah could clearly detect a rhyming pattern as her eyes scanned the first sheet of creased yellowing paper. Patrick had said that Michael Cafferty was a poet. This was amazing!

The next envelope contained something wrapped in tissue. A sob caught in Hannah's throat as the contents were revealed. Two locks of hair lay merging together in a final token of eternal love. One was a mid golden colour and the other 'marmalade'. The family traits were all there; her own fair hair and complexion and her father's Celtic characteristics.

She carefully returned each item to the box in the order in which she had found it. She needed time to peruse the poetry and to appreciate the artwork, and this was not the right time. The family would be returning soon and the second part of her Holy Grail was waiting in the Glory Hole. She put the precious box under some folded clothes in the bottom of her wardrobe and went down her little staircase into the kitchen. The vegetables would have to wait, she decided, her customary sense of duty tugging in her mind.

Moments later she returned to the easy chair by the range and sank down into the soft cushion. The cover of the sketchpad gave no indication of the contents. She turned the pages over, marvelling at the detail in sketches of objects so familiar at Willow Cottage. Each page revealed a marked improvement in the child's ability. A number of unused pages followed and she turned each one hoping for further revelations, suddenly gasping in astonishment. Looking out at her were the faces of her parents. They were not a copy of the pre-war photograph which had come to light in the old chest of drawers at Eastfield cottage; the only one she had of her mother, or of recent photographs of her father taken before his death back in the early days of her marriage. Yet they were unmistakably likenesses of Martin and Sylvia Flynn. She was loath to lose sight of them and hesitated before turning the page. Two children looked out at her. She recognised Lucy, her late granddaughter, from photographs sent over from America in Mark's letters. The little boy, she guessed, was Nigel, Aunt Kate's and Uncle Harry's son, who had died at such an early age. Leigh had mentioned him, and now he was communicating with Elphine. This was amazing. She could not stop looking at these little faces from the past somehow so real in the present. The next page revealed the images of Kate and Harry Churchill and their dog Winston. Hannah felt the colour flooding into her cheeks. It was like looking at a time before all the heartache of Aunt Kate's death and the following bitterness when Harry's sister caused so much trouble. All these years later she still felt anger, yet here they were, all together and still at Willow Cottage.

A page had been ripped out, and she guessed that Elphine had destroyed her drawing of Zacc Pound. However the next page immediately held her attention. There she was in all of her glory – old Mrs Knight! Hannah had forgotten what her face was like. She was only nine years old during that brief stay in the old woman's cottage. She remembered the long black dress covered in sequins and the black wig, but now she remembered the face, old and wrinkled, and her real hair, grey and close cut like a man's. Elphine had drawn several cats sitting around her, and on a shelf at the back of the picture there was an unmistakeable image of the Mooncat.

Hannah's thoughts returned to the sight of the Mooncat looking back at her this morning and of her excited anticipation. She turned the pages back to her parents and to Kate and Harry Churchill. There was no Ella with her or him, but then there was no Jack or Mark either. She quickly turned back to the end. The pages were sticking together. Suddenly, there he was – Michael Cafferty. This was Elphine's latest drawing Hannah thought, remembering her holding the orange crayon. The two coloured strokes across his hair indicated her intention to make this a feature. But there was no need to establish the identity in this way; the resemblance to the photograph in the box was unmistakeable. Underneath the child had written in sprawling capital letters, MAN IN THE MOON.

Hannah was puzzled for a moment, but then recalled how Elphine had said that it was the man in the moon who had told her that Molly's friend was called Sean. She and Alice had not taken much notice. Elphine was always quoting nursery rhymes especially when Jane had been looking after her. Still she had wondered afterwards about Molly's friend. Was he really called Sean or was Elphine making it up? So, was Michael Cafferty communicating with her, and if so, why did she call him the Man in the Moon? A sudden explanation came to her. Perhaps she had thought that it was the Mooncat talking to her in Mrs Knight's parlour, but then Jane had read her the nursery rhyme, and now that his appearance had been revealed sufficiently for her to add his face to the other images she must be convinced that he was the Man in the Moon. How often did he speak to her she wondered, and how much did Rebecca Lickis know, when she talked about the dots joining together?

She had never forgotten how Mrs Knight had explained that the Mooncat was as real as everything else. 'It's made of what we are made of,' Hannah remembered her saying. 'The dust from shooting stars, the bones of a dinosaur. Everything going round and round.' She had gone on to explain that the soul could go anywhere, and now here is my grandfather Hannah thought, already a voice in Elphine's ear before she herself knew that he had even existed.

She was loath to put the precious sketchpad out of sight again in the Glory Hole, but she knew that Marie would be on her way home with Simon and expecting the vegetables to be prepared. Minutes later, as she peeled the potatoes, her thoughts returned to the missing page and to the child's fear. There were such powerful forces at work. She wondered again why Jack, Mark and Ella were not included. But could she bear it? Could Leigh bear it? One day perhaps he could come to terms with the unhappiness experienced by his mother at the death of her daughter Lucy and the infidelity of her husband. They had never really considered her anguish, only their own at the loss of a son. Perhaps Sarah was seeking forgiveness when she tried to communicate with Leigh and Alice through the Ouija board. Each of these deaths was still so close in her memory. Perhaps that is where their images should be until the wounds had healed.

By the end of the week, both Emma and her son had been given a clean bill of health. Hannah was convinced that they had got the dates wrong. The child certainly looked full term. 'He is just impatient to get on with life,' Emma laughed. Greg was back from Zurich and her happiness knew no bounds. They registered their child at the city office. In spite of them not being married Greg had no objections to being declared the father, but Emma wanted to retain her identity in her son's name. The entry declared him to be Gary Emmett Clayton-Mear. The hyphenated name implied joint ownership. Hannah inwardly suspected her daughter of lack of trust in the future of their relationship. It would be easy to reject the second part and the hyphen. However, she reserved judgement chiding herself for suspecting the worst. She still remembered Rachel's two attempts at wedded bliss with some bitterness, blaming herself for not recognising the state of her daughter's well being.

'It's as though everything has suddenly moved into the next gear,' Hannah said. She was watching Emma easing her son's arms into a tiny pale blue hand-knitted jacket, and admiring her for sticking to her principles. The denim could wait but not for long, she guessed. Children seemed to be fashion-conscious at reception class level these days.

Emma smiled. It had been quite a bombshell to learn that her mother's family name should have been Cafferty. 'Did you see a photograph or anything,' she asked.

'Just family groups. So what about your future then? Are you going to get married?' She hesitated. She had promised herself that she would not interfere, but her mind veered away from discussing her own secrets.

'We're not in a rush to do anything. The wounds are still raw for him. He doesn't say much but the death of his wife was a terrible shock.'

'What happened to her then? Was it cancer?' Hannah screwed her eyes up into a frown and shook her head as though in denial of the word itself.

'No. They were on a cruise and there was a dreadful outbreak of food poisoning. She was one of a number of casualties.'

'How awful. When was this then?'

'About two years ago. She was very lovely. I don't know what he sees in me. There you are. All spick and span again.'

Hannah smiled at her latest grandchild looking for family characteristics, and wondering if there were Cafferty genes in his make up. She was reminded of Emma at this age but then Emma is his mother she thought. She had only met Greg twice, and the beard concealed the shape of his face.

'So what do you think of his name? I thought you would like Emmett. I think it is Irish and sounds a bit like Emma. Greg chose Gary so that we had our initials side by side and we thought that both of our surnames would give him a choice in the future, or sound quite posh really.'

'What's in a name as they say? I should have been Hannah Cafferty until I became a Clayton. At least Gary will know who his father is, not like Poppy.'

'Oh well, can't be helped, Mum. Anyway I must get on. I have promised Daisy that I will sort out the care plans this afternoon.' Emma stood up and transferred her son into the Moses basket.

'I'll leave you to it then. Don't forget I am here if you need me. It's good that you can slot in work around the baby. Daisy is very accommodating, bless her. By the way, don't say I told you, but I think she has a date. No doubt I will be hearing about it.'

Bad news travels fast they say, and it certainly was bad news as far as Hannah was concerned. Daisy's date turned out to be a meeting with Greg to discuss his proposed purchase of Daisy Cottage with a view to changing it into a country club with leisure and business facilities. Daisy could not get her words out fast enough in her excitement to impart the details to her friend.

'Of course,' she said 'we will not be taking in any more residents and the three oldest ones will be well looked after. I am sure we can come to a good solution for the other six. It has been such a worry with new regulations, and families expecting all the latest mod cons. I really can't afford to keep the place open for much longer.'

'But where will you go, and what about everybody's jobs?'

'Greg has got it all worked out. He will need a staff to run the place. Emma is a born manager and Rachel is in need of employment now that she is no longer committed to church work. Then of course there are the twins. Greg foresees a big future in physical health pursuits with a gym and sauna and a swimming pool, and plans to let out the units for weekend breaks.'

'What about Jane and Clive, and where will you live?'

'It will all be sorted and as for me – I'll be on the next world cruise as soon as the money is in my bank account.'

Hannah replaced the phone and shook her head. She went into the kitchen where Marie and Simon were sharing morning coffee. 'That was Daisy,' she said.

'Oh. She couldn't wait to tell you.' Simon smiled and Marie nodded in agreement.

'What? You knew about her selling up then?'

'Well, we knew it was on the cards. I'm sure she saw Greg as her saviour and was knocked down when Emma became pregnant. But really all she wanted was to get the nursing home business off her hands. Knowing Greg, he probably sweet-talked her when he first came on the scene.'

Hannah sighed. She felt sidelined by all of this. Suddenly life seemed to be fast-talking and fast acting; computers, mobile phones, e-mails and text messaging. She had congratulated herself on developing basic skills on the computer, but now progress was engulfing her. She was drowning in a digital world. She thought of her magic box as she called it. It was another little world where time stood still. She knew now that she could never disclose its secrets. They belonged to her grandmother and to herself.

20

Molly Put the Kettle On

Time passed both quickly and slowly, it seemed, as everyone became caught up in battling with cold winter days, the frenzy of pre-Christmas sales and the complicated plans and regulations regarding the changes to be made at Daisy Cottage.

Another year had passed since the millennium disaster, and now with Spring firmly on the horizon, thoughts were turning towards the promise of a bright new future. Daisy's departure on her world cruise strangely coincided with the need for Hannah to venture once more into the sky. Molly was the bearer of bad news, although its arrival had been anticipated over the last few months with reports of Patrick Flynn's declining health. Now with his death, Hannah welcomed the thought of returning to Ireland. Since her last visit she had felt a great nostalgia for the land of her father's birth. Alongside this was a sense of loss of identity as the world she had known for such a long time was going through major changes. Simon and Marie, spurred on by the dynamic personality of Greg Mear, were planning more diversification, and Marie's dream kitchen was now moving from the initial ideas into reality.

Leigh accompanied her on the journey, and later to the funeral, the only representatives of the family, Patrick's brothers long since dead and his nephews and nieces at too great a distance to travel.

Molly of course was there, her eyes swollen with crying. Her tenuous links to him through her daughter Alice seemed to put her on a level with his great nieces and nephews. Leigh welcomed the company of a younger person albeit she was Alice's mother and could one day be his mother-in-law. So it was that this small gathering of people made their way to the graveyard and watched as the coffin was lowered into the ground. It was a long time since Hannah had witnessed a burial, and the tears flowed unchecked down her cheeks. For her, he was the last link with her father, and thoughts of her own mortality crept through her like the dampness of the morning mist

Another night spent in Molly's cottage dampened her spirits further. The next day they had been directed to hear the last will and testimony of Patrick Flynn. The solicitor's office was situated in Belfast and involved a bus or a taxi. Molly assured Hannah that it was not far to walk at either end and Leigh was all for exploring the city streets. However, a taxi was summoned. The previous night spent on Molly's hard single bed had left its mark on Hannah's anatomy.

Her back ached as she sat on the hard wooden chair in the solicitor's office watching him opening the document, and then wincing as he noisily cleared his throat.

Molly gasped as he announced that she was to have ten thousand pounds in recognition of her care and concern for him and for brightening his life. Also she was to benefit from his furnishings, keeping anything she would like to own, and arranging for the sale of the remainder. This would not only help her to furnish her cottage, or a house she may choose to live in at a later time, but would also increase her bank balance. The solicitor explained that there was a limited time for the house clearance to be completed in order for the house to be marketable. Molly nodded and burst into tears.

Then it was Hannah's turn to cry out in astonishment. It appeared that Patrick had left the remainder of his estate to her, his niece, to make amends for the great injustice done to his brother Martin who had received nothing in the past. The solicitor explained that the three brothers had inherited everything when their father died except for a small amount of interest on an investment to be used for the basic requirements of their mother until she died. 'Of course,' he said, 'they regularly sent money to their mother, and I, as a family friend as well as their lawyer, made sure that she had what she needed.'

'But what about all his other nephews and nieces? Surely they will expect to have a share,' Hannah suggested, a frown creasing into a well-established line between her brows.

'I can assure you they were well provided for by their parents and will not want to go against their uncle's wishes. Besides, this is his will and your entitlement. Enjoy it my dear. Patrick has honoured the name of his mother and is exonerated in some measure from the guilt he felt for never trying to discover the whereabouts of his brother Martin. Of course, the house has to be sold and all of his investments and cash totalled, before we come to the final figure, but it will be considerable.'

They made the return journey in the taxi passing Patrick's house on route. Hannah was aware of Molly's pointing finger and Leigh's exclamation of 'Wow! Some house.'

She caught sight of the leprechaun sitting quite forlornly she thought at the side of the front door step. Where was Uncle Patrick now and what was she going to do with all of this money?

The whole family discussed the windfall, as it was known, usually when Hannah was not present. Simon fired on by the ambitious plans of Greg and Emma was surging ahead with ideas to bring in more revenue, and his proposals indicated big changes at Willow Cottage. Rachel was focusing all of her energies on her son and daughter and their possible future at Daisy Cottage, and Jane and Clive were prepared to expand their vegetable retailing business to include supplying a large range of foodstuffs for the hotel and leisure centre.

Hannah waited for news from her late uncle's solicitor and Molly. A large parcel delivered by registered mail and containing the bible belonging to her grandmother's side of the family gave her huge pleasure, and she chatted for nearly an hour to Molly, thanking her for such a lovely surprise. She traced her fingers over the signatures of her great-grandmother Hannah Mary and of her grandmother Kathleen Hannah, carefully adding her own with the date of entry.

The solicitor informed her that the house was now in the process of being sold and she would be advised shortly as to the final amount of her inheritance.

Meanwhile at Willow Cottage the finishing touches were being put to Marie's new kitchen. Hannah had always loved painting and decorating in the past, but none of it seemed to involve her any more. In spite of the fact that she had encouraged her daughter-in-law to put her own mark on Willow Cottage, the bland colours and sheer lines of the kitchen units were in her opinion too clinical. The small front kitchen still remained, but the solid fuel range had been removed to make way for the new entrance into the back kitchen. Apparently the Glory Hole with its accumulation of clutter as Marie called it, was next on the agenda to be sorted.

'It's like the heart has gone out of the house,' Hannah told Sally. 'I have a feeling that my little bedroom will be the next to go. Marie is talking about a split level dining room, with the wall, the stairs door and the crooked stairs being taken out.'

She and Sally were sharing a coffee in a department store in Hull. Sally had invited her friend over to her bungalow in Anlaby to share in her excitement. 'You are not the only woman of substance,' she had yelled over the phone.

It appeared that she had had a wonderful offer for her publishing business as a going concern. 'I don't know where I am going from here,' she said as she sipped her coffee. 'I would like to get back to writing. I haven't had time for years now, but I really need some inspiration. My dreary little place needs a complete makeover and quite honestly I don't know where to start. I may take myself off on a huge adventure. I might disappear into the Outer Hebrides.'

'That's a bit drastic,' Hannah laughed. 'I can't imagine you living like a kind of Mrs Crusoe. You would soon have to import a Man Friday, or perhaps a Woman Friday.'

'Do you fancy a world cruise like Daisy then?'

Hannah wrinkled her nose and shook her head. 'I don't like the way the world is going,' she replied. 'I feel as though I want to disappear down the rabbit hole. A comfy one I mean.'

'That would probably inspire me as well. Let's find a rabbit hole to disappear down then.'

'What? Do you mean move in somewhere together?'

'Yes. There must be a place waiting to inspire us. You could go to town on all the quirkiness, and I could soak up the atmosphere and write a bestseller. I know exactly how you feel about Willow Cottage. It's never been the same since Jack died. Gosh I'm all of a tingle.'

Hannah was also sensing the charges around her. Sally had always been her closest friend, in spite of the long periods in their lives when they had been apart. They had planned to live together in London. She could almost sense Jack's disapproval now. But then that was another lifetime away. Now they both had the funds to buy a substantial place with enough space each to follow their own pursuits.

'It must be old.'

'Of course. I need inspiration to write an historical novel. Neither of us wants to live in some kind of sterile new development.'

'It must be detached with a garden all around it.'

'That's fine, as long as you organise the garden.'

'It must have open fires and lots of rooms.'

'Oh Hannah! I can visualise it already, but let's not get too carried away. Even you can't summon somewhere onto the market with your witchcraft or your guardian angel. Do you have an estate agent angel? Golly that was hard to say! Or do you only communicate with Polly the parking angel? Oh! That reminds me of The Mermaid Inn, and I've got goose bumps again. That place was a bit too spooky!'

Hannah was on the point of saying 'Selina Constable', but stopped herself. She had never told Sally of her night-time experience and nodded instead. 'Yes we must get around to the estate agents. There are bound to be plenty of eager ones even if they don't qualify as angels.'

21

Edge of Square Nine

They could not believe it. After searching through the available properties on the market in Lincolnshire every day for a week, an agent, in what would seem to be a back street, rather run down establishment, said 'Eureka'. He was an odd-looking man, and Hannah and Sally exchanged glances, their mouths lifting at the corners with amusement. However, amusement changed to astonishment as he produced the details of an old cottage on the edge of a hamlet about ten miles from Norbrooke.

'It sounds like what you are looking for if you don't mind a bit of hard work and some renovation. It has been on the market for some time and there is no chain. The previous owner left it to his nephew in his will and that gentleman wants to get his hands on the cash of course. He lives in London and has no desire to move to the wilds of Lincolnshire.'

Hannah felt a little surge of guilt as she thought of her uncle's house.

'He hasn't finished clearing it out and there may be items of furniture that he will include in the sale. So, here are the specifications.'

He read out a long description of what seemed to be a strange collection of rooms. Some were specified as living rooms, four as bedrooms with a study cum bedroom as extra space, and two small rooms from converted stabling with low-beamed ceilings and no given function. The area of the land it occupied was approximately half of an acre, and a small woodland area adjacent to the garden was available as a separate purchase.

'It really does need closer inspection,' he advised, his small blue eyes regarding them and waiting for their reaction.

'Is there a photograph of it?' Sally asked.

'No. The light was very poor. I have been meaning to go back but I've been so busy. But I'm sure you will like it. Why don't you take the key and have a look for yourselves? I'll give you the directions. In any case you can't miss it. There are only a cluster of houses near by.'

'We didn't ask him how much it was, Sally. He kind of mesmerised us, didn't he?' Hannah said, as they found themselves walking away from the office and back in the direction of Sally's parked car.

Sally nodded. 'And why was there no photograph? I don't believe that bit about him being too busy. His place looks as though it has come out of the ark. There were cobwebs on top of cobwebs. I don't want to hark on about it, but he reminds me of that funny little old man at the Mermaid Inn. Do you think funny little old men are attracted to us?'

They both began to laugh and had to sit for a few minutes when they reached the car to get their breath back. The key weighed heavy in the old stained envelope, which the man had pushed into Hannah's hand. She drew it out, together with a list of instructions on how to find the cottage. 'What a big key,' she commented.

'And what a draughty keyhole no doubt,' Sally replied.

After a few wrong turns and reverses they found the tiny hamlet of Cotesby along a lane leading from a busy roundabout feeding the main route to the Humber Bridge.

'We must have been within a stone's throw of this a good many times. We really should know more about our environment.' Sally had pulled up on the side of the road, and their eyes rested on a group of brick cottages pressing together on the left.

'I can't see a 'For Sale' sign anywhere. Had we better go and ask somebody and get the lie of the land? We should know a bit about the neighbours, shouldn't we?' Hannah opened the car door and heaved her complaining back into a straight line.

They walked up to the door of the first house along the lane and rang the bell. The place looked deserted and unappealing. Hannah sighed and turned away. Sally rang the bell again and pressed her face to the glass panel in the door before joining her friend who was retracing her steps back along the path to the road. Suddenly a high-pitched voice broke the silence, and a head appeared at an upstairs window.

'What do you want?'

'There's a cottage for sale. Is it this one?' Sally yelled.

'No. It's not here, ducky. It's old Arthur's house you want. It stands on its own along the lane. You can't miss it.' The head disappeared and they heard the window latch drop into place.

'That's what the estate agent said. "You can't miss it." We might as well drive. It doesn't look as though we will be in anyone's way.' Hannah eased herself back into Sally's car.

They certainly could not miss it. It was on the left hand side of the lane about a quarter of a mile from the other houses, and dominated the surroundings.

'Crikey! It's huge,' Sally exclaimed. 'I bet they are asking a lot. Perhaps that is why he didn't mention a price.'

'I think we assumed that it was a rundown place and therefore a bargain. It still may be a bargain if this London bloke wants a quick sale. We'll look around and then come up with an offer.' Hannah's eyes were already beginning to sparkle with excitement.

The front garden had an air of sophistication in spite of outcrops of nettles and couch grass encroaching into the herbaceous borders. Bricked pathways carved up the space into geometrical shapes, each edged with slate tiles stood on end, and mature lilac and laburnum trees formed a border along the field side.

A wider path of stone slabs led to the front door through a gothic arch that in turn created a shallow porch. The garden disappearing from view along each side of the building invited inspection, but Hannah was brandishing the key and making a beeline for the ornately carved front door, already intrigued by the contrast between the fine artistry and the rustic ruggedness. It was obvious that previous owners had had good taste and a strong sense of history.

The door seemed reluctant to open, creaking out its protests.

'Nothing a can of oil won't cure,' Sally said wryly

Their gasps of amazement overshadowed the complaining hinges. They stood on the other side of the door looking in to a square entrance hall. A shaft of coloured light entered this space from above and drew their attention to a staircase with a large window on the first landing. A figure of a knight in armour on horseback surrounded by a geometric design all in stained glass immediately brought the poem of the Lady of Shallot and Sir Lancelot to Hannah's mind, and she suddenly felt that this house was her Holy Grail, no matter whether the rest of it pleased or not.

Nevertheless, she turned her attention to the lower levels of the room, joining Sally in admiring the stone slabs covering the floor.

'Some thick rugs on here I think,' Sally was saying, and Hannah murmured in agreement, looking through an archway in the opposite wall where a refectory table extended beyond the eye line.

'That's handy. A downstairs cloaks. Oh and amazingly a big corner shower!' Sally was investigating beyond a doorway on the left side of the entrance hall. 'Where are you Hannah? Come and see.'

However, Hannah was staring up at the wall beyond the arch. It was a small internal room dominated by the table and eight chairs. Unusually a strong source of light came from a row of windows set high in the wall. Each window had a geometrical border of stained glass, casting patterns in different colours onto the white plastered walls.

Sally had flung open a door on the right and revealed a kitchen. A window opposite faced out on to the side garden, an area dark in shade with overgrown shrubs and trees grown unchecked over a long space of time.

'Some pruning there for you, Hannah. You did say it must have a big garden.'

Hannah nodded. She was turning the big brass knob on another door on the right. The knob felt wobbly in her grasp and gave a protesting kind of squeak she thought. The varnished floorboards surrounding a threadbare and faded carpet square seemed to echo the complaint, creaking under her tread.

'This must be the study cum bedroom,' she said, pointing to the large captain's writing desk. It was positioned in a square, deep bay window with a view of more tangled garden. It was a substantial piece of furniture; solid oak by the look of it, the top covered in red leather with the corners curling up and ink stains recording past writing endeavours. 'There you are, look, Sally. It's waiting for your next best seller.'

Sally was examining the old fireplace. It was constructed of very small red brick, and in need of some repair; the mortar crumbling in the joints. The remnants of a recent fire were there in the grate, and charred sticks of firewood had spilled out onto the hearth.

'All the luck has come out of that!' Sally laughed, pointing to a horseshoe hanging upside down on a hook on the chimneybreast. A tall thin arched window on each side of the chimney hinted at more stained glass decoration under the grime. A window seat had been constructed on either side and Sally lifted the lids disappointed to find only the remains of wood and coal inside.

'This must be some of the furniture for sale,' Hannah said, pointing to the oak bureau sited on the opposite wall. 'It has certainly seen better days.' Three large drawers revealed nothing more than old newspaper lining the bottoms, and a slight smell of mothballs.

A large ornate mirror with a dark oak frame to match the furniture hung to the left of the door and reflected the tall windows and the fireplace. Here and there the image was marred where the silver backing had flaked off. Some old pictures remained on the walls above wooden wainscoting, hung with cobwebs spreading across on to the cream painted plaster.

'How strange that this room is almost as it was when in use and yet everywhere else seems pretty empty.' Hannah was staring at the curtain fittings, brass rings slotted on to a tarnished brass pole and supporting old velvet curtains which trailed onto the floor.

'Perhaps it was to save fuel. You know. Just ending up living in one room. That is one thing we must think about. I doubt there is a gas supply here and there are no signs of central heating.'

A sudden gust of wind blew against the branches of a tree growing close to the bay window, scraping them against the glass.

Sally shivered. 'Let's find the living room,' she said.

They retraced their steps through into the dining room and crossed over to a door opening up into a large well-lit room. French windows gave a view of an expanse of lawn and borders. The walls were plastered, with an area of exposed brick here and there, and a stone-lined fireplace with deep alcoves on either side dominated the room.

'That must be the stabling area he mentioned,' Sally said, pointing through an open doorway into an old cobbled floored space, supporting beams and roof timbers clearly visible. 'Let's just take a quick look. We've got all the upstairs yet.'

The quick look revealed further stabling facilities to the right. There was an air of dereliction about it all and they turned around to retrace their steps back to the staircase in the front entrance hall.

On closer inspection the stained glass window on the first landing was dulled with what seemed to be dirt and cobwebs of many years. Cleaning it would be a pleasurable future task, they both decided. The top landing was square and spacious. A large bathroom on the right was obviously positioned over the shower room downstairs, and four bedrooms, one over the sitting room with views of the side garden; one above the reception hall; another one which seemed to be over the study, the window giving views of the overgrown garden on the right; and a fourth one in the middle of the house with a small window looking down onto a bricked and cobbled area.

'How strange,' Hannah said. 'We didn't see that bit, did we? Have a look. It's like a little courtyard.'

They took it in turn to put their heads out of the small casement window. The walls of the house rose up on three sides. On the fourth side was the stable block; a low single story building. They remembered seeing a section of it from the main part of the house, and noticed now how the various areas fitted together like a jigsaw puzzle almost enclosing the little courtyard. Treetops showed above the pan-tiled roof directly ahead of their view out of the window.

'They could be in the little spinney the man mentioned,' Hannah said, pointing them out.

Sally took her turn at the window. 'It doesn't get any sun by the look of it,' she said, and grimaced as a shiver ran up her spine. 'We ought to be getting back. We'll come again tomorrow and explore that bit and the garden.'

They retraced their way along the lane and past the rest of the houses in this tiny hamlet of Cotesby.

'You are unusually quiet,' Sally remarked. 'Has it worn you out? I must admit it was a lot to take in.'

'Oh no! It's amazing. There are so many interesting features. Quirky I suppose you would call it. I feel as though I am on the edge of square nine.'

'Square nine! What's that, for goodness sake?'

'It was a board game we used to play. Didn't you ever play it? '

Sally shook her head.

'It was a kind of journey through life. In fact I think it was called The Journey, but we used to call it Square Nine. There were fifty squares from start to finish and dice and a number of characters to identify each person's position as they moved along. Landing on square nine was supposed to be a hazard with a pathway leading off the beaten track into all kinds of strange places where creatures from myths and legends were hiding, and turns to throw the dice were lost by falling under magic spells. The children loved to land on square nine. I bet Simon will remember it and I am sure Alice and Leigh played when they were kids. It's somewhere in the Glory Hole. Oh gosh!'

'What now, Hannah? You made me jump!'

'I've just remembered. They're clearing the Glory Hole out today to get at the wall at the back. It may be knocked through by the time we get back. There is a lot of my stuff in there.'

They arrived back at the cottage where the demolition work was still underway, and the brick dust and rubble took their minds off everything, until the family sat down to an evening meal well after seven o'clock. By this time their initial enthusiasm had waned and they prompted each other in descriptions of the salient features of each room.

'Is there an attic?' Simon asked. 'That's where people find priceless treasures.'

'There must be, mustn't there, Hannah? It has a steep high roof. I didn't notice any trapdoors in the ceilings, but then there was so much to see that we could easily have missed them.'

'That's one thing that could cost you a lot. A new roof,' Simon said. 'Anyway what's this guy asking for the place? A Londoner, did you say? Perhaps he is desperate to sell. It may be about to fall down.'

'We don't actually know the price do we, Sally?'

Simon raised his eyebrows.

'By the way, Grandma,' Alice suddenly said. 'I've rescued Square Nine from the skip.'

Alice and Leigh took Elphine through into the living room leaving Sally and Hannah to finish their cups of coffee. Marie was clearing the table around them and piling the plates and dishes into the sink.

'You will soon be in your new kitchen, Marie,' Hannah said. She suddenly was feeling guilty at dominating the conversation with hers and Sally's future plans.

'It was a grotty kitchen in that house, wasn't it?' Sally said. 'We really should be careful. And it was a bit creepy, especially looking down into that mouldy-looking area. Simon could be right, and what if it is haunted?'

'Oh Sally! Don't start getting cold feet now. I tell you what. That lady I know who does readings had an advert in the paper last week about a kind of spiritual house clearance. I could get her to give it the once over. She has been right every time so far with me. At least dropping hints. I don't think she likes to be too graphic about the future, but I bet she would soon suss out a ghost, and would know if the place was falling down.'

Simon grunted, and Marie turned both the water taps on at the same time.

Simon took the matter into his own hands the next morning by ringing up the estate agent and enquiring on the price of the cottage for sale at Cotesby.

'It has been sold,' came the reply.

'Could you give me the price all the same? My mother is interested in buying it.'

'Oh I see. She has already indicated a purchase. We are prepared to negotiate around two hundred and fifty.'

'Mother, have you agreed to buy this cottage?' Simon called up the kitchen stairs to Hannah at the end of the telephone call.

Hannah came down shaking her head

'He seems pretty sure that you have. By the way, the price is around two-fifty. Sounds a bit steep for me. I would offer him two hundred.'

'OK. We'll see. Emma is coming with us today with Poppy and baby Gary, and Elphine is desperate to see it. It's a lovely day for exploring the garden. The fresh air will do the children good. They spend far too much time watching the television.'

'The car seems to know its way already,' Sally said. 'It isn't far from Willow Cottage. Well not as the crow flies.'

'But we are not crows Auntie Sally. It will be too far to walk.'

'Turn left! Be quiet, children. Auntie Sally easily gets lost.'

Sally glared at her friend. 'Bossy Boots. She thinks she is still a school teacher.'

The two girls giggled, and Hannah muttered, 'Sorry.'

The cluster of houses on the right came into view and Elphine began to wriggle with excitement. A few minutes later they pulled to a halt on the grass verge outside the old cottage. It now had a relaxed air about it, sunning itself in the strong August light. The texture of the brickwork with its multi tones of oranges, reds and browns and the grey-slated roof reminded Hannah of an impressionist painting. She could see now how the garden spread out along the left hand side of the house, an old greenhouse reflecting the sunlight in sudden flashes.

'Is this your new house?' Poppy asked. 'It looks very old to me.'

Elphine was struggling out of her seat belt and reaching for the door handle. 'It looks very crooked to me,' she said. 'Shall I push the buggy?'

Her offer was declined, and the baby slept on oblivious to its new surroundings. They decided to explore the garden whilst the sun was shining. It came up to Hannah's expectations as wildly beautiful; expanses of lawn broken by shrubbery and borders. A pond, choked with iris, invited excited inspection, and the small spinney at the far end of a mud path reminded Hannah of her little 'Brigadoon'. She vowed to herself that she would plant a black poplar and watch a new Whispering Tree reach its branches towards the sky.

'Why do you keep looking at your watch, Mum?' Emma asked.

'Well actually I have asked Rebecca Lickis to come and check the place out for us. You know.' She nodded towards Poppy and Elphine, and mouthed 'Spiritual cleansing.'

'When did you do that?' Sally frowned.

'This morning first thing. I knew that you were having second thoughts and Simon was doing his best to put me off.'

'Well then we had best look at that funny little courtyard we spotted from the back bedroom window before she comes. It seems that the only way into it is through the stable block over there. It looks as though we can get through this door from the garden.'

The cobbled floor made way for a stone slabbed one at the far end. The first part appeared to be an area for storing gardening items. Two old wheelbarrows were propped against the sidewall, and an assortment of tools was hung on large rusting nails sticking out from the crumbling brickwork. Then Hannah stared in astonishment at what, to her practised eye, was obviously a large kiln. It was like a scene frozen in time. A long shelf housed items of biscuit ware awaiting the final glaze before a second firing and large tins and pots were stacked along a worktop, their labels indicating varying stains and glazes. It was as though the potter had left things to dry and gone in to get a meal or to have a rest.

'I might have known,' Hannah said quietly, suppressing the huge excitement she was feeling. 'This house with all of its quaintness had to belong to some kind of an artist. I have always wanted to get back to pottery. Do you remember, Sally? I was going to night class when we first met up before you disappeared to Australia. I don't know much about the firing process but how wonderful to learn something new. You can write your books and I can work with clay inside and soil outside.'

The children were calling them from the direction of the small courtyard. They had discovered a doorway into the shaded enclosure. The house walls rose up on either side to the rooftop, windowless but with a strong growth of ivy clinging to the stones. Elphine was already investigating a strange face on the wall. Green mould had gathered in the cracks and water was dribbling out through the mouth and collecting in a stone bowl underneath.

'That's Medusa,' Poppy said. 'Everyone who looked into her eyes was turned to stone.'

The little girl jumped back and clung to Hannah. 'I don't like her,' she said. 'I don't like this place.'

'It's only a story. Look, there's a magic mirror on the wall.' Poppy turned the little girl's attention to a large mirror half hidden by ivy and creating the illusion of being a window into another space.

Sally gazed up the wall facing them and pointed to the small sash window through which she and Hannah had viewed this dark shaded area on the previous day. A metal table and two chairs occupied a space in the middle of the courtyard and Emma remarked that this seemed an unlikely place to sit and relax with a cup of tea or a glass of wine. However a door to the left indicated a function of some kind. Emma grasped the handle cautiously, remarking on its resemblance to the head of a cobra. The door had a zigzagged gap at the top and a large space at the bottom. It reminded Hannah, in a flashback to her childhood, of the earth closet at Eastfield Cottage and of her great fear of rats. However, it appeared that a toilet no longer existed, although rusting capped pipes were a witness to its earlier use. Instead, dried flowers hung from large hooks in the beam, and packets of seeds were stacked on a shelf along the wall. A half full bag of seed compost occupied a corner, and Chinese Lanterns and

Honesty grown faded and marred by the passage of time, were still waiting to be transferred to vases.

'It's a glorified potting shed,' Hannah said. 'This is a little working area with a table and chair for comfort. Mystery solved.' She looked at her watch again, and turned to go back into the stable block and through into the living area. The children began to explore the rest of the house, and the three adults sought out the dining chairs and sat down, resting their elbows on the long refectory table.

However, their rest was short-lived. The clanging of a bell summoned attention to the front door. 'It'll be that woman,' Sally said. 'You'd better go.'

Hannah gave her a long look before she made her way to the door.

Rebecca had her hair dyed black again and cut into a fashionable bob. She was wearing a bright pink blouse together with a long multi-coloured skirt.

'What an incredible place,' she remarked loudly, her eyes darting around to view the entrance hall and the staircase. 'This all seems fine. Upstairs is drawing me.'

'Are you coming, Sally? Emma, do you mind staying with the children?' Hannah called.

She hurried after Rebecca Lickis who was already halfway up the long staircase and admiring the stained glass window. She reached the top and looked at the various doors leading from the landing as she waited for the two ladies to catch her up.

'This is the one,' she said, pointing to the little room with its view over the courtyard.

Hannah and Sally exchanged anxious glances.

'There's an attic, isn't there, which you haven't yet found and that's the reason why.' The medium pointed to an old wardrobe. 'Do you think between us we could pull it away from the wall?'

It was no easy task. The wardrobe was wide and solid, testing their strength to its limits. At last they had moved it sufficiently to reveal a small door in the wall.

'Goodness me!' Sally explained. 'Shades of Narnia here, I think.'

Rebecca lifted a latch securing the door and pulled it open. In the dull light coming through the tiny bedroom window they could make out two steps indicating a staircase.

'There we are. I thought so.' Rebecca's fingers had located a light switch and now the wooden tread of this attic stairs was revealed. Sally shuddered, brushing away the cobwebs hanging in big clumps as they tentatively trod on each creaking step.

Hannah was beginning to doubt the wisdom of her actions in inviting Rebecca to the cottage, but then reassured herself that her clairvoyant friend would already know what to expect.

Wires looped along linking the electricity supply to another bulb at the top of the stairs. This illuminated the beginnings of a long attic both floor boarded and ceiling boarded. A glimmer of light was forcing its way through a window in the gable end, ivy penetrating through from the outside and hanging in long pale tendrils.

As their eyes became accustomed to the gloom, they could make out strange shapes covered in dustsheets, and tentatively lifted the edges to reveal first a birdcage on a stand, then a rocking horse, and further along a glass dome covering a stuffed bird. A large oblong shape indicated a picture, and as the dustsheet fell to the ground, an oil painting came into view. It seemed that the colours, protected from the glare of the sun, had retained their original freshness, many shades of blue glowing in the subdued light.

'This is a picture of the Blue Angel,' Rebecca said. 'I was told that I would find her here. She is the guardian angel of this house, and will always protect you. You may be aware of her from time to time, particularly if you are in the midst of great creativity.'

Hannah was entranced, and then suddenly caught sight of her own reflection in a cheval mirror standing along side of the picture. As she stared at herself noticing the deepening shadows around her eyes, another face appeared, briefly obscuring hers. She felt a huge surge of emotion travelling through her and knew that she was experiencing a spiritual encounter.

She turned to speak to Rebecca Lickis but, as their eyes met, she realised that the experience had been shared.

'So, no problems, my dears. Shall we join the rest of your family?' Rebecca's high-pitched voice broke into the silence.

After a brief chat with Emma and the children, Hannah accompanied the lady, who had already played such an important role in her life, to her car.

'I want you to put a guitar into the little boy's hands as soon as he can hold one,' Rebecca Lickis advised. 'He is surrounded by music both in this world and the next, and will share with his sister in a great future. Elphine is like a little candle burning in the night. Some burn for a shorter time than others but then very often with greater intensity like the May fly dancing non-stop through the only day of its life.'

'Where are you going to put the Mooncat, Great-grandma? He will need to look out of the window.' They were returning to the estate agents to make purchasing plans and Elphine as usual was one step ahead. Hannah looked at her dear little crooked face and a sob caught at her throat.

'I am sure we will find the right place for him, darling,' she replied. 'I don't think he really needs a view. After all, he looks into time, doesn't he?'

Epilogue

The Mooncat looked into the past and the future, occasionally noticing fleeting significant moments as they passed by, each disappearing into history.

He recalled how these two friends set out at the age of nine on the great adventure that would change their lives forever.

He mourned the loss of all of those so dear to Hannah, yet ensured the links binding them together in eternity.

He witnessed the restoration of Blue Angel Cottage year by year, and the accomplishments of Hannah with her creative hands in both clay and soil. He rejoiced in the publication of Sally's two novels, and her success in needlecraft as she carefully completed a cross-stitch tapestry of The Lady of Shallot as part of the Holy Grail and destined to hang on the staircase wall close to the stained glass scene of Sir Lancelot.

He applauded the success of both Poppy on the piano and Gary's universal recognition on the guitar.

He saw the business successes together with the trials and tribulations of the members of Hannah's extended family, and the increasing maturity and dedication to duty of the younger members. He was not surprised to see Daisy sunning herself on deck with her latest conquest.

He watched Hannah re-site the rose bush, Sweet Dreams, close to a stone angel that she had chosen in the gift section at Willow Cottage Garden Centre, and knew that Jack, in spirit, shared all of the house and garden with her.

He foresaw the terrible sadness of Elphine's death when she was ten years old, yet welcomed an ally into the spirit world.

He watched over every one of them, each on their own journey, with an occasional visit to Square Nine when they felt the need to escape into a special dream.

THE END

Lightning Source UK Ltd.
Milton Keynes UK
UKOW03f1309270714

235844UK00003B/46/P